Praise for *Painting the Corners Again*

"With these stories, Bob Weintraub has executed a triple play: savvy baseball writing, unforgettable characters, and a home run ending for each tale. By all means, read this book."

—W. P. Kinsella, author of *Shoeless Joe* (the basis for the film *Field of Dreams*)

"Imaginative baseball stories for long rain delays and hot stove league nights."

—Darryl Brock, author of *If I Never Get Back* and *Two in the Field*

"Unique and wonderfully twisted

—Ed Asner, actor

"Great storytelling for fans and r ...ue talent."

—Dan Shaughnessy, author of *The Curse of the* ... .st for the *Boston Globe*

"The prevailing trend seems to be to reduce baseball to numbers, to take out the adjectives and hyperbole, eliminating the descriptions of facial tics and personal travails and sunsets, to treat the game as some algebraic problem stretched across a blackboard in the basement of stats guru Bill James or some other math junkie. I myself prefer my baseball with the imagination left in, thank you very much. This collection of deft stories by Robert Weintraub takes us back to the bleachers and locker rooms, to the people who actually play and watch the game. Very nice. Very nice, indeed."

—Leigh Montville, *New York Times* bestselling author of *The Big Bam: The Life and Times of Babe Ruth* and *Ted Williams: The Biography of an American Hero*

"The world might have had its fill of good stories 'about' baseball, but I'm not sure it has had any that are 'like' baseball, until now. Bob Weintraub's sly, slippery tales carry within them something of baseball's very own cockeyed relationship to reality—the real game within a reality of artifice. They also convey, in a singular, accessible language, those acts of grace, coincidence, and improbably heroics that keep America tethered to its pastime. These stories are as faithful to the spirit of a ballgame as a box score, yet with all the color of a yarn told in a clubhouse during a rain delay."

—Michael Coffey, author of *27 Men Out: Baseball's Perfect Games*

"Like lots of good stories set in baseball, the entries in *Painting the Corners Again* are less about baseball than they are about people and the curveballs they throw each other. Of at least one of the stories, O. Henry would have been proud."

—Bill Littlefield, host of NPR and WBUR's *Only a Game*

Other Books by Bob Weintraub

Best Wishes, Harry Greenfeld (2002)
My Honorable Brother (2014)
Painting the Corners (2014, 2017)

Painting the Corners Again

A Collection of Off-Center Baseball Fiction

BOB WEINTRAUB

Skyhorse Publishing

Skyhorse Publishing books may be purchased in bulk at special discounts for sales promotion, corporate gifts, fund-raising, or educational purposes. Special editions can also be created to specifications. For details, contact the Special Sales Department, Skyhorse Publishing, 307 West 36th Street, 11th Floor, New York, NY 10018 or info@skyhorsepublishing.com.

Skyhorse® and Skyhorse Publishing® are registered trademarks of Skyhorse Publishing, Inc.®, a Delaware corporation.

Visit our website at www.skyhorsepublishing.com.

10 9 8 7 6 5 4 3 2 1

Library of Congress Cataloging-in-Publication Data is available on file.

Cover design by Tom Lau
Cover photo credit: iStock.com/CSA-Archive

Print ISBN: 978-1-5107-2533-1
Ebook ISBN: 978-1-5107-2535-5

Printed in the United States of America

DEDICATION

I dedicate this book to the game of baseball, our national pastime, that binds one generation to both the next generation and the one after that. Baseball gives the Dad a sense of pride and joy, and his young son a memory to cherish for life when they go together to the boy's first major league game at the local stadium. It introduces the child to that marvelous habit of checking the box scores each day to see how his heroes performed the day before, and then learning how to keep score of a game himself. By then he is anxious to be taught the basics of the sport in Little League or just hang out at the nearby ballpark, and gains confidence as he spends those long summer days hitting and fielding the baseball with his pals from just after breakfast to just before sundown. It gives the young man who has practiced hard and often the chance to be a teammate (and perhaps even a hero) in high school and college, learning about loyalty, grit, and determination, while Dad takes an afternoon off whenever he can to sit in the stands, root for his son and hope the game gives him a reason to shout, "That's my boy!" Soon enough that same young adult, the New Dad, will be taking his own son to *his* first game and setting the process in motion again. Dad (now Grandpa) will hardly be able to wait until that grandson is old enough to wear the mitt that *he* wore as an adult, including his midlife switch to softball. But before finding a place for it on a closet shelf, he'll rub it down with neats-foot oil and tie a baseball snugly into its pocket. If he's nimble enough, Grandpa will take the boy aside, even in the living room, to show him how certain plays should be made and, of course, how to hold the bat to lay down a successful bunt. And all too quickly, the little boy who on that beautiful day was brought to the big league ballpark by his Dad will be taking his "old man" to a game now and then while the opportunity is still there. They'll talk baseball for a few hours, enjoy the hot dogs and beer, reminisce about the games and players they remember best and love every minute of their time together.

CONTENTS

A Dog Day in Dyersville • 1

The Right Pitch for Cuba • 27

Matters of Principle • 37

Just One to Go • 53

Wives and Lovers • 61

When the Spirit Moves You • 87

Bobby and Me • 103

A Corner for Love • 119

Little League Home Run • 129

All in the Family • 145

Hot Corner Blues • 195

Trade-Off • 201

Her Beauty Was Just Skin Deep • 209

Catch Me, Catch Me • 225

A DOG DAY IN DYERSVILLE

"The other day they asked me about mandatory drug testing. I said I believed in drug testing a long time ago. All through the sixties I tested everything."

—Bill Lee

IT WAS DURING the cab ride to the airport Sunday evening that Albie Knox first told his wife about his plans for Wednesday, the last day of baseball's three-day Major League All-Star Game break.

"We can sleep late tomorrow morning, and then I'm due at the ballpark by one o'clock. They'll have a bus to take all us American League players there. There's two hours scheduled for pictures and interviews, and then each team has an hour for batting practice. All the wives and girlfriends are supposed to be at the park at the same time for the lunch they're throwing you. They may have another bus to take you there, but you'll find out for sure tomorrow morning. And after lunch you're getting a tour of a couple of museums in the city."

"Sounds good," she said.

"Yeah," he answered. "Anyway, the players will eat dinner in the clubhouse because everyone's supposed to stick around for the home run hitting contest. That starts at seven and goes about two hours. The whole thing's on TV. So I don't expect to get back to the hotel until about eleven. You don't have to stay for the contest, honey. I know you'll root for me wherever you are, and watching it is boring as hell. Go back to the hotel and have dinner in that new restaurant you read to me about."

"Casa Roberto," she said.

"Yeah, that's it," he said, "and the game starts Tuesday night at eight, so I'm guessing we'll have to be in uniform by four. I'll rest up in the room until it's time to go, and you can take a taxi over to Comiskey whenever you want. Just don't start out too late because there'll be a lot of traffic in that direction and you'll owe the driver a fortune if the highway turns into a parking lot." He turned toward the window and took a deep breath. "Then Wednesday we'll take a morning flight to Dubuque, Iowa and . . ."

She cut him off. "What are you talking about? I've told you a hundred times I'm going shopping along the Miracle Mile on Wednesday. It's my only chance before I go home Thursday. What in the world is in Dubuque?"

"It's not what's in Dubuque, hon. We've got to rent a car there and drive to a town called Dyersville. That's where the Field of Dreams is."

"The Field of Dreams? Do you mean that baseball movie a few years ago, the one with what's his name?" She closed her eyes for a few seconds. "With Kevin Costner?"

"Yeah. I've watched it in the clubhouse three or four more times and I want to go there. I want to see my father."

"Albie, you can't be serious. That's just a nice story someone wrote. Those players aren't real. That's just the movies. They can do anything like that."

Albie turned toward his wife, his arms moving up and down as he spoke. "I know it was a movie but I believe it. You can make things happen if you want them bad enough. I'm sure I can see my father and talk to him. He was a great minor league player, and a couple of the guys told me they heard the minor leaguers come to that field and play an all-star game the day after the major league one. I've got so much I want to say to him."

Nothing was said as they stared at each other for several seconds, she in disbelief, he in searching for something more to tell her to advance his proposal. "Besides, honey," he continued, "you can shop during the day on Tuesday while I'm at the park, or you can change your ticket and go back on Friday."

Gloria Knox knew her husband well enough to realize the die had been cast. One of the things she loved most about him was his ability to express his emotions on things that mattered to him and to her also. She had learned to live with the fact that some of what he said or did in response to those emotions was unreasonable or incredible.

"Okay Albie, we'll go there on Wednesday. And I'll leave it to you to get me a nonstop flight home on Friday."

Albie leaned closer to his wife, waited for her to look at him again and brushed a kiss across her lips. "Tuesday night in the game I'm going to hit one out for my father," he said, then took her hand and held it until they reached the airport.

Their flight to Dubuque didn't leave O'Hare until 10:45 a.m. on Wednesday morning. That gave Albie ample time in the Continental Airlines lounge to read what several columnists had to say about the All-Star game played the night before and about his own heroics. Voted into the starting lineup in the outfield, he was in the game long enough to have three at bats. In order, Albie flied out to left field, forcing the outfielder to retreat to within several feet of the wall to make the catch; hit a line drive bullet off the center field wall that reached its destination so fast he had to hold up at first with a single; and then drove a ball to left, officially measured as travelling 432 feet, that the left fielder simply watched all the way without taking a single step toward the outfield fence. The home run drove in two runs in a game in which the American League was eventually victorious by one. Albie finished second in the voting as the game's most valuable player, that honor bestowed on the team's shortstop who had three singles, including the hit that drove in the winning run. But he was satisfied that the power he showed at the plate made up for the fact that he finished a disappointing sixth out of the eight players chosen to participate in the home run hitting contest two nights earlier. Albie felt that the pitcher throwing to him, a last minute substitute for the one he'd chosen but who had taken ill suddenly, put too few balls in his power zone, cutting down the number of chances he had to put the fat part of the bat on the baseball.

He and Gloria rented a car in Dubuque and drove the twenty-five miles into Dyersville, home of the Field of Dreams, stopping on the way for lunch at Bellevue's Castle. Albie thought it was a good sign that the Inn and Restaurant dated back to 1893, exactly one hundred years earlier.

"What's in that gym bag you brought?" she asked.

"My uniform shirt and cap," he answered. "I'm going to put them on. I want my Dad to see I'm a major league player. And I've got my glove so he and I can play catch while we're talking."

"Well just don't feel too bad if you don't see him or any other players out there."

"I'm going to see him, honey. I'm sure of it."

It was one thirty in the afternoon when they arrived at the Field of Dreams. Only one other car was in the parking lot, and as they walked toward the field Albie saw a man and woman sitting in the bleachers along the first base line. He was surprised that the bleachers behind third base that he remembered seeing in the movie were no longer there. A sign on the walkway notified visitors that the farmhouse adjacent to the field was privately owned and not part of the attraction.

"That's too bad," Albie said. "I wanted to see what the whole scene looked like from the porch over there, from higher up."

"At least you've got all that corn growing out there," Gloria said. "I thought this time of year it might only be about a foot high. It looks beautiful from here."

A small building, below the level of the farmhouse and painted red on the outside, bore a "Souvenirs" sign on the door. "Let's go in here, hon," Albie said. "Maybe they've got a picture of my father I can buy."

It was a small shop, hardly satisfying with its lack of variety. Albie had no interest in looking at the jackets, caps, and bats that took up most of the space. The woman behind the cash register informed him that the only baseball cards they had on hand were ones for Shoeless Joe Jackson and Moonlight Graham. "They're the only ones people are interested in," she said. She confessed that she didn't know the names of any other players shown in the movie, and was unaware of any occasion, in the three years she'd been employed there, on which any visitors claimed to see ballplayers on the field. Gloria looked at her husband, expecting to see disappointment written on his face, but he smiled at the clerk and told her there was always a first time for everything. He purchased two dozen baseball cards, intending to give one to each of his Orioles teammates, and they left the shop.

"Come on," he said, "let's take a seat in the bleachers."

The older couple Albie had seen earlier were still the only ones there, seated in the top row, just five rows up from the ground. He and Gloria made their way up to the same level and exchanged greetings with them.

Who'd you come to see?" Albie asked the man, smiling at him.

"I don't really expect to see anyone, but I keep hoping whenever we come here. If I had my choice, it would be Ty Cobb, Lou Gehrig, and the Babe, of course. Saw them all play when I was younger. That was in the twenties and thirties, a little before your time." He took off his cap and showed it to Albie. "The 'W' on there's for Washington.

My dad bought this for me for less than two bucks the day we saw Walter Johnson outpitch Lefty Grove. If I could choose a pitching match today, it would be Satchel Paige against Warren Spahn, but Spahn's still breathing so I'll go with Lefty Grove. How about you, come to see anyone?"

"Yeah, my dad. He was a hell of a minor-league ballplayer, but never made it to the majors. I've seen him come out of that cornfield a few times in my dreams and I'm sure it's going to happen today. They're supposed to be playing a minor-league all-star game this afternoon."

The man seemed slightly confused as he looked at Albie. "I didn't know they were putting out schedules for this," he replied, but he was curious about what Albie had said and didn't wait for a response.

"What was your father's name?"

"Arthur Knox. He was in the Milwaukee Braves system, a third baseman, damn good fielder but a light hitter. His last three years were in Triple-A with the Louisville Colonels, but he wasn't going anywhere with Eddie Mathews at third for the Braves."

"I don't recall the name," the old man said. "But Knox, are you Albie Knox from the Orioles?"

"I guess I am," he answered. He turned the other way to look at Gloria and wink, happy to be recognized.

"Well, I saw you on TV last night hit that ball out of the park. Four hundred something feet, the announcer said. The Babe would have been proud of you on that one."

"Yeah, I caught it real good. I was guessing slow curve and that's what he threw me. Last time I saw him he fanned me on the same pitch." Albie opened the duffel bag, took out the uniform shirt and cap and put them on.

"Well, I think we ought to introduce ourselves. I'm Preston Hollander and this is my wife, Daisy. We're from St. Joe, Michigan, right on the lake."

"And this is Gloria," Albie said.

The two men shook hands, and the women, who were in the bookend positions, smiled and waved at each other.

"How many times have you been here?" Albie asked.

"This is our third, and it will be the last if nothing happens today."

"How come you came back again?" Gloria asked.

"To give it one good chance," Hollander said. "The first time we stopped at a couple of places along the way and got here to the field late in the afternoon, when the sun was starting to set. There was no one on the field when we reached the bleachers, but I could see some of the corn stalks moving in just one place out there, where left center field is, where they went in and out from in the movie, and I figured we had just missed seeing them. There was no wind at all that day, so there was no other reason for that corn to be swaying like it was. And you know, it stopped after just a few seconds. Daisy saw it too, although she doesn't believe in any of this."

"I told Preston I thought I saw it, but that I wasn't sure," Daisy said, looking directly at Gloria, as if needing to find a way out of being included in her husband's certainty.

"The second time," Hollander continued, "we'd only been sitting here about half an hour on a beautiful day for baseball when two buses showed up, full of kids with their own bats and balls who took over the whole field. We waited a while, but they looked like they weren't going anywhere soon, so we left. I knew the players wouldn't come out if they couldn't have the field for themselves. So I'm hoping we picked the right day today. If not, that's it, and no regrets. Tomorrow we'll be on our way to see our kids in Kansas City."

By four o'clock the two men had already discussed, and lightly argued at times about the pennant race in the American League and the sad status of Albie's Orioles. Both agreed that Toronto would maintain its lead over the Yankees, but disagreed as to whether the Blue Jays or the Western Division leading White Sox would advance to the World Series. Albie acknowledged that the Orioles were going nowhere, but refused to point out faults of any of his teammates.

"I'm telling you, Preston," he said, "we've got a good nucleus on the club with Ripken, Buford, Brady Anderson, and Mike Mussina. We can do a lot better next year if we pick up a couple of good free agents. Look at what Molitor has done for Toronto."

As they spoke, they seemed to take turns glancing out at the outfield to check on whether any players were emerging from the cornfield onto the baseball diamond.

"It's cooled off a little," Hollander said, "more comfortable for playing out there. It was too humid before."

"You're right," Albie answered. "I wouldn't mind being out there myself right now."

Daisy and Gloria had moved away from their husbands to the other end of the row. In anticipation of what she was sure lay ahead that afternoon, Daisy brought her knitting with her and worked easily on lengthening a scarf she was making while talking to Gloria. From time to time there were other visitors to the Field of Dreams who walked over to view the site for a short time and then departed. Some stopped at the souvenir shop on their way out while others were more anxious to get on their way.

"The girls are coming back," Albie said, as Gloria and Daisy moved down the row toward them.

"Preston, how long do you intend to sit and wait for something to happen?" Daisy asked. "Gloria and I are thinking of going into town for some iced tea."

Hollander was slow to reply, and looked at Albie.

"I'm staying until six," Albie said. "I'll keep Preston company at least until then. They're not going to want to start a game after that. So you gals go on and enjoy yourselves. Here's the car keys, honey. You do the driving."

The two men got up to stretch and walked up and down the row several times until they saw Albie's rental car leave the parking lot and drive off. They were the only tourists remaining. When they sat down again, Hollander told Albie that the longest home run he'd ever personally seen was hit by Frank Thomas.

"Daisy and I were in Boston for a weekend last year at a family thing and I got tickets to a Red Sox game on Saturday afternoon. Well, when Thomas hit that ball out over left field, it looked like it could have cleared two Fenway Parks if one was right behind the other. I saw it from the first base stands and I couldn't believe how high up in the air it was when it went out of there. It was almost like a rocket."

Albie shook his head in agreement without saying anything, and Hollander continued. "There seems to be a lot of home runs being hit these days, and plenty of them a long ways. I guess it's the baseballs. I've read where the company turning them out can do something with the rubber or whatever it is inside the balls to make them more lively. Even sewing the stitches tighter helps it go further, they say."

"That's right, I guess," Albie said. He looked down at his feet as he spoke. "I've heard players say the same thing."

"Some folks believe the commissioner ordered them to do it because that's what the fans want to see. It pushes up the attendance and that makes the owners happy." Hollander waited for Albie to answer or to dispute what he had said, but when he didn't, Hollander continued. "Me personally, I can't say I go for all those home runs and the high scoring games. I'd much rather see two pitchers going at it, with a lot more suspense. I like it best when every pitch could decide who wins." Albie's continued silence and the fact that he still had his head bowed, as if eyeing something on the ground below the bleachers, irritated the older man. He felt strongly about the opinion he had offered and thought he was being ignored. "Well, *you* play the game," he said, indicating he expected an answer. "Do you agree with me, or how do you feel?"

Albie raised his head, and almost in the same motion jumped to his feet, pointing to the field. "They're coming," he said. "Look out there, Preston. The players are coming out of the cornfield."

"Yes, they are," Hollander shouted. "Holy cripes, they really *do* come here to play. There's about thirty of them out there. Look at those different uniforms they've got on. Must be the ones they wore for their last minor-league clubs."

As they watched, the players split into two teams. Half of them gathered on the third base side of the field, in foul territory, about twenty feet off the base line. Nine of the others took up the defensive positions on the field, leaving a handful to sit between the first base foul line and the bleachers. The pitcher on the mound began warming up, using a flick of his wrist to signal the catcher what the next pitch would be.

"Albie, I thought you said this was all minor leaguers. That's Lefty Grove out there. I saw that big Philadelphia "A" on his shirt and then recognized his delivery. Watch him kick that left leg up in the air. You're looking at a guy who won 300 games in his career and 31 in one season. They used to say all he had was a fast ball and everyone knew it was coming, but no one could hit it. I know for a fact he pitched over 250 innings in 11 seasons out of 12. Back then they weren't counting on having eighth inning set-up guys and ninth inning closers." Hollander turned to look at his new friend. "Did you find your father out there yet? I want to see him as soon as you spot him."

Grove struck out two hitters and retired the side on eight pitches in six minutes. When the other side took the field, Hollander had another surprise thrown at him. He wasn't certain at first as he watched the pitcher get loose. "Do you know who I think is out there now, Albie? If it's him, you're looking at maybe the greatest pitcher of his time, white or black. I know he was over forty years old before they let him play in the majors. And he wouldn't have gotten in if the Dodgers didn't sign Jackie Robinson first." Hollander turned to look back at the field. Several seconds later his excitement burst forth again. "It *is,* Albie, it's Satchel Paige. The two pitchers I wanted to see, and they're both here today. It's like someone knew what I wanted and my wish was granted. If anyone else told me this happened to them, I never would've believed it." Still watching the field, he said, "These minor-league guys will be lucky to get a hit off either pitcher."

Hollander suddenly remembered why Albie was there and saw that he looked distressed. "What's the matter, can't you find him?" he asked.

"No, he's not out there. If he was, he'd be playing third. And he's not one of the guys waiting to hit."

While they spoke, Paige matched Grove's efficiency, disposing of the three batters he faced in six minutes also.

"Well, if he was as good as you say, he'd be playing. So chances are it's the same as with some of the major-league all-stars. He probably got picked for the team and then got hurt or sick and had to pull out. That's what I think, Albie, and maybe you can find out for sure when the game's over."

There was no scoring by either team in the first six innings, and luck had allowed each one hit off the opposing pitcher. In the seventh, the last inning they would play, Grove's thirteenth strikeout victim reached first base on a passed ball by the catcher. A sacrifice bunt moved him to second and he advanced to third on a ground ball out. Grove seemingly got out of the inning with yet another strikeout, but his catcher mishandled the ball again, allowing it to roll far enough away for the speedy runner on third to cross the plate safely. His team now needed a run in the last half of the inning to avoid defeat. Although Hollander was secretly hoping that Paige would repeat his legendary feat of intentionally walking the first three batters to load the bases and then striking out the three that followed, Paige shortcut that route and fanned the first three men he faced.

As soon as the last out was recorded, the players all began a slow walk back toward the cornfield, signaling to their two spectators in the first base bleachers that the game was over.

"Go on, Albie," Hollander said. "You can catch up with one or two of those guys."

Albie quickly made his way down from the bleachers and jogged out past the infield until he crossed paths with one of the players heading toward the cornfield from the third base side.

"Hey," the player said, waving an arm in Albie's direction.

"Hey," he answered, and began walking beside him. "Can I ask you about someone? I expected to see him in the game today, but he wasn't there."

"Sure, go ahead," the player said. "I saw you sitting there the whole game and figured you might be looking for someone. You're an Orioles fan, huh."

"I play outfield for them. My name's Albie Knox."

"Oh, then you're Arthur's son."

"Yes, I am. You know him?"

"Of course I do. We all know each other." He smiled at Albie. "How did you like the game?"

"I loved it. The guy sitting with me couldn't believe it. Grove and Paige were the two pitchers he wanted to see the most."

"Yeah, we knew that. And they didn't mind coming out and pitching to us minor leaguers."

"So can you tell me why my dad wasn't out here today?"

"Yeah, I can, but you ought to talk to him. See that spot where the guys are walking into the cornfield? It looks like I'll be the last one in. Just wait a few minutes after that and then call your dad. He'll hear you."

"That's great. Thanks a lot. Hey, I'm sorry, I didn't ask your name."

"It's Jocko Kantor. I caught for the Durham Bulls a couple years. I saw your old man play a bunch of games. He was as slick a third baseman as they come."

When they reached the edge of the cornfield, Kantor stopped and turned to Albie. "Good luck," he said. "I hope things work out for you." He turned quickly, stepped between several stalks of corn and disappeared.

As Albie and Kantor approached the cornfield, Gloria and Daisy returned to the bleachers.

"Where's Albie?" Gloria asked as they reached the top row where Preston was standing. "Looking for a bathroom?"

"No, there he is in the outfield, walking with that ballplayer. He wants to ask about his father."

"I see Albie," Gloria said, "but he's alone. There's no one with him."

"Of course there is," Hollander answered. "The guy has on an orange shirt and a blue cap, and he's carrying a catcher's mask in his hand."

"Preston, you've had too much sun today," Daisy said. "Gloria's right. He's out there all alone."

Hollander knew *he* was right, but now was beginning to understand what was going on. He and Albie could see the players because they *wanted* to see them and believed they *could.* The women didn't care at all. They were just patronizing their husbands, letting them have their fun. The players and the game meant nothing to them, so they saw nothing and wouldn't believe anything they were told. He realized there was no sense filling Daisy in about everything that took place in her absence, or she might think he was beginning to show signs of senility. When he looked out again, Albie was standing alone at the edge of the cornfield.

It felt strange to Albie to be calling his father by his full name. "Arthur Knox, Arthur Knox, it's Albie, your son. I want to see you and talk to you. Dad, Arthur Knox, please come out."

"I hear you, Albie, but I can't come out. I'm not allowed on the playing field or even where you can see me."

Albie heard the familiar high pitch of his father's voice and felt closer to him immediately. In his mind's eye he saw images of his father talking to him from across the dinner table and coaching him on the baseball field that was located just a block from their home.

"Why not?" he asked.

"Because of you, because of the way you've disgraced baseball. The players here know about it and they're taking it out on me."

"What do you mean?"

"You know darn well what I mean. You take steroids to help you play better. You're willing to cheat to hit home runs and pad your statistics so you can make more money. Everyone here played the game honestly, even though they knew steroids would help them get out of Triple-A and up to the big leagues. All their lives they dreamed of making it to the majors, me included, but no one here would shame themselves like you've done to get there. When a hitter suddenly goes from fifteen home runs a year to 45, there's no secret what he's up to. And the players here are taking it out on me because they figure I didn't teach you how to respect the game."

"But you had nothing to do with it. You never encouraged me to cheat." Albie realized in that moment that he was openly confessing to cheating for the first time.

"You and I know that, but that's not going to change their minds. The only chance we have of being together and my getting back into the all-star games is for you to stop taking the stuff. Can you do that or are those home runs and the money more important to you?"

Albie's emotions took over. "Of course I can stop. I want to see you. I want to sit down and talk to you about a lot of things. I can't wait to throw a ball around with you. I'll stop the stuff, I promise. You're going to play in that next all-star game, Dad, you can count on it. And I'll be here to watch."

"Thanks, Albie. I was sure you'd give it up as soon as I spoke to you about it. I'll let everyone here know."

"Tell them I apologize for what I did. I let the pressure get to me because my contract's up this year and I wanted to make as much as I could in the next one."

"Okay, Albie, I understand, but now you know it was a mistake. Listen, I've got to get back, but I feel terrific because I know I'll be seeing you soon. Goodbye, son."

"Goodbye, Dad."

On the drive back to the airport Albie told Gloria everything that happened that afternoon. She listened to all of it without interrupting once to ask a question. Her feeling was that if it made him happy to invent that kind of story or to be imagining those things, there was no reason for her to dispute it and risk starting an argument over it. As they neared the airport, however, she couldn't resist letting Albie know that during the time they waited in the bleachers while he walked to the edge of the cornfield, and even while he made his way back to them, Preston never said a word about there having been a ballgame played on the field.

"Surely he would have said something to Daisy if what you say was so. After all, she came here with him three times because he was so sure he'd see some players on the field. If he did, I don't think he could have kept it to himself." After a short pause, Gloria added, "Preston did point to you in the outfield and tell us you were walking with a baseball player who wore an orange shirt, but both Daisy and I could see you were alone. Anyway, Albie, I wasn't aware you were taking steroids. Is that dangerous?"

"It doesn't matter. I feel fine. The stuff's in Baltimore and I'll get rid of it as soon as I get back."

Gloria was satisfied. "I can hardly wait to shop that miracle mile tomorrow," she said.

On July 17th, an article in the sports section of the *Baltimore Sun* indicated that Albie Knox, whose contract expired at the end of the season, had made up his mind to test the free agent market. The information was attributed to Knox's agent who was successful each year in negotiating the most lucrative contracts for his clients. The team owner pleaded poverty to the media consistently whenever he was questioned about any player signings, but always concluded his reply with the pledge that "We'll do everything we can to keep him an Oriole." In this case, he knew already that Knox's demands would be more than he'd be willing to pay.

A week later, an hour before the start of the rubber game between the Orioles and the Mariners in Seattle, Albie was called into the manager's office and told he'd been traded to the San Diego Padres.

"The GM said he spoke to your agent and there's no way the club can match what he says you'll be looking for in free agency. The Padres think they have a decent chance to make it into the playoffs, but need a hitter like you in the middle of the lineup to drive in some runs and help win the close ones. They're giving us a frontline pitcher in Hal Rodgers and a couple of good prospects in Double-A, so it looks like a good deal for both clubs. They want you to report right away, Albie, so you probably ought to say your farewells to the guys now and catch a flight down the coast. I'll miss you and I'm damn glad we won't have to pitch to you ourselves." The two men shook hands and fell into a mutual hug.

That night, after arriving at his hotel in San Diego, Albie phoned Gloria and told her about the trade. Later on, as he was enjoying a room service dinner, he had an unexpected visit from the Padres general manager who welcomed him to the city and the team.

"We gave up a lot to get you, Albie, but we expect it to be well worth it. We've given our fans an exciting season so far—something they're not used to—and we want to make it a memorable one by getting into the playoffs. Our pitching is as good as anyone else in the division—that's why we could send Rodgers to the Orioles—and it's what has carried us to this point. We're only five games out of first with plenty of time to catch up, and we've still got ten games left with the Dodgers. They beat us six of the first eight we played them, but we didn't drop a single one by more than two runs. A long ball at the right time here or there and the results would have been reversed. That's where you come in, Albie. You're on a pace for 45 to 50 home runs, the same as last year, and that's what's going to win ballgames for us. I never interfere with what the manager does, so it's up to Glenn where you'll hit in the order, but you'll *hit* and that's why we brought you here."

When the GM left, Albie wanted to call Gloria again in Baltimore and talk about his "problem," but realized that with the time difference between the two coasts she'd be asleep. He had promised to stop taking steroids, but now his new team was counting on his hitting ability and had paid dearly to get it. How could he let them down? The bottle, still half full, that he had picked up in Baltimore after the All-Star game, was in his suitcase. Albie reasoned that the next all-star game for his father was a year away and that he could postpone acting on his pledge until the current season was over. But he vowed that he would go into spring training and the next campaign free of steroids, certain that his father's community of ballplayers would know it.

In his first three weeks with the Padres, Albie hit six home runs, one a grand slam, and the team won thirteen of its nineteen games. Three of the early victories were a momentum-building sweep of the Giants in Candlestick Park. On the team's next day off, he had a call from his agent who informed him that the Padres wanted to extend his contract.

"I proposed a three-year deal for a total of twenty-one million," he said, "but they don't want to go beyond two. That's okay, Albie, because they're willing to pay sixteen million for the two years instead of the fourteen you'd get in the first two years of a three-year deal. And you'll probably end up better off when it comes time for your next contract. I don't think you'd do any better in free agency because word has it that the owners aren't going to be throwing a lot of money around this fall. And remember that it's all guaranteed as soon as you sign the extension. Without it, if you got hurt between now and the end of the season, you might have trouble getting a good offer."

All Albie could say was that it sounded good but that he wanted a couple of days to think about it.

"How can I agree to it?" he asked Gloria on the telephone. "That's eight million dollars a year. When I stop taking those vitamins I told you about, my hitting could go back to what it was two years ago. If it does, I won't be giving the ballclub what they're paying me for. Fifty home runs may become fifteen again, and that'll mean half as many RBI's, or even less. The fans will be booing every time I leave men on base, and blaming me and my fat contract for every close game we lose. What should I do, Gloria?"

There was no hesitation on Gloria's part. She was too practical to allow her husband to let the opportunity he was being given get away.

And if that meant acknowledging his belief that he could watch a game between old-time ballplayers at the Field of Dreams, she was up to it.

"Listen to me, Albie," she said. "So far, your father has missed playing in only one all-star game. If you extend the contract, he'll miss just two more. But he's always going to be with those players, so not getting into three of those games is nothing. I'm sure he'd want you to take advantage of this and get us financial security, especially now that we know I'm pregnant. You've got to listen to your agent, Albie, and do it."

Albie Knox took Gloria's advice and gave the Padres everything they hoped for and more. From the time he joined them in the last week of July through the final week of September, his hitting kept them in the race. And when the Padres beat Colorado at home on the last day of the season, while the Dodgers blew a lead in the ninth inning to lose to the Giants, the two teams tied for first in the division. The joy of Padres' fans lasted less than twenty-four hours, however, when the team, hosted by the Dodgers the next day in Chavez Ravine, saw its pitching fall apart in an 11–6 drubbing.

In the 1994 pennant race, in which Albie reached his peak of 53 home runs and 141 runs batted in, the Padres won the division but encountered disappointment again when they were knocked out of the playoffs in the final game of the first round by the Atlanta Braves. The mood in the losers' clubhouse was somber until Albie called for silence and then shouted, "Next year we're going to the World Series." He was certain the next year would be his last, and his goal was to be a member of a world champion team before his playing days were over. "We'll get 'em next year" were the words of encouragement that filled the room after Albie spoke.

And "get 'em" in '95 they did. The Padres ran away with the division, swept the Mets in the first round and beat Cincinnati in the next, four games to two, to capture the National League pennant. They were in the World Series, ready to challenge the reigning world champion

Minnesota Twins. Albie had batted just .250 against the Mets, with no home runs, flying out to the deepest parts of Shea Stadium on several, occasions, but came back to hit .381 against the Reds and be recognized as the MVP of the series.

The Twins won the first two games played in Minneapolis, and Game Four, in San Diego, pushing the Padres to the brink of elimination. In Game Five, Albie batted with two outs in the tenth inning and hit a walk-off home run to send the Series back to the Metrodome. The team carried the momentum into Game Six and squeezed out a 6–5 win thanks to a two-run double by Albie in the seventh inning and the performance of its closer who pitched the last two innings without allowing a Twins hitter to reach base.

Albie saw the final game of the Series as his swan song in baseball because he continued to doubt his ability to produce what was expected of him without his use of steroids. For a reason never adequately explained when it happens, especially in a situation where adrenalin is supposed to take over and push the athletes to greater accomplishments, Albie and the Padres came out flat for Game Seven. They fell behind early by four runs and never caught up, losing 9–4. During the quiet flight back to San Diego, Albie made it a point, without mentioning what he saw as his impending departure from baseball, to try and make his teammates see what a successful season they had.

During July and August the Padres had made overtures to Albie's agent about a new extension of his contract. In each case, although the agent boasted that the deal he could finalize would make him one of the highest paid players in baseball, Albie put off any discussion of it. He insisted that he wanted to concentrate on playing without losing his focus in any negotiations. When the season ended, and Albie became a free agent, the Padres quickly put a proposal for a new three-year contract on the table. It was an offer they felt their star right fielder wouldn't refuse.

"I'm not going to sign a new contract, Gloria," he told his wife as they dined in a restaurant overlooking the city of San Diego. "I don't have any of that stuff left and I'm not buying any more. I went along with what you said two years ago, but not now. I want to see my father play in that all-star game with the other ballplayers and there's so many things I want to talk to him about. What I've got to do now is let the team know I'm not coming back next season."

Gloria had been preparing herself for this conversation with her husband. She paid rapt attention to him as he spoke, and took her time, when he finished, before replying.

"Albie, this is one of the most important decisions of your life, and we're going to do what you say," she began, "but first tell me, do you think ten million dollars is a lot of money?"

"Of course it is, but I'm not going to take it under false pretenses."

"That's because you think you'll be a lousy hitter without the steroids."

"That's right."

"But you can't be certain until some pitcher is throwing the ball and you're trying to hit it."

"Look, Gloria, the year before I went on steroids I hit thirteen home runs and batted about .260. I had just 57 homers in my first five years with the Orioles. If they were a better team, they wouldn't have kept me around. And I was younger then than I am now."

"But you're more experienced now."

"Just tell me your point."

"Albie, we've got the twins and I'm due again in April. It would be wise for us to have you play another year and get us the additional financial security."

"I told you I'm through with the steroids. I'm not changing my mind on that."

Gloria realized she had to make her position clear to Albie. *"I don't want you to.* I just want you to play next year and do the best you can. If you can't hit and want to leave the team, I won't try to stop you. But if your experience helps you, you can earn a wonderful salary and still get to see your father in July."

Albie stared at his wife, thinking about what she had said.

Gloria broke the silence, recognizing she had Albie on the ropes. "Tell the Padres you only want a one-year contract. When that gets announced and the media starts asking 'Why?' you can say you've been thinking of retiring—after all, you're thirty-six—and want to take it one year at a time. Then, if you're not hitting home runs and think you're hurting the team, you can retire and it won't be such a shock to everyone."

"What reason would I give for retiring?"

"What did you plan to say if you quit now?"

Albie thought for a few seconds. "I'd say my goal was always to play in a World Series, and now I want to stay home and be a family man."

"You can say the same thing later, and in the meantime you'll be getting paid." Gloria sensed that it was time to make the sale. "We can always use the money, Albie. Who's to say we won't have four children or even five?"

In the fourth week of spring training, Albie fractured his ankle on a late slide into second base. At the time he was batting just under .300 in the five games he had played, and had one home run and a long double to his credit. The injury kept him in rehab in Arizona when the Padres opened their season, and his recovery, including several games with their minor-league affiliate there, wasn't complete until the last week of May. When he took his place in right field, batting fifth in the lineup instead of his customary third ("Just 'til we're sure you've got your swing back," he was told), he was surprised to find himself with a hot bat. He hit three home runs in his first thirty trips to the plate, maintained an average in the .260 to .280 range, and had twelve home runs at the break for the All-Star game. Albie was proud of the fact that the fans voted him onto the team for what he had accomplished in the two prior seasons. He declined to participate, however, offering a flimsy excuse about resting his ankle. In fact, it was because the game was being played in Tampa Bay on Tuesday night and he was afraid of not being able to make the necessary flight connections to get him to the Field of Dreams by Wednesday afternoon.

Gloria didn't want to make the trip to Dyersville and attend the minor-league all-star game that Albie had been talking about for weeks. She envisioned the boredom of sitting in the bleachers for hours, knowing that nothing would be taking place on the field, and ultimately witnessing her husband's disappointment at not seeing his father. Still, she knew the sacrifice he had made for his father in giving up steroids, and his willingness to agree to play for the Padres another year, at her request, despite his own reluctance to do so. Of course, as Albie would have to admit, it had worked out well and he had received a paycheck every two weeks while not having to suffer any embarrassment over his performance thus far.

So she arranged for her regular nanny to stay with the twins while she and Albie flew from San Diego to Dubuque on Tuesday, rented a 1996 Mercedes convertible there on Wednesday and headed toward the Field of Dreams. Gloria was pleasantly surprised when Albie offered to drop her at Bellevue's Castle and pick her up later, after the game and his meeting with his father. She had brought a book with her, and would be able to relax in the comfort of the hotel, with an iced tea available to her whenever she wished. She protested at first, not sure if that's what he really wanted, but was happy when he insisted upon it.

Albie joined about eight others in the bleachers and watched the continuing parade of tourists coming and leaving as the afternoon wore on. Several stopped where he was sitting, wearing his Padres shirt and cap, and asked kiddingly whether he brought the baseball glove he was holding because he hoped to catch some hitter's foul ball. He was pleased this time that no one recognized him and that he didn't have to sign any autographs.

Only minutes after the last two visitors climbed down from the bleachers, saying nothing to Albie on the way, and drove out of the parking lot, the ballplayers came jogging out of the cornfield. Most of them paired off and began playing catch in the outfield and along the baselines. Albie thought he saw his father when he spotted the number "14," his father's number, on what he thought was a Louisville shirt, but it turned out to be a Nashville uniform. After warming up for about ten minutes, one group of players took their defensive positions on the field and the game began.

Albie couldn't understand why his father wasn't among the twenty-six players he counted on the field. But his concern was relieved somewhat when he saw a handful of players come onto the field after the third inning, replacing the same number who returned to the cornfield. Additional replacements emerged after the fourth inning, and more after the sixth, but Arthur Knox was not among them. One last group of players came running out just before the eighth inning began, causing Albie's disappointment to reach its zenith when his father wasn't there.

The game itself held no interest for Albie, but near the end he saw that Jocko Kantor was again behind the plate for the team in the lead. When the final out was made, Albie caught up with Kantor as he headed for the cornfield.

"You're Arthur's son, aren't you?" Kantor said as soon as Albie fell in stride with him.

"Yes, I am. Albie Knox. And you're Jocko Kantor."

"I remember you from when you were here before. It was three years ago."

"You're right, and you told me how I could get my dad to talk to me that day, and he did. I was sure I'd see him today, but he never came out, and there must have been almost fifty different players on the field at one time or another. Why didn't he play?"

"I think I can answer that," Kantor said, "but be patient with me because I want to get it right." He took off his cap, and Albie saw him close his eyes as they walked along.

"When you left here that day, Arthur told us that you had promised to go off the steroids, and everyone was happy about that. Then we heard you had been traded to San Diego and were still hitting home runs at the same pace as in Baltimore. We suspected that the trade changed things for you and that you may have been forced, so to speak, to continue what you were doing, so we weren't holding that against Arthur. Then we got word of your contract extension with the Padres, saw those fifty-three home runs you hit the next year, and almost as many last year when you gave your team the hitting it needed to get into the World Series. That put Arthur in a bad position again with the players, but he kept saying you'd made a promise to him and he was sure you'd keep it. Since we knew your contract was up last year, we waited to see what would happen. Then when the team announced that you had signed a new deal—but just for one year—and you'd be paid ten million dollars, we knew you'd have to stay on steroids to hit enough home runs to justify getting that much money. Arthur was devastated by that news."

"But I *did* give up the stuff after last year," Albie said, stopping to face Kantor as he spoke. "I *did* keep my promise. I signed the contract, but I was ready to retire right away if I couldn't hit without loading up."

"Yeah, well nobody here knew that, and when you were able to keep hitting them out after that injury you had, it sure looked like you were still getting help. So when the lineups were announced for the all-star game, your dad was left off again."

"That stinks, Jocko. I stopped just so he could play. He must feel terrible. I want to talk to him and let him know I kept my promise. At least he'd be able to look forward to next year."

They had reached the edge of the cornfield. "Wait here," Kantor said. "Don't go anywhere."

A few minutes later, Kantor returned. "Listen, Albie," he said, "you can't see your father. When he found out he couldn't play in the game this year, he told us it was no fun hanging around for nothing, and that he had decided to retire. He left a couple of weeks ago."

"Where did he go?"

"I don't know. Nobody knows. When guys leave here, they never say where they're going. And you never get any mail from them."

Kantor saw a few tears running down Albie's cheeks and felt himself losing some control of his own emotions. "Listen, before Arthur left, he brought me this baseball and asked me to give it to you if you ever came back here."

Albie took the baseball from the large catcher and looked at it. On one side, his father had written his name. On the other, it read "To my son, Albie, with love, Dad."

He thanked Kantor for the ball and told him that maybe he'd return some day and watch another all-star game. "At least I'll be able to show this ball to my wife and get her to admit that you guys really exist."

"No, you can't do that, Albie. You're the only one out there who'll ever see what's written on it. Everyone else will just be looking at a plain old baseball. Good luck with your hitting." Kantor winked, turned around, and disappeared into the cornfield.

THE RIGHT PITCH FOR CUBA

"I was never nervous when I had the ball, but when I let go I was scared to death."

—Lefty Grove

H E WAS NINETY-NINE years old, just a wisp of a man, when I first heard him tell that amazing story. But don't let yourself take any of it lightly on account of that. Believe me, Russ had all his marbles. He was playing with a full deck and the joker to boot.

I'd been an aide in the nursing home just a short while back then—it was 1981, in San Diego—but it didn't take long to see that Russ was easily the smartest person there. He could talk on any subject at all and tell you things you'd never heard before. When he spoke, you listened, because you knew he had something to teach you every time. Russ read magazines like *National Geographic* and *Smithsonian* from cover to cover and watched a lot of videos his family brought him. Operas and documentaries about history were his favorites, and his TV never moved off the education channel. Russ had bad hands, very arthritic, but all he had to do was press a few buttons on his remote to get things going.

"So what do y'all know 'bout Teddy Roosevelt?" he asked me one afternoon when I was in his room to get his pills ready. "You must have studied him back in school, Arthur."

He was the only one who called me Arthur. Everyone else knew I preferred Art or Artie, but Russ had this thing about formality that made him use a person's full name. He even learned how to pronounce the names of the aides who came from foreign countries, though everyone else had nicknames for them to make it easier. The funny part was that no one ever called him by his full name, which was Russell, and he didn't seem to care.

"Not too much," I answered. "I know he was president sometime in the early 1900s, but I couldn't tell you which years. And he fought in one of the wars, the Spanish-American I think it was. I remember seeing pictures of him on horseback, charging up a hill. But I forget whether that was in Mexico or where it was."

"That's damn good, Arthur," he said. "Roosevelt became president in 1901, when McKinley got himself assassinated. He served in office for not quite eight years. The Spanish-American war broke out before that, and was fought mostly in Cuba. And Roosevelt was a big American hero by the time it was over. He sure was. It helped him no end getting elected after that. The picture you're thinking 'bout was the one showing him leading his men up what was called San Juan Hill."

Russ stopped talking for a minute and just stared at me while I put the pills he needed in a small cup. When I finished, he motioned for me to sit near his wheelchair, on the side of his bed. "Like lots of things," he said, "there's a story 'bout that, one worth telling."

"What do you mean?" I asked.

"I'm going to spell it out for you, Arthur. Just be patient." He rolled his head back and looked up at the ceiling for a minute. He smiled while he was in that position and you could tell he was seeing something in his mind's eye that made him do it.

"In 1898," he began, and lowered his head again, "I was already sixteen years old. I lived in Texas, in a small town 'bout forty miles outside of San Antone called Fenton. My father had grown up as a cowboy in Oklahoma and still made a living for himself that way. Neighbors who owned cattle had him come 'round to rope them and brand them, and sometimes he was paid to break broncos. I used to love watching him do that. After school I worked different jobs in town, but in the summer most of us boys from 'round there had little to do. School let out early in June and we had three months to just take ourselves over to the ball field every day and razz each other 'bout girls at night.

"In May that year we had the greatest thing happen to us. Today, it'd be like the whole Barnum & Bailey Circus suddenly showing up to perform in some town out in the middle of nowhere. What a time it was. And that's when I first heard 'bout what they called the Spanish-American war."

"What was it, Russ?" I asked. "What happened?"

He smiled again. "We suddenly had all of a thousand soldiers set up camp right near our town, 'tween us and San Antone, and start training for going to war. It was either land the Gov'ment must have owned, or maybe they leased it from someone, I can't remember. But they put up them tents all over the place. When I say soldiers, Arthur, I mean most of them were cowboys, just like my old man had been, and they came to that camp from places you'd expect, like Arizona, New Mexico and Oklahoma. Of course those states were still Indian Territories back then, and there were some real Indians, straight off the reservation, in camp too. All of them had spent most of their lives on the back of a horse and had been brought together to form a cavalry regiment. We went over there lots of times after school and they'd let us stand around watching them ride and do marching drills and take shooting practice with their Springfield rifles. We heard the fighting was going to be in Cuba and they'd be up against some bad foreigners from Spain who'd taken over the island."

"That's right," I said. "I remember now that it was Cuba, not Mexico. An American ship got blown up in the harbor, in Havana."

"A ship called the *Maine*, Arthur, and that's what got this country into the war. They said it was the Spanish who did it."

Russ seemed to be waiting for some kind of an acknowledgement from me. I shook my head up and down and he continued.

"One day one of the officers came over to talk with us. Seeing him come near, we all would've sworn it was Mr. Wyman, who taught English and Geography in school and coached the boys in sports. We figured he must've joined the regiment. I think one of us even said, 'Hello, Mr. Wyman' before this fellow told us his name was Theodore Roosevelt, and he was a lieutenant colonel, second in charge of the regiment. I mean he and Mr. Wyman could've been doubles for each other, with the same walrus mustaches and little round eyeglasses. He even kept rubbing his mustache with his thumb the same way Mr. Wyman always did. Roosevelt saw how we were looking at him, sort of scared like, and must've thought it was on account of how important he was.

"Anyway, he told us they'd prob'ly be training there a few more weeks and then ship out to some port city in Texas or Florida for the trip over to Cuba. That's when we found out the regiment's name officially was the First Volunteer Cavalry, but everyone had started calling them the 'Rough Riders.' Roosevelt liked that name—you could tell from the big smile on his face when he said it—and he let us know they all couldn't wait to go fight and help Cuba get independent from Spain."

"But Roosevelt came from New York," I interrupted, "and was just a politician. How could they send him out west to lead a cavalry regiment?"

"Good question, Arthur," Russ said. "I didn't know it then, but turned out he'd spent two years in the North Dakota Badlands when he was younger. That was after his wife died giving birth to their first child. He must've wanted to go off by himself and think about things. Started from scratch and became quite a cowboy."

Russ let those last words sink in and then picked up the story.

"I guess he noticed a few of us carrying what went for baseball gloves back then and asked where we played. I told him 'bout the field in our town and he asked if we'd like to play some games against his men on the weekend. We said sure we would and agreed they could use our gloves while they were in the field. So right then we arranged to play two games that Saturday and Sunday.

"Well, we didn't know what to expect though we figured most of those cowboys didn't know too much about playing baseball. But come to find out the regiment had guys in it from the East Coast, and a bunch of them played one sport or another in college. On Saturday they walloped us by better than ten runs, against Billy Johnson who was the best pitcher in our school. And on Sunday it prob'ly would've been by twice as much except for Roosevelt mercifully ending the game after six innings, saying his men had to get back to camp for an early dinner. We were totally embarrassed and said we wanted to play them again the next weekend. He said that'd be fine and he'd try bringing more cowboys and fewer Easterners with him.

"School let out for the summer that week and so we practiced hard every day 'til almost dark, getting off the field for just a couple hours starting at noon when the sun beat down the worst. We'd asked Mr. Wyman to run the practices for us and he'd agreed because he still wasn't sure if he had a summer job in San Antone or not. I played third base for the team but I had a real good arm so Mr. Wyman had me doing some pitching too. We'd already let him know how he looked just like Colonel Roosevelt and he was nipping at the bit to see it for himself. He could ride a horse as good as Roosevelt—we all knew that from the times we'd seen him in the local rodeos they had in Fenton. In fact, next to my old man, he was the best in town.

"Before the Saturday game got started, we brought Mr. Wyman over to the Colonel and you could see they hardly believed their eyes. They shook hands and laughed and you'd have sworn there was a mirror there 'tween the two of them. Roosevelt told us this was the last weekend we'd be playing because they'd received their orders to ship out and would be leaving by train for Tampa on the following Thursday. The game that day was a lot closer than the first two, but they still had a few of the college guys with them and beat us by two or three runs right at the end. I smoked a home run in that one, a line drive over the left fielder's head he was still chasing when I'd finished rounding the bases."

"Did Teddy Roosevelt play at all?" I asked.

"I was just getting to that," Russ said. "But you ought to understand back then no one called him 'Teddy.' He was 'Colonel' to everyone. Wasn't 'til long afterwards that some newspaperman started the 'Teddy' business. Anyhow, for the first three games he sat on their bench most of the time but every so often went out and coached at one of the bases. He was about forty years old then, prob'ly twice as old as most of the soldiers who were playing. But after three innings or so of the final game, Roosevelt put himself in and played right field where he must've figured he wouldn't have much to do. He laughed when he went out there and hollered over for Mr. Wyman to get in the game too. 'Come on, Tyler,' he said, 'let's show these young bucks a thing or two.' Mr. Wyman laughed right back at him but shook his head and said he'd stay where he was.

"On his first time at bat the Colonel hit a dying quail into center field for a single and was happy as heck about it. We actually got ourselves the lead in that game and built it up to 'bout five runs with a couple innings to go. Then, when the 'Rough Riders' started a rally and were getting closer, Mr. Wyman put me in to pitch.

"They cut us down to just a run ahead and had a couple men on base when it was Roosevelt's turn to bat again. He stood real close to home plate, not leaving much room for a pitcher to throw inside. I figured I had to move him off a little by aiming the ball at his belt buckle. I never intended it to be any higher, but that's where it went. Well, he just froze right there when he saw the ball coming at him, then turned away at the last second but not in time to keep from getting hit on the back of the head. He sort've twisted 'round a little and then just flopped right down in the dirt."

Russ stopped talking for a few moments and I knew he was reliving that scene again.

"Well, natur'ly," he went on, "everyone came running over to him. I was one of the first and was scared to death seeing him lying there with his eyes closed, his glasses on the ground, and him not moving at all. Mr. Wyman took charge and began asking Roosevelt a few questions to see how he'd answer. I guess he didn't like what he heard because after that he hollered for a soldier to ride into town with one of us boys and bring back Doc Lacey and a wagon as fast as we could. I figured I should go since I was the one who hit him and we got Doc back to the field in no more than half an hour.

"The short of it is it took Doc Lacey only a few minutes to know Roosevelt had himself a severe concussion. He wanted to treat him in his office, where there was a bed in the room next door, so he got some of the soldiers to move the Colonel there in the wagon, slowly and carefully. The game never picked up from that point, as you'd imagine, so we always said afterwards we'd won it."

Russ took a second to chuckle at that.

"On Monday morning I went over to Doc Lacey's office to see Mr. Roosevelt so I could apologize for hitting him in the head. But Doc told me he was sleeping and prob'ly wouldn't be able to have any visitors for several days. He said he might even have to move him to the hospital in San Antone. I repeated what Roosevelt had said 'bout heading for Tampa on Thursday with his regiment. But Doc just shook his head, saying there was no chance of that and telling me the Colonel wouldn't leave his office to make the trip unless it was over Doc's dead body."

"So what happened?" I asked, probably raising my voice a little too much.

Russ winked at me, as if to tell me to calm down, that it was all coming out. "On Wednesday," he continued, "I went back there again to see if there'd been any improvement. Just as I got to the office, the door opened and I was almost bowled over to see Mr. Roosevelt coming out with another soldier, an older man with white hair and gold stars on his uniform. But then I realized it was really Mr. Wyman when he said,

'Good morning, Russell,' told me Doc wasn't letting any visitors in and said he wanted to see all the boys at the ball field at four o'clock that afternoon.

"Well, most of us showed up and were sitting 'round and talking instead of practicing, but we had to wait 'til close to four-thirty before Mr. Wyman got there. He came on horseback, riding in hard, and was dressed in old clothes and a long pair of boots you could tell had just been shined. A job had come through for him in San Antone, he told us, if he could be there by Thursday afternoon, so he was leaving early the next morning. He said he'd be back teaching in September, God willing, and told us we should have a good summer and play lots of baseball. Then we were all surprised when he shook hands with everyone there before mounting up, saluting like the soldiers did and riding off.

"After baseball practice on Thursday, just 'bout noon, I went back to Doc Lacey's office again, hoping to see Mr. Roosevelt. But when I went inside, no one was there. The bed he kept in the next room was empty when I looked in and the mattress was gone. I hollered up the stairs to the second floor, first for Doc and then for Mrs. Lacey, but there was no answer. I went over to the food and grain store Sam Jenkins ran and asked if he'd seen Doc. He had, he told me, 'bout eight o'clock that morning when he first opened up and was sweeping in front. Doc and Mrs. Lacey drove by slowly, with their own horse and a borrowed one pulling the wagon. He said Mr. Wyman was with them, riding with Doc up front. Doc's wife was sitting in back on a pile of blankets, and there was something else in there with her but it was mostly covered up and Sam couldn't make out what it was. Doc said he and the missus were going to see some friends in San Antone and Mr. Wyman waved at Sam as the wagon passed on by."

I guessed it was Roosevelt lying in the wagon on that missing mattress, but I could see Russ wanted to keep on with the story without my interrupting again.

"The next week, when I went to Doc's and asked him 'bout Mr. Roosevelt, he told me the Colonel had made a remarkable recovery from his concussion and went back to his regiment on Thursday morning in time to ship out with all the others. I reminded Doc what he'd said on Monday 'bout Mr. Roosevelt having no chance of leaving, but he cut me short and said there was no sense asking lots of questions, you couldn't always be just right in predicting how well or poorly a patient would respond to treatment.

"When September came, we had a substitute teacher for the better part of three weeks before Mr. Wyman returned. He looked more tanned than he ever had before, and when he wore a short-sleeved shirt with no jacket on, you could see several places on his arms where it looked like long cuts were still healing. He told us we all looked a foot taller than when he'd seen us last and asked whether we'd enjoyed the summer. Everyone said 'Yes,' of course, and then I asked him 'bout his. 'Work is work,' he answered, flashing us a smile, 'but it was totally interesting and I'll tell you more about it some time.' He never did, all that year, and then moved to another school way down in Houston just after my class graduated. That was the last I saw of him.

"Being where we lived, we never heard anything about the Spanish-American war while the fighting was going on. But a couple years later, when Roosevelt was running for vice president on the ticket with McKinley, I was living at Southern Methodist University in Dallas. That's when I read all 'bout how he'd been such a hero in the war, leading his troops on a charge up San Juan Hill on horseback and helping kick the Spanish army out of Cuba. And in one of the pictures that caught my eye in a book 'bout the war, there was Colonel Roosevelt, the leader of the 'Rough Riders' posing with some other soldiers, bandages showing on both his arms.

"And you know what, Arthur? Ever since that day, when I saw that picture and thought about the baseball I threw hitting Roosevelt in the head and all, I've always said to myself, 'Good job that summer, Mr. Wyman, a damn good job over there in Cuba.'"

Russ winked at me again. "Now what do y'all think of that, Arthur?" he asked.

And all I could say was, "I don't know, Russ."

I stayed in that nursing home for four years. When I left, Russ was a hundred and three years old, sharp as ever, and still figuring the story was worth telling to every new nurse or aide that came there to work.

MATTERS OF PRINCIPLE

"There is always some kid who may be seeing me for the first or last time. I owe him my best."

—Joe DiMaggio

THAT'S RIGHT, EVERYONE knows North Dakota doesn't have a city big enough to get itself a major league baseball team, but there's a lot of baseball playing that goes on here. In the time you're asking me about, back in the mid-fifties, Devil's Lake—where I've lived all my life—was one of four towns in our corner of the state that had a professional team. The teams were in what was called the North Dakota–Minnesota Independent League. Minnesota had four teams across the state line from us, and the eight clubs played their entire schedules against each other. It was usually still cold in May, and then too cold for baseball after about midway into September, so the teams played a 75-game season during the months of June, July, and August. Then the first place team in each state played each other to see which one could win four games and be the league champion. We all called that the "little world series," just to make it seem more important.

Although all the players were professionals, their pay was very low in those days and some of them had part-time jobs away from the ballpark. They were given a small expense account by the owners and had to find themselves room and board in the town. None of them could afford the Empire Hotel in downtown Devil's Lake or even the Palace, out there on the highway, which had only eight rooms. So they had to find a family with an extra bedroom or two that could take them in and feed them. We never did that in our house, although we could have, but I'll explain that to you as we go along.

Marion Houston, whom you asked about, played in Devil's Lake for three years back then. He was tall and strong, with a full head of curly red hair going in all directions and a smile that could change your mood even if you'd just come from a funeral. He was the left fielder for the Demons and could hit the ball farther than anyone else on the team when he connected. Once in a while a player from our league was bought by a major league team and assigned to one of its minor league clubs. Marion didn't have enough all-around talent to figure that would happen to him, but he was young enough to still hold on to that dream.

There was a story once in *The Prairie Times*, our local paper, in which he talked about his name. He said that his great-great-grandfather was part of the Houston family that gave the City of Houston its name. They had moved into the eastern part of Texas from Louisiana about fifteen years before the fight at the Alamo, and one of the Houston daughters actually died there along with her husband. As for his first name, according to what he told the paper, his folks fell in love with the name Marion for some reason and decided they would give their next child that name whether it was a boy or a girl.

In his first summer in Devil's Lake, Marion lived with the Dondelinger family. They had a couple of teenage sons who were fanatics about baseball, and I guess the boys were always all over Marion to practice with them whenever he wasn't at the ballpark. He's the kind of guy who couldn't say "No" to that, but I would hear from one friend or another that Marion wished Eric Dondelinger would set up some rules so that the boys would know when to leave him alone.

The Demons finished third in the North Dakota standings the first summer that Marion was here. He hit twelve home runs, averaging one every week, but he struck out an awful lot and wasn't considered the player you'd like to see up at bat in the ninth inning when you really needed a hit. At the end of the season, though, Marion was given a contract to come back the next year.

Before he left Devil's Lake to return to Texas, Marion looked around to make arrangements for a different place to stay. I guess he heard somewhere that the mayor of Devil's Lake had a large house for his wife and himself, with a daughter away at college. He made an appointment to see the mayor in his office and asked about renting a room for the next baseball season.

"I've seen your home on Maple Avenue, Mister Mayor, and it sure looks like you'd have an extra room I could stay in. I'm a quiet person, I'm sure I'd like anything your wife cooks for dinner, and Eric Dondelinger can assure you I always pay my rent on time. I'd even be willing to see your grass gets mowed without you having to pay me for it."

The mayor was not a big man—the body of a second baseman you'd probably say—with a ruddy complexion and a thin salt and pepper moustache. He wore a light-colored sports jacket made partly of silk over a blue buttoned-down shirt and a striped tie. "I could have saved you a trip over here, Mr. Houston, if I knew that was on your mind," the mayor told him. "The fact is I never rent out rooms to baseball players."

"Is there a reason for that?" Marion asked.

"Yes, there is, and I'll be honest with you about it. I've lived in Devil's Lake for over thirty years, and I've seen the players come and go for about twenty of those years. Too many of them have been drunk in the streets, or out of control at parties, or doing something they shouldn't be doing. I often have to get involved just because I'm the mayor here, but I don't want anyone living in my house who could be acting that way. You may be a fine young man, Mr. Houston, but I refuse to take any chances, so I just don't rent to ballplayers, period."

Marion was considering whether to just get up and go, or plead his case further, when the mayor added, "And besides, I have a daughter who has been spending this summer with friends in Michigan, but she'll be home next summer and I don't want any strangers living in the house with her. It's out of the question, Mr. Houston. The most I can do for you is have my secretary make up a list of folks in town who do rent to ballplayers and I'll check off the ones I think you should try first. Would you like that? I can probably have it for you in half an hour."

"Yes, thank you, I would," Marion said.

He picked up the list a short while later, and by the end of the day he had rented a room with his own bathroom from the Kretchners. It wasn't big or beautiful, but it was clean, the price was right, there were no children in the house, and he and the Kretchners had taken to each other while they discussed his living there. As if anyone could have a hard time getting to like him.

After Marion went back to Texas, we had our usual dreadful winter which I've never gotten used to as long as I've been here. That was followed by an exceptionally wet spring, and there was even some flooding in a couple of the towns around us. But in the middle of May, all the baseball players on the Demons began arriving back in Devil's Lake and working out at the ballpark to get ready for the start of the season. The park is called Randolph Finderson Memorial Field, by the way, and it's located just two blocks east of Main Street, right near the shopping district.

I can't tell you where they met for the first time although I'm sure Marion didn't know that Gail was the mayor's daughter when he saw her and fell head over heels for her right from the start. I even suspect Gail may have seen him at Finderson Field and arranged to be at whatever nightspot she heard the ballplayers frequented. I can tell you that Marion had come back to North Dakota a little broader and handsomer than ever. In any event, Gail fell just as hard for him, and in no time all their friends recognized that they were a couple. I know now that it didn't take long before the two of them began talking about getting engaged and marrying each other a year later. They were going to wait until after the next baseball season, when Gail would be out of college.

Things started happening one evening when Gail said to him, "I know it may be a little old-fashioned, Marion, but you've got to speak to my father and get his blessing for us."

"I don't think that's a good idea," he told her. "He already let me know once that he doesn't trust baseball players. If he wouldn't let me have a room in his house, I don't think he's going to want me to have his daughter."

"Well, he knows I've been dating you steady and hasn't said anything to me about it."

"But he may be thinking that nothing will come of it. He's waiting to see if you'll eventually feel the same way about ballplayers that he does. There's no reason for him to talk to you about it now and maybe have an argument."

"Please, Marion, do it for me. I'm sure my dad will say it's okay."

Several days later, Marion had the mayor's first appointment in the morning. The mayor's secretary had allotted it a half-hour's time, but the meeting took no more than ten minutes. The mayor was friendly and commented on the fact that the team had not gotten off to a very auspicious start in its first twenty-five games; but he was visibly upset when Marion said that he had come to ask for his daughter's hand in marriage.

"I've said this before, Mr. Houston, that you appear to be a nice young man, but you already know how I feel about ballplayers, and I don't think my daughter would be making a wise choice in marrying one. It's my hope that she finds someone who has a professional career ahead of him, who can offer her a secure future and who is respected in the community. I'll tell her exactly how I feel when I see her this evening."

Marion reported on the meeting to Gail. She was disappointed, but expressed confidence that she would be able to change her father's mind.

"I definitely want us to have his blessing, Marion. I wouldn't feel right about getting engaged and married without it." But even as she spoke, Gail knew she would do anything—even elope—to be Marion's bride.

"Does that mean you won't marry me if he's stubborn about it and won't accept me?"

She wanted to say, "Of course not, I'll marry you no matter what." But she had to make Marion understand how important it was to her. "I don't know," Gail told him. "I think I still will, but I just don't know."

At the halfway mark of the baseball season, the Devil's Lake club was in third place of its four-team division, and appeared to be going nowhere. Then, on the very day that Marion was moved from fifth to third in the batting order—a desperation move, the manager later confessed—he got hot. He began having multiple hit games almost regularly, and his sudden burst of home runs provided the winning margin in many of the team's victories. In the space of three weeks the Demons moved from near the bottom to the top of their division. And they got there, finally, by sweeping a three-game series with the Blue Beavers, the team from Warren that was leading the Minnesota division.

On the first game back in Devil's Lake, Finderson Field was almost packed. Marion kept the winning streak going with a double in the ninth inning that drove in two runs to end the game. When he returned to the dugout and was shaking hands with all his teammates, he heard a fan close to the field shouting, "Keep it up, Houston, and you'll be mayor of Devil's Lake one of these days." A short while later, Marion was resting in the clubhouse before taking his shower and recalled Gail telling him that her father would soon begin campaigning for reelection. He was completing his third term and had been in office almost twelve years. Although there would be a primary election in the middle of September, her father was quite certain, she told Marion, that he would be running without competition from any other Democrat. On the Republican side, two candidates would contest that party's nomination to run in the general election.

At City Hall the next day, Marion learned that the only require-ment in running for mayor was to submit an official nominating paper along with the signatures of one hundred people who were then living in Devil's Lake. He took the necessary paperwork with him to the ballpark that day, explained his intention to his teammates and within three days had all the signatures he required. He returned to City Hall and became a Democratic candidate for Mayor of Devil's Lake.

With one week remaining in the season, Devil's Lake was tied for first place in its division with the Foresters, the team from Grand Forks. Although they had continued to play well, the Demons had been over-taken for the joint lead when the Foresters won ten of their last eleven games. Marion had continued to be the main reason for the Demons' success, hitting at a .360 average with five home runs in the two weeks that had passed since he began running for mayor. The crowds at the ball-park had become progressively larger as the season wound to an end with the Demons in the fight to get into the little world series. As Marion's hits won ball games, his popularity throughout Devil's Lake continued to grow by leaps and bounds. Unlike the mayor, who had campaign signs up on front lawns all over town, Marion had only the posters with which he decorated the roof and sides of his 1949 Chevrolet. He had asked the team's general manager for permission to hang a campaign sign across from the ticket booths at the ballpark, but his request was turned down. I'm sure the team's front office didn't want to chance offending any of the Demons' paying customers who may have favored a different candidate.

"Marion, my father wants to talk to you," Gail told him late one afternoon as they walked hand in hand from the ballpark toward the downtown shops. She had felt from the start, when she first learned of Marion's political aspirations, that she would be somehow caught in the middle between the two men. When she asked him why he was entering the mayoral contest, she was surprised to hear Marion tell her that it was one way he could get her father's blessing for their marriage.

"I think I can win," he said, "and as the former mayor he would have to respect my new stature and not think of me simply as a ballplayer. It would certainly show that I have the respect of the community." Marion told Gail that he was prepared to give up his playing days with the Demons after the season and that he would be happy living in Devil's Lake if he were elected mayor.

The two opponents agreed to meet at the ballpark several hours before the start of the next game. The mayor's secretary, whom Marion had called, said that the mayor felt it wouldn't look right for Marion to be seen going into his office at City Hall.

"I'll be brief, Mr. Houston," the mayor said as soon as they sat down on a bench in the upper grandstand. "I don't think you understand everything that's involved with being mayor of this town, and for that reason I don't believe you'd do a good job. Believe me when I tell you that there's much more to do than cut ribbons and attend Kiwanis meetings. That's exactly what I've been telling the folks in Devil's Lake when I'm out campaigning. But I respect the fact that you were willing to run for the office and that you haven't tried to tear me down in any way. In fact, as far as I know and from what I'm told, the only campaigning you've done is with that baseball bat of yours. I truly believe that if you were to defeat me in the primary—which I don't think will happen, but anyway—you would lose the general election to the Republican candidate. Whoever that is—and they are both powerful men in this town—will tear into you like a power saw into a sapling. You've been nothing more than a summer visitor here for the past two years and you wouldn't have any answers for the issues in the election, for all the things we fight about in Devil's Lake the rest of the year."

The mayor paused a few seconds, loosened his tie slightly and continued. "Right now, it's a popularity contest between you and me. You're popular because you help win games for our team. The better the Demons do, the more people like you. But if the team doesn't get into the little world series at the end of this month, your popularity will have a lot of time to fade away before the primary election on September 19th. Instead of waiting to see what happens, I'd like to make an agreement with you now. I confess that my daughter has told me why you entered this race. So I've come to ask you to withdraw from the election and to tell you that I'll welcome you into our family if you do."

Marion was silent. He looked around the ballpark, empty except for one groundskeeper filling in some bare spots with white chalk along the left field foul line. He knew instinctively what his answer would be, but realized that the man making the unacceptable proposal might soon be his father-in-law. Were there no such possible connection, he probably would not have been thinking about keeping his temper in check.

When he answered, it was in a low voice. "My folks always told me to be sure to finish whatever I started. That way, if I knew I had an obligation to get it done, I'd think hard about it before I jumped into it. I entered this race to get your blessing, but as much as Gail and I want that, I can't accept it as a reward for withdrawing. Win or lose, I've got to see it through to the end."

"I'm sorry about that, Mr. Houston." The mayor stood up, hesitated a few seconds as if getting ready to say something else, but turned away instead and left.

As fate would have it, the Demons played their last three games of the season at home against Grand Forks. The two teams were still tied for the division lead, so whichever club won two of the games would go to the little world series.

The first game was a pitcher's duel, and the score was tied 1–1 when Marion batted first in the last half of the ninth inning. The infielders were aware of his power and always played back for him. But this time he surprised them by bunting a ball toward third and getting a hit. On the first pitch to the next batter, Marion stole second base and went to third when the throw from the catcher sailed over the shortstop's head into center field. The Forester's manager came out and ordered his pitcher to walk the next two batters to fill the bases. By the way, that was only the second Demons game I had ever been to, and all the strategy had to be explained to me by my daughter, with whom I went. She had become a very big fan that year and quite knowledgeable about the game. But the strategy didn't work when the next player hit a fly ball and Marion scored the winning run after the catch with a beautiful slide into home.

The second game was as different from the first as you could get. They all called it a "slugfest," and the Grand Forks players were doing most of the slugging. They won the game by a score of 13–7, and had four home runs to none for the Demons.

Well, you can imagine all the anticipation for the final game and the tension around town. It was a Sunday, and that morning the minister in our church said a prayer for the Demons. But it was clear he wasn't totally convinced his prayer would be answered when his sermon dealt with different instances in which the noblest or the most deserving of men or women didn't achieve what they desired the most. It started with Moses leading his people through the desert for forty years but not going into the promised land himself, and ended with Gloria Swanson not getting the Academy Award a few years earlier for her role in *Sunset Boulevard*.

Of course, as you may know, that third game belonged to Marion. He had two home runs, four hits altogether, and scored more runs himself than all the Foresters. Devil's Lake won the game 7–3, and there's no doubt that if the election had been held the next day, Marion would not have just been victorious, he'd have won in a landslide.

The way the little world series was set up that year, the first two games were to be in Warren, Minnesota, at the Blue Beavers' park. They had won their division easily. The next three were at Finderson Field, and then back to Warren if one or two more games were necessary for either team to reach four victories.

Warren's best pitcher—he was signed by the Cincinnati Reds the next year—had a whole week to rest before the first game, and he beat the Demons 8–1. It seemed like everyone in Devil's Lake had the radio on that afternoon to hear the game, and I heard there was a caravan

MATTERS OF PRINCIPLE   •   47

of cars that drove over to Warren in hopes of being able to buy tickets
and get in. No player on the Demons did anything worth mentioning
that day, including Marion who struck out three times. I went to the
movies that night with my daughter who was feeling quite distressed,
and I was surprised to see so many people there on a work night. But I
guess that was the best way folks had of getting their minds off something that bothered them.

The second game was a lot better. This time it was the Demons' best
pitcher's turn to be the star, and he didn't let the Beavers score any runs
until the last inning. By that time our team had scored five runs and we
won it 5–2. Our second baseman, who had one home run all season, hit
one over the left field fence with two runners on base and that gave us
the lead early in the game. Marion had no hits in the second game either,
and struck out two more times, but no one cared about that as long as
Devil's Lake won the game. The team now had momentum, folks started
saying, and all the talk was of winning at least two of the next three
games at home.

The weather for the third game, two days later, was absolutely beautiful. The sun was shining brightly, there wasn't a cloud in the sky, and
the temperature was about ten degrees warmer than what you'd expect
for the second week in September. My daughter had purchased two
tickets for all the games at Finderson Field, and since my husband was
too busy to attend, she insisted that I accompany her. It was one of those
games where everyone felt that one run would probably make the difference. When it's like that, I find more people expect the home team to
lose than to win. If that's true, then those folks came out on top because
Devil's Lake lost the game by a 4–3 score. We were ahead 3–2 after seven
innings, but in the eighth inning Warren had two runners on base and
they both scored when Marion lost a fly ball in the sun out in left field.
The Demons couldn't get that run back in their last two at-bats. You
would have thought my daughter was responsible for what happened
from the way she reacted. She didn't speak a word to me on the way

home from the ballpark, and not until she said "Good night" and went to bed.

I thought the spirit in the grandstand for the fourth game was good, considering what had happened the day before. The same man was sitting next to me again and kept saying things like "Don't worry, we'll get them today," and "Houston's due for a big game. I can feel it." The nine-year-old girl who sang The National Anthem was delightful, and Karl Ekland, who had earlier managed the Demons for ten years, had the honor of throwing out the first ball. He got a big round of applause from everyone there.

It turned out to be an afternoon on which every player on the Devil's Lake team had at least one hit, except for Marion. The big problem for the Demons was that whenever Marion came to bat, except for the first time, there were runners on base and two outs. In both the third and fifth innings, when the team had its chances to go ahead, he struck out with the bases loaded. And in the sixth inning, after the Demons scored four runs to answer the five runs that the Beavers had scored in the same inning, Marion popped out to the first baseman with the two tying runs on base. That's as close as our team got for the rest of the game. We were five runs down by the time Marion batted again in the eighth, so even a three-run homer at the time wouldn't have turned things around. Marion hit the ball back to the pitcher and was easily out at first. At that point the man sitting next to me said, "Houston's a bum," loud enough for everyone around us to hear. My daughter just glared at him as he stood up to leave and edged his way onto the stairway that was already crowded with people leaving the park.

That meant, of course, that the Demons were down three games to one and the little world series would be over if they lost one more. As the saying goes, you could cut the tension with a knife at Finderson Field that day. The crowd was quiet, even before the game began, knowing that the Blue Beavers' best pitcher would be facing the Demons again. In that morning's *Prairie Times* the Demons manager was quoted as saying that the most important thing was for his club not to fall behind early, but to stay in the game with the Beavers and try to make something good happen at the end. The players spoke of how "their backs were to the wall," and how important it was "to focus on winning one game at a time." We all hoped they would win and avoid the embarrassment of losing three straight at home.

For eight innings, things went just the way the Demons manager had hoped. The Beavers twice took a one-run lead but the Demons tied it each time. In the last half of the ninth inning Marion was on first base with two outs. The next batter hit a ball to right field and it landed just fair, down the line. You could see the white chalk flying in the air when the ball hit the ground. Marion was racing around the bases with the winning run as the right fielder retrieved the ball and threw it toward home plate. Everyone in the stands was on their feet, waving their arms and urging Marion on with their shouts, confident that he would score. And there was no doubt he would have beaten the throw to the catcher had he not tripped just a few steps beyond third base. He fell hard to the ground and rolled over several times before he could bring himself under control and get up again. But by then he found himself trapped between third and home and was tagged out in a rundown.

You could feel the crowd's enthusiasm totally collapse, like air rushing out of a balloon. The *Prairie Times* wrote the next day that fate was sending us a message at that moment that the Demons were dead and that Marion was digging their grave. Before the Devil's Lake fans were emotionally ready for it, the tenth inning got under way. And I guess the players felt the same way because before the Demons came to bat again in their half of the inning, they were three runs behind. No one reached base, and the series ended with a 5–2 defeat.

There were eight days between the end of the baseball season for the Demons and the Devil's Lake primary election. And four days after the primary, Marion was in his Chevrolet heading back to Texas.

The mayor had kept up on all the details of the games played in the little world series. He wanted Devil's Lake to win, of course, and had made a much-publicized bet with the mayor of Warren that involved the movement of certain farm products from the loser to the winner. But as the losses mounted, he could not help feeling some comfort in the fact that Marion was playing so poorly. He fully realized at the start of the series that if Marion continued to perform as he had against the team from Grand Forks, and led the Demons to victory over Warren, his popularity could win him the primary in a town enamored with its success. But as he told Marion several weeks earlier, the opposite was also true, and he knew that Marion's vote-getting ability was diminishing with every game. For his part, Marion didn't have to be told—or read in the *Prairie Times*—that he was the "goat" of the series. So it came as no surprise to either man that the mayor received sixty-eight percent of the vote cast in the Democratic primary.

Marion and Gail sat at a small table in Reinlander's ice cream parlor on Main Street the night after the primary. They had shared a hot fudge sundae without much conversation, and were now beginning to unwind and discuss the decisions they had to make.

"I've thought about it, Gail, and I want to play one more year with the Demons. They've already told me they'll give me a contract. I don't want to give up baseball with the kind of series I just had. It would haunt me the rest of my life."

"What about after next year?" she asked.

"I want to get into TV," he said. "It's going to grow bigger and bigger and there'll be room for a lot of people. Announcing sports on TV is what interests me the most. I know I'd be good at it, and I can still get in on the ground floor. But when we get married, we'll probably have to leave here and go live in a big city like Chicago or New York or Los Angeles. That's where most of the jobs are going to be."

"Marion, you're overlooking the fact that there's still the matter of getting my father's blessing."

"I don't know what to say about that," he answered, shrugging his shoulders. "He didn't like me before I ran for mayor and was pretty upset when I told him I wouldn't withdraw. He's your father. What do you think I should do?"

"I think you should meet with him again. Now that he's won the primary and is pretty certain he'll be reelected, he's more relaxed. I'm sure it will be easier for him to accept you. He took the rest of this week as vacation, so why don't you come to the house tomorrow afternoon, about three o'clock, and I'll let him know you'll be there."

"Congratulations, mayor," Marion said as soon as they were alone together in the mayor's small office off the living room.

"Thank you," the mayor answered. "Frankly, I expected to hear that from you Tuesday night after they counted the votes."

"You're right. I'm sorry about that. My only excuse is that I went to bed early that night. I knew I didn't have a chance so there was no point staying up and waiting for the results."

"What do you intend to do now, Mr. Houston?"

Marion's gut told him that the "Mr. Houston" greeting on this occasion was not a good sign. "I'm going to Texas the day after tomorrow and I'll be back here in May for one more season with the Demons. I just signed my new contract this morning. In the meantime I'm going to look into TV announcing and take any speaking or writing courses that would be helpful to me. I've made up my mind to go for a career in television."

The mayor seemed to be thinking about what Marion had just said. He was biting his lower lip and had tilted his head to one side.

Marion spoke again. "I want to marry Gail next year, after she finishes college and when the baseball season is over. We love each other, and it's important for her to have your blessing." He hesitated, then added, "And it's important for me, too."

"You may recall, Mr. Houston, that I offered to give you my blessing several weeks ago, and you rejected it. You did so as a matter of principle, you told me. I could never fault you for that, but matters of principle are a two-way street. And for me, now, that means I'm not going to do something for which I earlier asked something in return but got nothing. I hope you can understand that. That also is a matter of principle."

The fact is that just after Marion had gone in to meet with the mayor, I opened the door a crack to listen in to what was being said. And when I heard those last words, that was too much for me. I went into the room and walked straight over to where they were sitting, the mayor in his padded rocking chair and Marion on the short sofa, across from him.

"Frederick," I said, "this has gone far enough. I think you've forgotten what it was like to be young. Your daughter and this fine man are in love with each other. They're making plans to get married, and what a wonderful thing it is in this day and age that they're asking you for your blessing. They want to become engaged right now, even though they know they won't be able to see much of each other before next May. I'm all for it, Frederick. Our daughter knows she has my blessing, and the only matter of principle is that unless you want to start finding out what a very unhappy wife can be like, I suggest you tell Marion right now that we are thrilled and anxious to have him become part of our family."

The mayor looked at me in silence for several seconds, his mouth hanging half open while he probably was remembering how stubborn I could be about things that upset me. Then he gave me one of his best election campaign smiles and I knew everything was going to be fine.

That was quite a while ago. I hope you can understand why we're so proud of Marion now that the CBS network has made him the head of all sports on television. And even though he doesn't walk so well, the mayor—everyone still calls him that around here after twenty-four years in office—always insists on our getting on a plane to New York each year on our anniversary so we can visit with the grandkids. With him, it's a matter of principle.

JUST ONE TO GO

"You don't save a pitcher for tomorrow. Tomorrow it may rain."

—Leo Durocher

DEAR ANDREW,

Thank you for your letter, nephew. I wish you didn't live all the way across the country so I could see you more often, but maybe your Mom will let you come here to Florida during one of your school vacations and spend a little time with Honey and me.

Sure, I still have a bunch of those glossy photographs showing me swinging the bat, and I'll toss a few in with this letter. Once in a while some fan who remembers me gets my address from the Indians' front office and asks for a picture. If they say something nice about me in a letter and throw in a stamp, I'll send them one, but not if it's just a "hello, send me a picture, goodbye."

The statistics you got out of that baseball encyclopedia are right. In thirteen years with the Indians—that was my whole career—I could always be counted on to have a batting average somewhere around .300 and to hit twenty to twenty-five balls out of the park. I've been retired now seventeen years, Andrew, and it still bothers me to see and talk about how those two stats ended up. There's a story behind it which I'll tell you now in case your Mom never did. Of course, she only knew part of it anyway.

My last year with the Indians was 1960, the same year that Ted Williams called it quits with the Red Sox. He was the best hitter I ever saw, Andrew, the absolute best. And that includes all the "M" guys they compared him with, May, Mantle, Maris, and Musial. My rookie year with the club—1948—was a real fun time. We won the pennant in the American League and beat the Braves in six games in the World Series. The Braves were in Boston back then. I didn't get much playing time, but I learned a lot sitting on the bench, listening to Lou Boudreau, our player manager, and the coaches. The worst time for the Indians while I was there was 1954, but only when we got to the World Series again. We had the greatest pitching staff going that year and won something like 110 games. Everyone figured we'd stomp the Giants in the Series, but Willie Mays made a catch off Vic Wertz in the first game that seemed to take the life out of us; and a pinch hitter named Dusty Rhodes just killed us every time he came to bat. We got swept in four games and couldn't pack our bags and get out of Cleveland fast enough. As that encyclopedia would tell you, I got only three hits and no home runs in those four games.

But back to 1960. That was a crazy year for the team because of everything that was happening. Rocky Colavito got traded to Detroit for Harvey Kuenn, and Norm Cash was sent to the Tigers too, just a week into the season. Both of those deals worked out better for Detroit. But the wackiest thing was in August when our club and the Tigers traded managers. Joe Gordon went over there and Jimmy Dykes took his place with the Indians. I don't know if anything like that ever happened before, and I'm pretty sure it's never happened since. But Dykes couldn't get us to play any better than Gordon, and when we got to the last game of the season we were 76 and 77, one game under five hundred. Don't forget that back then we played a 154-game schedule, eight games less than today. Before that last one with the White Sox at Comiskey Park, Dykes called a meeting in the clubhouse. He told us how important it was to him and the ownership to win so that we didn't finish with a losing record. Either way we were going to end up in fourth place. Some of the guys thought Dykes was pleading for his own job, figuring he wouldn't be back next year if we didn't win as many as we lost.

Dykes didn't particularly like me. Or at least he never had much to say to me. Once in a while he let me start in the outfield, or even, to give Vic Power a day off, at first base; but he knew I was retiring at the end of the season and I usually had to pinch hit to get a bat in my hands. Gordon had put me in the lineup more often, sometimes in left or right field, depending on the park we were playing in. He respected the fact that I could still hit. I'm pretty sure I had about eighteen home runs that year.

Before we left Cleveland to end the year with three games in Chicago, some reporter at the *Plain Dealer* did a story on me. He showed how my lifetime batting average right up to the minute was .299 and that I had 299 career home runs. That meant I needed just one more hit to get to .300, and that I'd have three hundred homers if I could put one more over the fence. I didn't know if Dykes had seen the story or not, but I figured he hadn't when I got to sit on the bench for the first two games of that series.

Now we had a guy on that club named "Speedy" Juniper. His first name was Jim or Joe or something simple like that, but everyone called him Speedy because he could run like a deer. He was a kid at the time, maybe twenty years old, tall and wiry, like he was held together with hinges. He'd been called up to the Indians from the AAA Toronto club in September so they could take a look at him and see if he was ready for the big leagues. He got to play only when it was a tight ball game and Dykes needed a pinch runner for one of the regulars who got on base in a late inning.

It happened that Speedy and I were sitting next to each other in the dugout for that last game of the season, and we were talking back and forth as the game moved along. He asked me what I'd be doing when I was out of baseball, which was really going to start the next day.

"I'll go back to Texas and work my ranch for about ten years," I told him. "Then I'll take the wife and move to Florida somewhere. Probably near Orlando. I like that area." It occurred to me while we were talking that I had no idea what position this kid played. He'd never been out on the field when the other team was at bat, and I guess he just hadn't caught my eye in practice.

"What do you play, second?" I asked him.

"I could," he said, "but center field's my position. With my speed I can catch most everything that's hit out there unless it's in the stands."

"How about stealing bases?" I asked. "I know you've got a couple since you've been here."

"Four," he corrected me. "Four for four, so far. And in Toronto I had 53 out of 58 before they called me up."

I think I whistled when he told me those numbers. "What happened those other five times?" I asked, but I sort of just meant it as a joke.

"Bad umpiring," he said, and shook his head back and forth as if he was picturing each of those occasions.

In the seventh inning we were down by a run to the White Sox. Speedy moved a little closer to me and spoke in a low voice, "I hope you get a chance to hit today. I read that story about you in the paper. It's a shame the manager hasn't already played you so you could try to reach .300."

"He may not even know about it," I answered. "Most managers don't bother reading the sports pages because the beat writers are always second-guessing them. They don't want to look like they're making moves on the field because some writer said that's what he should do."

"I hope you're wrong," he said. "I want to see you hit one out and get to three hundred both ways."

I told him I appreciated how he felt. "But listen, we're just one down," I said. "Early Wynn's one smart pitcher. You'd better start watching him carefully because you may be running for one of the guys before this one's over."

"I've been watching him all game," Speedy replied. "I always do. That's one reason I'm so good at stealing bases. Wynn's got a routine with men on. He always throws over to first before his second pitch to the plate. If the manager puts me out there and wants me to steal, it should be on the first pitch. And I'll make it to second easy."

Someone got a hit off Wynn in the seventh and someone else drew his only walk of the game in the eighth. In both those innings I watched Wynn closely when the runner was on first. Just like Speedy had said, each of Wynn's pickoff throws to first, to hold the runner close, came before his second pitch to the plate. We didn't score in either inning, but neither did the Sox, so it came to the ninth inning with our club needing one run to tie and two to go ahead.

I can still see that inning like it happened yesterday. Woodie Held, a clutch hitter for us all season, led off. He hit one on the ground ticketed for center field, but Aparicio caught up with it, whirled around, and threw him out by half a step. Vic Power was up next and hit a long drive to left field on the first pitch. When the ball left his bat, we all hustled up to the top step of the dugout, thinking it might leave the park, but Minoso raced back to the fence, leapt up at the last second and pulled it down.

That's when Dykes called my name and told me to get a bat. "If Keough gets on, you hit for Phillips," he said.

"Why in hell doesn't he have you hit for Keough?" Speedy whispered. "I don't believe what I'm seeing. What's wrong with this guy?"

I grabbed a bat and went out to the on-deck circle to get loose. My one chance to get the hit I needed depended on a teammate with a .240 average getting on base.

We were down to our last out, and to our last strike after Keough fouled off a couple, but then he came through with a looper to center that fell in for a hit. Dykes hollered for Speedy to go in and run for

Keough. Speedy was out of the dugout in a flash, and as he ran past me, he wished me luck. "Make it happen, old man," he said. "Just think of that number three hundred and make it happen. I prayed for you to get the chance, so don't let me down."

I was announced as a pinch hitter, took a few more swings, and walked to the plate. For a minute or so, it was like old home week. The umpire, Joe Paparella, had been in the League almost as long as me, and knew he wouldn't see me again. He wished me luck and then reminded me of the time he threw me out of a crucial ball game against the Yankees when I argued about a called third strike. I had used a few choice words back then in making my point. "Maybe, as I think about it now, that pitch you complained about was a little low," he said, grinning at me.

"Thanks, Joe," I answered. "You were always one to admit your mistakes."

The White Sox catcher, Sherm Lollar, had gone out to the mound after I was announced. When he got back behind the plate, he said, "Early's going to give you a retirement present, a fastball on the first pitch, right down the middle."

I knew that was just to get me thinking, to wonder if he really meant it, so that I might be sitting on a fastball while he came in with a slider or a slow curve. "Sherm," I said, looking down at him, "you tell that SOB pitcher of yours I'll never forget him for being so nice to me today." Early Wynn had been my roommate for three years during the time he pitched for Cleveland. Now he was moving in on winning 300 games, and I knew he'd do anything to get there. He'd make me look like a fool up there if he could.

I rubbed some dirt on my hands, took one last practice swing, and stepped into the batter's box. As usual, Wynn had the brim of his cap pulled down low so that most of his face was in shadow. I took a long look at the third base coach to see if there was anything on. Dykes wasn't telling Speedy to steal second on the first pitch, but he was giving him the green light to go if Speedy thought he could get a good jump. I knew he'd take off as soon as that first pitch was thrown. Wynn put his right foot on the rubber and Speedy took his lead off from first. Wynn bent forward and stared into the plate for a long time to get the sign from Lollar. Speedy lengthened his lead, inches at a time, as Wynn raised his arms and got set to pitch. It seemed like forever to me, wagging the bat back and forth, before Wynn moved again; and as he did I could see Speedy, out of the corner of my eye, turn toward second and start running. But Wynn wasn't pitching to the plate; he had thrown to first and had Speedy picked off cleanly. Roy Sievers, their first baseman, fired the ball to Aparicio at second and Luis tagged him out as Speedy went sliding into the base. The game was over, and so was my career in the major leagues. For eternity I would be a lifetime .299 hitter with 299 home runs.

As I was walking toward the dugout, still holding my bat, Wynn shouted over to me. "Hey, hitman," he said, using the name he always called me. "I wanted to pitch to you, but that kid runner had 'pick me off' written all over him. I really was going to throw you that meatball. I bet you would have mashed it." I tell you, Andrew, I'm sure he didn't mean it, but I wish he hadn't said a word to get me thinking.

That's all for now. Love to you from me and your aunt Honey. Let us hear from you again soon.

Uncle George

WIVES AND LOVERS

Dedicated to the Memory of Robert S. Fuchs

"Being with a woman all night never hurt no professional baseball player. It's staying up all night looking for a woman that does him in."

—Casey Stengel

IT ALL STARTED on a beautiful July Fourth afternoon, during the Great Depression, just after an eleven-inning game between the visiting club from Scranton and the home team Harrisburg Senators in the New York-Penn League. Before the extra innings began, the crowd in Island Park had been treated to a full fifteen-minute fireworks display in case the game ran too late to celebrate the holiday within the Sunday curfew restrictions. Mickey Doolin had fallen hard for Lenore McHugh a long time before, but watching her in the first row of boxes all afternoon from his position at first base had pushed him over the edge. He wanted her desperately. Lenore was his ideal woman, and had been for the season and a half he had played for the Harrisburg Senators. The problem was that she was married to Davey McHugh, the club's center fielder.

Doolin felt motivated and inspired by her appearance at the park that day, an infrequent one, and had, in fact, secured the victory for his team with the hit that drove in the winning run, one of three he had that day. On his way to the dugout, surrounded by several of his happy teammates, he winked at Lenore and received a wave and smile in return. "Take me, I'm yours," the smile said to him. It promised everything he was certain he wanted.

As soon as he had showered and dressed, Doolin walked over to McHugh's locker. "Can we talk a minute, Davey?" he asked.

McHugh grinned at his friend. "I thought you'd be hurrying outside to give the scribes an interview. You're today's hero. They deserve it. And it never hurts to get written up on a good day."

"This is more important, Davey." Doolin reached for the stool in front of the adjoining locker and sat down. "It's about your wife."

Davey McHugh was the last player to leave the Harrisburg locker room that afternoon. He had sat and listened quietly while Doolin told him how sure he was that he loved Lenore and had to be with her. His attraction to her and their flirtation with each other had begun during the prior baseball season, Doolin said. "Whenever the four of us were together, Davey, I always wished I was going home with Lenore, not Estelle." And his desire had been growing by leaps and bounds since spring training brought them all together again. "All winter I was looking forward to baseball again, not for the game but just to see Lenore."

When Doolin finished describing all the details of what he considered his "love affair," he took a deep breath and exhaled it loudly. "I hate to be saying what I'm saying to a teammate and a good friend, Davey, but I can't help it. I've been attracted to her like a moth to a streetlight."

At first, McHugh felt his blood boiling inside him and was sure his face was flushed with the same scarlet color. If it had been anyone but

Doolin talking to him, he would have already struck the first blow. But as Doolin's confession continued, McHugh reminded himself that his marriage to Lenore had not been ideal. In fact, his understanding of what made her content—what she revealed of herself when he courted her—had been totally jarred by her current need to be "doing something" or "going somewhere" a good deal of the time. She was no longer the stay-at-home wife he thought he married, and their differences had given rise to frequent arguments.

Now, calmed down, McHugh tried to look sympathetic. If Doolin thought Lenore was the woman for him, it might benefit McHugh in the long run. "I understand, Mickey, I understand. We've all been there," he said. Then, after a long pause, "Have you told Lenore how you feel?"

"No, not yet, but I know she's waiting for you outside and I'm going to let her know as soon as I leave here."

"And what about your wife, Mickey? Does Estelle have any idea what's going on?"

Doolin didn't speak, but he bit his lip and shook his head from side to side.

"So how do you figure to handle it?" McHugh asked, again as amiably as he could. Anyone passing by and hearing just those words and the tone in which they were spoken might have assumed that one player was telling the other about the rent that had gone unpaid.

Doolin's silence continued a while longer. Finally, rising from the stool and kicking it over on purpose, he replied, "We've got no kids, Davey, so it's not like I'll be leaving her in a big hole or anything. She's still a good looking broad. She can find another guy."

It was at that precise moment that Davey McHugh realized how much he had always liked Estelle Doolin. And in a flash it occurred to him that if he were looking for a bride for the first time and could choose between the two women they were discussing, he would propose to Estelle. But events were moving too quickly and he needed time to gather his thoughts and his feelings.

"You go speak to Lenore," he told Doolin. "I'll still be a while getting dressed. If you two are gone when I leave here, I'll understand that Lenore feels the same way about you that you do about her. Tell her I'll take a bus back to the apartment and talk to her later."

Doolin was obviously relieved. He had no idea what he would have said or done if McHugh had warned him to stay away from his wife. "You're being a real teammate here, Davey. I wasn't sure how you'd take it."

"These things happen, Mick. Life plays funny tricks on you, especially when you're not expecting it. Go see how Lenore feels. Maybe she thinks she'll be happier with you or maybe we're just wasting a lot of breath right now."

A simple "thanks" would have been called for, but Doolin grabbed McHugh's hand and shook it vigorously. "Yeah, you're right," he said.

Lenore McHugh was tingling. She felt that her big smile at Mickey Doolin that afternoon, along with a wave of her hand, had sent a message. He excited her, and she wanted to be with him.

Lenore had become bored with her marriage to Davey McHugh. She admired him for the man he was—kind, considerate, and protective of her—but what she wanted out of life ran counter to his nature and style. In the magazines she read, beautiful women went to parties and had fun. They dressed well, danced a lot, and were always seen laughing over something with their husbands or friends. Lenore knew she was beautiful also, but her life with Davey was very different from what she discovered in her reading.

She was almost twenty-one when they married after a two year courtship. Both were from a small town in Missouri and met at a YMCA function there. He never swept her off her feet, but she had realized that McHugh was her best ticket if she was serious about getting out of that town. Davey had proposed to her just after he signed a contract with the Braves to play in a Class C league in Florida. Anticipating the proposal, she had thought of making him wait overnight for an answer, but decided that the risk involved would make the wait more difficult for her than for him. The wedding took place three months later.

Lenore had enjoyed being a new bride in Florida. McHugh's team played its games in a park just south of Miami, and she had enjoyed sitting in the stands, knowing that fans around her were aware she was the center fielder's wife. The apartment they rented, though small, had had an ocean view, and the sound of waves breaking on the beach under a moonlit sky helped Lenore feel some romance in the moment. One of Davey's teammates who was also married had owned a car, and the two couples found much to enjoy in the area.

Although she didn't say anything at first, Lenore was disappointed when McHugh had gotten promoted to play in Harrisburg. For her, it was as if she had been brought back to Missouri, being in the middle of nowhere with nothing exciting to do. She had come to realize that Davey relished what she saw as monotony, that his life was the five hours a day he spent at the ballpark, and that staying home at night was both restful and pleasant for him. Her own restlessness, however, had led to arguments between them when he consistently balked at going to the movies, to a restaurant, or to a local theatre production as often as she liked. The disagreements had intensified on days when weather forced the cancellation of a game and Davey used the conditions as an excuse not to make the drive to Baltimore or even Lancaster where some event that Lenore was interested in was taking place.

When they returned to Harrisburg for the next baseball season, Lenore had begun to feel trapped in the life she was living. She knew that something had to change, and that's when she had begun going out to the Senators' ballpark to watch the players. It wasn't long before she made eye contact with Mickey Doolin, whose position at first base put him closest to the spectators sitting on that side of the field.

Lenore had spoken to Doolin at other times when the couples bumped into each other after one of the team's games or met by chance while shopping in Harrisburg's main business district. She had recalled his fondness for telling jokes and his friendliness in general, but had never regarded him as a potential romantic interest. After she had caught him glancing her way enough times during the games to convince Lenore he was attracted to her, she appeared at the park less frequently, intending to arouse Doolin's passion for her by her absence. In watching Doolin, she saw a man with a big smile for whom baseball always seemed to be fun. Lenore had felt she could count on his wanting to have fun her way also, and she had intended to speed up the process of determining whether he was seriously interested in her or not. That day she had had a strong feeling that what she was looking for had arrived.

At home that evening, McHugh had no trouble remaining calm as he and Lenore discussed the unfolding situation. He had actually returned to their apartment before she did, even though he had stopped for a drink and some quiet contemplation on the way.

Seeing that Lenore was not waiting for him outside the ballpark, he assumed that Doolin's pleas had won her over and that she might even be anxious to talk about a divorce. But now, having honestly considered their three plus years of marriage and the direction in which he felt it was going, he was just as anxious to discuss their permanent separation.

"Mickey doesn't want to get a divorce right now because he can't afford it," Lenore told him, while drying dishes at the sink. "He just wants to move in with me, and he says you've already agreed to move out."

McHugh was momentarily startled by his wife's words, but realized that he hadn't given any thought to the cost of a divorce. Doolin was right, he told himself. The way conditions were, and with the little they were paid to play baseball, this was hardly the time to be spending money on anything that wasn't essential.

"Yeah, that's about it," he answered. "We don't have money for a lawyer either."

"And Mickey said you could stay at his place tonight, that he'll tell Estelle everything and she'll understand."

"What's the rush?" McHugh asked. "I could get my things together on Wednesday. We don't have a game that day. It's not like I had a month's notice from the landlord. Mickey just hit me with this a few hours ago."

"I told him that, Davey." Lenore hung the towel on a rack next to the sink and sat down across from him at the small kitchen table. "I didn't want to have to fight with you about any of this. But Mickey doesn't want us to spend another night together in the same apartment. He says that if it's over, it's over. He's afraid of you-know-what, even though I told him there's no chance of that."

"So he's coming back here tonight?"

"No, he said he'd bunk in with one of the guys on the team, but he made me promise that you wouldn't be here. I only agreed when he got Estelle to say you could sleep on their couch, so you wouldn't have to go looking around for another place."

McHugh was tempted to say, "He's such a sweet guy," but controlled himself because he realized he had no problem with the sudden arrangements for that night. "Okay," he told her, "Mickey's probably right, and it will keep us from fighting with each other over who's to blame for what's happening."

"No one's to blame," Lenore said, "or maybe we're both to blame."

"Whatever you say," he answered, and headed off to the bedroom to get a change of clothes for the next day.

Estelle Doolin, who came from a Polish family, grew up on a potato farm in western New York near the state's border with Pennsylvania. She was the oldest of seven children and had been taken out of school by her father after completing the eighth grade, the last year of junior high school. Her father had listened to the praise bestowed on his daughter by several of her teachers who recognized Estelle's talent for learning and wanted to see her continue her education, but he saw his wife's need for help in raising their family and felt his decision was the right one. Estelle had applied herself to what she was taught and became skilled in everything it took to run a large household. At the same time, she had taken correspondence courses by mail and was only one year behind her former classmates in receiving a high school equivalency degree.

Estelle met Mickey Doolin in Buffalo on the weekend of her nineteenth birthday. She had been there with her mother on a trip they had planned for months as a reward for her "graduation" from high school. The running of the kitchen had been placed in the hands of her sixteen-year-old sister for the three days they would be away. The two women were having lunch in a highly-recommended downtown restaurant, one that had begun serving beer and wine with its meals again, once prohibition had ended. The restaurant had been quite crowded, it being Saturday, and they had been suddenly asked by a tall gentleman if they wouldn't mind his sharing their table with them. They had politely obliged, and as soon as he sat down next to Estelle, he had begun a running conversation, asking them all about themselves and life on their farm. In short order, they had learned that Mickey Doolin was a baseball player, that he expected to be playing professionally when the next season came around, and that he'd been told by several scouts that he had the ability to be an exceptional player if he was serious about making the game his career.

The time flew by quickly as Doolin talked; and the conversation would have continued in the now nearly-empty dining room had Estelle's mother had not pushed her chair back from the table and said that they were already an hour behind schedule for what they intended to do that afternoon. Before Estelle could get up, Doolin asked if she would give him her address so that he could correspond with her by mail. The request had prompted an immediate sensation of butterflies in her stomach, but Estelle had maintained control and wrote out her full name and address for him.

The first letter from Doolin had arrived about two weeks later and other letters from Minnesota followed about a week apart. He had written about himself and whatever else held his interest at that moment. In every letter he had repeated his feelings about the wonderful time he'd had with Estelle and her mother in the restaurant and how he hoped to have more of such conversations.

Estelle's replies had been less frequent and much shorter. She had enjoyed Doolin's company at the restaurant, but didn't think of him as a serious suitor. For one thing, he lived half a continent away; for another, he seemed much too taken with himself; and for a third, his occupation would keep him away from home much of the time. Although Estelle had been taken with Doolin's good looks and his sense of humor, she refrained from intimating any desire for companionship with him.

Then, just a week before Christmas, Doolin had arrived at the farm with presents for everyone in the family. They found him a place to sleep in the house, and he had spent all of his time each day following Estelle around while she worked. He had talked about anything and everything, and his unending conversation seemed to bring them closer and closer by the hour. Estelle had realized that all of his talk about himself and his dream of playing professional baseball had been in the spirit of openness, not conceit. And she had found him to be sensitive to the things that meant a lot to her, including her desire to continue her education.

When he spoke of marriage, Estelle had told him she would have to think about it, but she knew she'd be able to leave the farm with a man she could love. On the day after Christmas the couple had informed Estelle's parents that they were engaged (although without a ring to bear witness) and wanted to get married before Mickey had to go off to play baseball. All the necessary arrangements had been made, and in planning the invitations Estelle had learned that an older sister, living in a house that had belonged to Doolin's parents in Minnesota, was all the family he had.

Doolin had signed his first professional contract with the New York Giants, and at the end of spring training in Florida, had been assigned to a Single A farm team in Charleston, South Carolina. He and Estelle had spent the entire season there, renting the second floor of a home just six blocks from the ballpark. Neither of them had cared much for the city, finding it uncomfortably humid most of the summer months. Doolin's play for the team, especially his hitting, proved disappointing, and at season's end the Giants had informed him that his contract had been assigned to the Boston Braves.

During the winter, Doolin had introduced Estelle to life in Minneapolis. The snow and freezing temperatures were nothing new to her, but the feeling of being housebound, with little to do for so much of the time, had disturbed her. Doolin had worked for the State as a mechanic in a garage that maintained snow removal equipment. Estelle had tried to find work in the city as a clerk of some sort, but no one wanted to hire her as soon as they learned she would be leaving the area in February. She had looked forward to their return to Florida, and they later celebrated their first wedding anniversary in Harrisburg, where the Braves had assigned Mickey after watching him hit good pitching in a number of Florida games.

Estelle's search for a job during the baseball season had been only partially successful. Positions had been very hard to come by, especially for someone who was new to the city and had no helpful contacts. Still, she had managed to find work two days a week, cutting out and filing newspaper articles in the file room of the *Harrisburg Herald*. She had checked into taking courses in nursing at the Hope Hospital in town, but was told that all courses started in September. Estelle had tried spending other afternoons at the ballpark, but was bored by the game itself and had felt uncomfortable listening to the chatter of some of the other players' wives, all of whom had seats in the same section. But had she continued to attend the games, Estelle probably would have noticed how well Lenore McHugh dressed whenever she appeared there, and might also have become aware that Doolin often seemed to turn his head and smile directly at Lenore whenever he had made a good play in the field.

It had been on their return to Harrisburg the next year and shortly after the celebration of their second year of marriage that Mickey expressed some dissatisfaction with their life together. He had found no fault with anything Estelle did, he said, but thought that maybe they had married too young in life. He was looking for some new spark, he told her, but couldn't put his finger on what it was and wasn't sure where it was going to come from.

Doolin's feelings had come as a surprise to Estelle who had thought they had been getting along well. Only several weeks earlier, in bed at night, they had talked about the right timing for having a child. Doolin had seemed enthused about the idea that night, but hadn't mentioned it again. Estelle had thought that perhaps the realization of what a commitment that would be had given rise to her husband's stress. She had considered phoning her mother and asking her advice, but realized that someone listening in on the two-party line might spread word of Estelle's problem to other farmers in the area. In the end, she had decided it was best for her to be patient with Doolin and hope that his attitude would change on its own.

Doolin had tried spending time with some of his unmarried teammates at night, drinking beer, playing pool, or joining card games, but he confessed to Estelle that none of it made him feel any better. "When what I want shows itself, I'll know it," he had told her, although by then he was already far into the web Lenore had been weaving. So it didn't come as a total shock to Estelle when Doolin came home from the ballpark that day and announced, hands deep in his pants pockets and eyes staring at the linoleum floor, that he was moving in with Lenore McHugh to see if that was what he was looking for.

"Davey understands what's going on and he agreed to move out. Is it okay if he stays here a day or two until he can find a place?"

"Mickey, I'm your wife," she said. "If that's alright with you, tell him he's welcome."

Estelle made McHugh feel comfortable as soon as he arrived. She had prepared steak and mashed potatoes, a ballplayer's favorite dinner, and an apple pie baked in the oven while they ate. She'd had several hours to come to grips with the fact that Mickey had left her for another woman. What was she supposed to do now? She asked herself whether she would take him back if he tired of being with Lenore, but she didn't have the answer. Eventually she decided that she would live her life with the understanding that Doolin was out of it. She broke the ice quickly with McHugh as she poured beer for each of them. "You can stay as long as you want, Davey."

"Or until Mickey decides to come back," McHugh said, watching her closely as Estelle first dropped her head and then raised it to look at him directly.

"Mickey's an emotional guy," she replied. "Lots of times he does things without thinking and then later changes his mind."

"Well, I'm not going back to Lenore. That's over and done with. You don't get thrown out like this and then make believe later on that it never happened." He hesitated, suddenly realizing that what he had said may have hurt Estelle. "Of course, there are always exceptions," he added. Then, during a short silence between them, McHugh told himself that it was probably the time to go all the way and let her know how he felt. "I'd be happy to stay here, Estelle, because I like you very much and have for a long time." He hesitated again, fiddling with the fork that was in front of him, placed there for the apple pie. "I mean that if we were both single and I was courting you, that's what I'd be saying because that's how I feel."

Estelle blushed. She smiled at him and got up to check on the pie. "Five more minutes and it will be ready." She returned to the table and sat in the chair next to his. "I like you the same way, Davey, and I'm pleased that you want to stay here." She leaned her head toward him and he put his arm around her shoulder.

"Mickey won't be thinking about a divorce anytime soon," she said quietly, "even if he stays with Lenore. He says we haven't the money for it."

"I know that. And it's the same with me and Lenore. We'll all have to wait until times are better and there's more money to spend."

"So does that mean we're just swapping husbands and wives for the time being?" Estelle asked.

McHugh smiled, and then there was laughter in his eyes. Estelle saw it and smiled back. "Don't say it too loud," he whispered, "the neighbors may hear you."

Doolin entered the locker room the next day just as McHugh was getting ready to go out on the field. "Davey, hold on a second," he said. McHugh stopped and waited for him to come closer.

"Is everything okay?" Doolin asked.

"Yeah, it's fine," he answered.

"No problems with Estelle?"

"No problems."

"You going to stay with her?"

"Yeah, that's what I'm planning to do."

"Glad to hear it, Davey. That's good; good for both of you. But I was thinking about you and Estelle, and how I just sort of messed things up all around . . ." Doolin looked down at the floor, closed his eyes, and seemed to be trying to remember what he wanted to say next. When it came to him, he continued. "I mean I'm the one who caused all this. This wife-swapping is on account of me, so I want to put a condition on it that makes it fair for both of us."

McHugh tensed up. He knew Doolin wasn't about to do him any favors, that he had to listen carefully. "What is it, Mickey?"

"Here's my idea. Let's agree that when next July Fourth comes around, if you still want to be married to Lenore and go back to her, or if I feel the same about Estelle, all either of us has to do is speak up, anytime within a week after the holiday, and whoever does it gets his wife back. But if it's you wanting Lenore, you have to tell me in person, face to face, no other way. Or I'd have to tell you the same way, face to face, if it was me wanting Estelle. But we've got to have a year to see if this works out. So it can't be before July Fourth, and it's got to be only the seven days right after the holiday or forget about it altogether and there's no swapping back, even if we're still not getting divorced. I hope that's fair enough, Davey. I owe it to you."

Even before Doolin had finished, McHugh could see the fine hand of Lenore in everything his teammate was saying. She was afraid, he knew, that things might not go all that well with Doolin after the passion had died down, and it would be a lot easier for her to toss him out if he still had Estelle to go back to. Lenore wasn't concerned about Doolin or Estelle, only herself. She knew that McHugh would never come back to her after what she had done.

"But what if a year from now you're through with Lenore and Estelle doesn't want you back?" McHugh asked.

"She's got no say in the matter, Davey, unless she suddenly comes into a lot of money. She can't support herself."

McHugh realized how unfair the situation was to Estelle, but he knew his teammate was right. He also knew that Lenore would be able to find another man after Doolin, if she wanted one. "It's a deal, Mickey." he said, trying to keep things light. "You get to speak up during that seven-day period in July or forever hold your peace."

Doolin grabbed McHugh's hand and shook it up and down several times before saying, "Let's shake on it, Davey. You're a good man."

The months that followed the wife-swapping arrangement were some of the happiest of Davey McHugh's life. He couldn't have imagined how well suited he and Estelle were for each other and how much joy she would bring him. It was impossible for him to understand why Doolin would have wanted to leave her.

There was little or no talk of Lenore or Estelle when the two team-mates saw each other at the ballpark. Once in a while, when they happened to be alone in the locker room or when one sat down next to the other in the dugout, Doolin asked, "How's Estelle? Is she treating you okay?" McHugh's answer was always the same. "Yeah, Mickey, things are fine." When the Harrisburg season ended on Labor Day, the two couples went their separate ways.

As winter neared its end and spring training for the new baseball season rolled around, McHugh and Estelle left the home in New Jersey they had been renting and made the long drive to the team's training site in Bradenton, Florida. He hadn't mentioned the agreement with Doolin to her, and only then began to worry that Doolin would take advantage of it in July. If that happened, he couldn't be sure how Estelle would react. She hadn't once said a bad word to him about her husband, and expressed concern several times when she heard about the fierce snowstorms that hit Minnesota, where Doolin still lived in the off-season. McHugh hoped to see his teammate and Lenore still showing a lot of passion for each other.

When he saw Doolin on the field the day they reported, McHugh asked how Lenore was doing. "She's looking great, Davey," Doolin said. "Minnesota was good for her." Later, when Estelle asked whether Mickey had inquired about her, McHugh said he had and that he sent his regards. He was sure Estelle would ask the question, and had decided beforehand to do both her and his friend that favor.

Several days later McHugh learned that Lenore had not accompanied Doolin to Florida. "She just couldn't come right now," Mickey told him. "She took a job in a factory outside Minneapolis and had to promise she'd work right up until May when things slow down for them. So she'll skip Florida and come to Harrisburg after I get there. I'm thinking the club will have us both back in Harrisburg for another year, or at least until one of us gets called up to the Braves in Boston. Hey, Davey, maybe we'll both make it this year. Wouldn't that be something?"

"Yeah, it sure would, Mick."

Doolin was right about the franchise's plans for both him and McHugh. A week before the parent team was to leave Florida for several more exhibition games on the road before reaching Boston, the two of them were reassigned to Harrisburg and given four days to report. At Estelle's suggestion, McHugh asked Doolin to ride with them in their car. But he rejected the offer, saying that he preferred taking a train so that he could move around as he wanted during the long trip from Florida to Pennsylvania.

May arrived and Lenore was still a no-show. "I haven't seen Lenore out at the park yet," McHugh said as he and Doolin were doing their stretches on the field before a game against the Wilkes-Barre Barons. "Still getting settled?"

"No, Davey, she's not here yet. What a gal. Her sister, the one in St. Louis, had to have some sort of operation and be in the hospital a while. So Lenore's there taking care of her husband and kid. She said you'd met her once, her name's Pauline. I guess she's a few years older than Lenore."

"Well that's too bad, Mickey. It's tough being alone. But I'm sure Estelle would like you to come over for a nice home-cooked meal. How about it?"

"Hey, thanks, and you tell Estelle I appreciate it, I really do, but I'm just not ready for that right now. I'd either lose my tongue or maybe say the wrong thing at some point without Lenore being there. Let's wait, Davey, okay? Maybe down the road, we'll see how things go."

At dinner that night McHugh couldn't help wondering aloud whether something else was going on. "It's possible they've already had enough of each other," he said. "Lenore's got another sister in Chicago and she could have gone to St. Louis if there's really a problem there. That sister's not married—at least she wasn't a year ago—and you'd think she'd be the one to help out and let Lenore take care of her husband." He quickly corrected himself. "I mean her boyfriend . . . Mickey."

"Well, we'll find out in time, so there's no sense wondering about it." As she spoke, Estelle pushed the last of the salad onto McHugh's dish. "Mickey's not the type to make up stories. That's not in his blood. And he's too bullheaded to come here for dinner. His sister told me once that he's just like his father was."

Not having Lenore around certainly didn't affect Doolin's play on the field. After six weeks he was leading the league in home runs, runs batted in, and walks, with a batting average hovering around the .300 mark. The Harrisburg players were beginning to rag him regularly about being called up to the Braves. McHugh worried more about losing Estelle back to his teammate with Lenore still nowhere to be seen. He had begun hoping that Doolin's success would soon be rewarded with a trip to the big leagues, putting a lot of geography between the two of them. It was already the third week in May and July Fourth was getting closer every day.

On Sunday, June 6th, the Senators played a doubleheader at home against the Williamsport Grays. Doolin's production for the afternoon netted him five hits in eight official at-bats, including a home run in each game and the hit that drove in the winning run just minutes before the Sunday curfew would have brought the second game to a halt. By Tuesday, word was out that Doolin had a ticket in his pocket and would be leaving that day to join the Braves, who were playing in Cincinnati. McHugh approached his teammate in the locker room as he was packing his bag.

"Congratulations, Mickey, you sure deserve it. You've been playing the game like a man possessed. I hope it keeps up when you're in Boston. In fifth place like they are, they can sure use a bat like yours." He watched as Doolin carefully untaped a picture of Lenore that hung inside the door of his locker. "Have you told Lenore yet?" he asked.

"Of course I have, Davey. You know, she's been sick herself, near pneumonia I guess, after doing all she did for her sister. But she'll be taking the train from St. Louis to Boston in a couple of days and she'll be with me as soon as the team gets back home from Cincinnati and Philadelphia."

They talked for a while, about nothing in particular, just two friends finding it hard to let go, until Doolin was packed and, as a parting shot, had torn off the strip of tape with his name on it from above his locker. "I don't want this up here waiting for me to come back," he laughed. "You'd better get out on the field for practice, Davey, or the old man's going to bust a gut. Tell Estelle I was asking for her, and I know I'll be seeing you real soon." With that, Doolin punched McHugh's arm lightly and headed for the door.

This time McHugh did not relay Doolin's regards to Estelle. Mickey's last words had sent a cold chill down Davey's spine. If he's going to be seeing me real soon, he thought, it's got to be about Estelle, and if it's about her, it's only because he wants out from Lenore and back to his wife. There was no reason for him to believe what Doolin had said about Lenore being on her way to Boston. After all, he'd been making excuses about her absence since the start of spring training, and before today hadn't said a word about her being sick, especially with something as serious as pneumonia. You could die from that, and he couldn't see Doolin being silent about it, just keeping it to himself day after day while they spent hours around each other, both in the locker room and on the field. He was convinced more than ever that Mickey and Lenore had called it quits some time ago and that Mickey was now waiting for that week in July to reclaim his wife. In that case, he certainly wasn't going to give Estelle any reason to feel good about Doolin by telling her that she was in his thoughts as he left for Cincinnati.

The next day McHugh went to the man they all called Fyooksie, the general manager, and checked both the Boston and Harrisburg team schedules for the week that would begin on July 5th. He was pleased to find that the Braves were scheduled to play every day but one that week, with games in Pittsburgh and St. Louis, while the Senators would be playing and traveling in upstate New York. It would be difficult for Doolin to have a face-to-face meeting with him. The only day he had to be concerned about was July 5th, the day after the holiday, when the Braves would be arriving in Pittsburgh for an off-day before the start of their series with the Pirates, and the Senators would be in Harrisburg all day until their overnight train departed for Elmira at eleven o'clock at night. That would be Doolin's only chance to find him in Harrisburg and still have time to get back to Pittsburgh for his game the next day.

By the time July 4th arrived, McHugh's plans were in order. He and Estelle left Harrisburg as soon as the Senators' game that day was over, and stayed overnight—under an assumed name—at a lakeside cabin colony a short distance from the city. They checked out of there late the next day and drove to Lebanon, which would be the first stop the train carrying the Harrisburg team would make on its way to Scranton and then New York State.

"You take the car back to Harrisburg," he told Estelle. "Go see Fyooksie at the train station when he's checking the boys in. Tell him I had an emergency call from a relative and that I had to leave first thing this morning. He'll get all excited at that, so let him blow off a little steam, but then assure him that I said I'd be in Elmira when the team arrived if I couldn't catch the same train at another station." McHugh put his hands on her shoulders. "Have you got that okay?" he asked.

"I do, Davey, but you haven't told me why you're doing this. What's it all about?"

"Just trust me, Estelle. It's something I'm doing for us, and I promise I'll tell you what it is as soon as I'm back from the road trip." McHugh knew from the silence that followed and the look Estelle gave him that she wasn't going to push him any further. "Now let's have a kiss and you drive back carefully." Estelle obliged but didn't start the car until McHugh pointed to the key in the ignition. "One last thing," he said, as he opened the passenger-side door and began to get out, "if you meet anyone at the train station we know, no matter who it is—even if Doolin of all people suddenly appears out of nowhere—don't tell anyone I'm getting on the train in Lebanon. Just tell Fyooksie or anyone who asks that all you know is what I said, that I'd be in Elmira for tomorrow's game."

As she drove back to Harrisburg, Estelle was bothered by what was going on. McHugh had surprised her that day by driving to Lebanon instead of returning home, giving her no reason for the detour. "You'll see," he said. Then he had added to the mystery by sending her back to Harrisburg while he remained there. He had asked her to tell Fyooksie about an emergency telephone call when there really wasn't one. And she couldn't understand how his strange conduct could be a way of his doing something for the two of them, as he had said. Estelle wondered whether there was another woman involved. Certainly McHugh had the opportunity to meet someone in each of the towns where the team played, and one of them might live in Lebanon. Why else would he send her home almost five hours before the train from Harrisburg was scheduled to stop there? And why would he caution her not to tell anyone else that he was in Lebanon?

Estelle realized that she had grown tired of living in Harrisburg. She was still unable to obtain any interesting employment and dreaded the days when there was no work available for her at all. She had no intimate friends from among the players' wives, avoided the ballpark when the Senators were home, and felt depressed when McHugh was on the road for a week or more at a time. "How long can I put up with all this?" she asked herself.

That night, when he boarded the train in Lebanon, McHugh wore a false mustache and beard that he had purchased in a joke shop earlier in the week. Instead of going to the first class dining car or to the sleeper car where the Senators would be bunking, he took a seat in coach class near the rear of the train. He also had on a gray fedora, the brim of which he tipped at an angle just above his eyes. He was afraid that Doolin might be on the train, ready to ride it as far as Wilkes-Barre, to see if McHugh got on anywhere between Harrisburg and Scranton. If so, Doolin might be checking each car, looking for him. But he was satisfied, having seen himself in the mirror, that Mickey would never recognize him from a quick walk-by down the aisle of the coach, and, in any event, wouldn't expect McHugh to be anywhere but with his teammates.

In Scranton there was a layover of about an hour as several cars were switched to a waiting train that would head directly north into New York State and on to a series of towns that included Elmira. McHugh waited patiently from a distance, and then, when the final boarding call had been announced, he entered the last coach car on the train. Only several seats in the car were occupied. He found some pillows and a blanket in an upper rack and made himself comfortable on a seat in the middle of the coach. He waited until the conductor came by to take his ticket, asked to be awakened if he were sleeping when the train approached Elmira, and then stretched out on the double seat for the rest of the trip.

The following morning, when the train arrived in Elmira, McHugh caught up with his teammates as they were leaving the terminal to board the bus waiting to take them to their hotel. Fyooksie, counting bodies at the entrance to the bus, stopped him.

"When did you get on the train, McHugh?"

"In Lebanon, Fyooksie. But I'd had such a long day I just collapsed in a coach car and fell asleep. Sorry for any trouble I caused."

"Okay, as long as you're here, but Sam wasn't happy about your not being in Harrisburg with the rest of the team. I spoke to him about it after Estelle told me your problem. It should be all right when he sees you in uniform."

That afternoon the Senators made easy work of the Elmira Colonels, beating them 6–2. McHugh had three of his team's ten hits, including a home run. When the teams reconvened for the second game of the 3-game series a day later, the Elmira club looked as lethargic as the day before, succumbing by an 8–3 score. McHugh had two more hits that afternoon, both doubles, and knocked in three runs.

It was obvious the next afternoon that the Colonel players had been admonished for their performance on the field. The spirit they showed during both infield and batting practice carried over into the game and they took a commanding 7–0 lead after four innings. The Senators rallied several times after falling into the hole, but couldn't get the key hits to sustain a comeback. McHugh had another double in the eighth inning that drove in two runs, but it was in vain as Elmira won the game 10–5.

That evening, after the Harrisburg players arrived by bus in Binghamton for the team's series with the Triplets, McHugh went off by himself to see a movie. He felt comfortable about the fact that the Braves would be playing in St. Louis for the next three days while his Senators were 1500 miles away. And once the series with the Triplets was over, he'd be able to return to Harrisburg and not worry about Doolin suddenly showing up to reclaim Estelle for himself.

When McHugh got back to his room at the hotel, there was a message waiting for him from Fyooksie that had been slipped under the door. "See me as soon as you get this note," it read. "I'm in Room 310."

Fyooksie opened the door and greeted McHugh with a big smile. "Come in, Davey, come in. I could have waited on this until breakfast tomorrow, but then you would have missed out on the great night's sleep you'll have tonight. Here's the good news. The Braves are going to have an opening on the roster the day after tomorrow and the club wants you to fill it. I guess they took notice of how you've been hitting lately. Anyway, that means you get on a train tomorrow and head out to St. Louis. You'll get there at night—it's about a twelve-hour ride from here—and be activated on Saturday so you'll be available for the two weekend games. Congratulations, Davey, you're going to be a big leaguer."

McHugh didn't know what to say. Fyooksie was telling him that his lifelong dream of playing in the major leagues was about to come true.

It was all he ever wanted, to be on the same field with the best players in the world. Natural talent played a big part in McHugh's success, but he had put in the long hours and done all the hard work to reach this point. He should have been jubilant at the news. But in fact he was devastated by it. He looked at Fyooksie silently while his head was reeling at what he had just been told. Moving up to the major leagues at this point wouldn't make up for losing Estelle to Doolin if his former teammate wanted her back. The only way McHugh could be certain of keeping her was to avoid Doolin altogether. And that meant staying away from St. Louis and the Braves for the next three days. He had to convince his general manager to let him do that. He had to come up with something quick.

"Fyooksie, it's great that the Braves want me. Getting to the big leagues is all I've thought about since my dad got me my first mitt and took me to a Cardinals game. I want to go desperately, but I can't go tomorrow. The problem is that Estelle isn't well. We don't know what's wrong, but she's got an important doctor's appointment first thing Monday morning when we get back from this trip, and I promised I'd be with her. She's worried sick about herself, and I can't let her go to the doctor alone. If I went out to St. Louis, I couldn't get back to Harrisburg on time." He was silent for a few moments before continuing. "Wait a second, where do the Braves go after the St. Louis series?"

Fyooksie pulled a schedule out of his jacket pocket. "Back to Boston, to play the Dodgers," he answered. "Tuesday, Wednesday, and Thursday."

"So I could leave Monday, after Estelle's appointment, and be in Boston in plenty of time for the Dodgers. I'd only be missing the two games against the Cards."

"I think you'd be taking a big chance, Davey. No manager likes to be caught a guy short on the bench in case he needs him. I'm sure Billy O'Connell feels the same way with the Braves. If you can't go, the club may call up someone else. Probably not from the Senators but from some other farm team. And if they do, nothing says they'll want you next week when they're back in Boston. You might be real sorry you didn't jump at the chance when you had it."

"Fyooksie, like I said, it's my dream, but there's nothing I can do. Estelle has to come first."

"Okay, I'll make a phone call and explain the situation. As soon as I know what the decision is, I'll let you know."

The next day McHugh continued his hitting streak. He had a perfect afternoon at bat, reaching base on three singles and a walk. Two of the runs he scored helped give the Senators a 5–3 victory over Binghamton. McHugh hoped that word of his performance would convince the Braves to hold off filling the roster spot until he could join the team in Boston.

But it didn't work out that way. While McHugh was eating dinner that night in the hotel, Fyooksie came by and gave him the bad news. "Sorry, Davey. Billy O'Connell told the owner he wasn't going to manage a man short if there was a body available. He was really upset with you. They decided to pull some infielder off the Toledo club. I suspect they'll hold on to him for a while. I can't say whether O'Connell will call you again. You'll just have to keep playing the best you can, try to keep that hot hitting going."

McHugh was in the locker room, slowly dressing for the game on Saturday afternoon. He was sitting on a wooden stool, facing his locker, when he suddenly felt a large hand on his shoulder. Before he could turn around and look up, he heard the familiar voice greeting him: "Hello, Davey boy, good to see you."

"Mickey," he blurted out. He got up and looked at the smiling Doolin. "Mickey, what the heck are you doing here?"

"Didn't Fyooksie tell you guys? I got sent down yesterday, and here I am. It was no surprise, the way I've been hitting the past few weeks, or not hitting is what it really was. Just stopped seeing the ball good all of a sudden, and I dropped about thirty points in my average. So Quinn told me the best thing was to take some time in Harrisburg and get my eye back. How you doing, Davey? You look like you just seen a ghost."

While McHugh was listening to what Doolin had to say, he was trying to think ahead, wondering if there was anything he could do, any way he could object if Mickey told him he wanted to go back to Estelle. But he realized that they were face to face, as the agreement had specified, and that there was nothing to prevent Doolin from calling the shot.

"I'm good, Mickey. It's just such a surprise seeing you." He reached out to shake Doolin's hand. "And I'm sorry you got sent down but you'll be back up in no time, I'm sure of it."

"Yeah, I'm still waiting for when we can both be up there at the same time, Davey. I was hoping it was you who'd get the call and fill my spot with the team. Quinn told me how you've been knocking the cover off the ball. But at least coming back here gives me the chance to talk to you about Estelle and Lenore. I tried to see you at the train station in Harrisburg Monday night when the team left for Elmira, but you weren't there and someone said you'd been missing all day. I came in from Pittsburgh because I wanted you to know how I felt. I was really afraid I might miss you this week. Good thing the Braves sent me back here, huh?" Doolin meant the last words just half in jest.

McHugh saw his best laid plans going up in smoke by Doolin's unfortunate demotion back to the minor leagues. He understood that the only reason Mickey would have been looking for him at the train station was to carry out the agreement in person and tell him about going back to Estelle. McHugh knew the ax would fall at any second. "You're right, Mickey," he said, "I couldn't make the train but I caught up with the team in Elmira."

"Anyway, Davey, here's what I want to tell you. Me and Lenore both feel we're hitting it off good and we're looking to stay together for a long time. At the point you can afford a divorce from Lenore, Estelle and I can split too, and then either of us is free to marry someone else if we want. I knew I had to let you know that during this week, like we said last year in that agreement we had."

The exhilaration he suddenly felt was overwhelming. McHugh wanted to wrap his arms around Doolin, to hug his friend as hard as he could. He was about to tell Doolin that he had their arrangement completely backwards, but then thought better of it. Let Mickey believe his demotion was fated, that it had come at just the right time so he could be there with McHugh to claim Lenore for his own.

"Well then, that's the way it's going to be, Mickey, and I'll give the news to Estelle as soon as we get back to Harrisburg. And the first night back you're coming over for dinner."

"I'd like to, Davey, but I'd have to be sure you had no hard feelings about what I just told you. Because if you did . . ."

McHugh interrupted him. "Mickey, no hard feelings at all. We made an agreement and we'll always be friends. You stay with Lenore and I'll stay with Estelle. Besides, I want you to tell me all about life in the big leagues. I didn't get there this time, but maybe one of these days I will."

When the team returned to Harrisburg, McHugh found a note on the kitchen table from Estelle. She told him that living in Harrisburg had become tiresome and depressing. She had decided to move to a bigger city and enroll in a nursing school. She was hopeful of finding a job to support herself and of receiving a scholarship to attend classes. She didn't say that life with McHugh was bad or boring, only that she needed to expand her horizons. "You've been good to me, Davey, and I'm grateful. I'll probably go to Boston. If playing baseball ever brings you there, you may want to look me up."

WHEN THE SPIRIT MOVES YOU

"When Steve (Carlton) and I die, we are going to be buried in the same cemetery, 60 feet, 6 inches apart."

—Tim McCarver

DARRIN CLARK'S NIGHTMARE began in the ninth inning of the rubber game against Baltimore. The visiting Orioles were behind 3–2, but had put runners on second and third with two out. When Carl Fullmer swung and missed at a low slider, putting himself in a two-strike hole, the Fenway Park faithful rose to their feet. Rhythmic applause heralded their anticipation of a game-ending strikeout, victory over the hated but more talented O's and a return to first place in the division standings.

Second baseman Clark pounded his fist into his glove and watched the catcher flash a series of signs that called for a curveball breaking outside. He relayed the signal to Hal Perris, playing a deep shortstop, and moved a few steps to his left just before the pitch was delivered. Fullmer, guessing fastball, lunged at the offering at the last instant and hit it on the ground between first and second. Clark glided over, scooped up the ball cleanly, and started to throw it to Mike Josephson at first. But halfway through his motion, it was as if an unseen hand had grabbed his shoulder and pulled on it. Clark hesitated before letting the ball go and then watched in pained disbelief as it flew wide of Josephson and into the Red Sox dugout.

The thirty-three thousand fans filling the ballpark were stunned by the sudden turn of events. Most of them cursed under their breaths as they sat down again; some did so more vocally. High fives greeted the Orioles' base runners as they crossed the plate to give their team the lead.

In the last of the ninth the Sox put the tying run on base with one out. But the disenchanted crowd failed to respond with its support and the rally fizzled. Boston's fifty-fifth loss of the season was in the books.

In the clubhouse, Clark was ignored by the beat reporters. They knew better than to ask him to explain the miscue. He sat on a chair facing his locker until the sounds in the room told him it was practically empty. Several teammates came by on their way out to offer encouragement. "Get 'em tomorrow, Darrin," was the message. He showered alone, dressed slowly, and was the last player to leave.

The next night's game was the first of three against the visiting Blue Jays. Toronto was in third place, three games behind the Red Sox. In the sixth inning, with one out and Toronto runners on each base, Clark was the middleman in what should have been a routine 6–4–3 double play. But as he jumped to avoid the sliding base runner, his arm poised to make the throw, he never followed through. By the time he landed on his feet and reloaded, it was too late to get the third out.

Clark couldn't believe what had happened. He knew that his arm had met some invisible resistance that prevented him from completing the play. He looked at Perris, ready to blurt out an explanation, but realized it would be useless. How could he expect his shortstop or anyone else to accept what he would say? To make matters worse, the next Blue Jay batter lofted the first pitch over the Green Monster, giving Toronto a three-run lead they never relinquished.

It was after midnight by the time Clark returned to his apartment. At twenty-eight and single, he lived alone in a town nineteen miles west of Boston. He snacked on some Swiss cheese and crackers, along with a glass of beer. The late night baseball coverage on one of the cable channels featured the winning Toronto home run, but not the play at second base that had set it up. He tried to sleep, but the drone of the air conditioner fighting the August heat and humidity kept him awake for a long time.

Clark's short rest ended just before three thirty that morning. He awoke suddenly, realizing that the dream he'd been having had pushed him into consciousness. It was still very vivid in his mind. He had been out on a lake in a rowboat. Another baseball player was with him, someone whose identity he was never sure of. Huge waves, coming out of nowhere, interrupted the tranquility of their day, rocking the boat violently. Neither man had taken a life preserver with him. In an effort to avoid being thrown into the water, they knelt down and wrapped their arms around the wood planks on which they had been sitting. After a short struggle, his friend fell into the lake and was quickly carried away from the boat by the surging waves.

Clark had never been a good swimmer. He felt that the only chance of rescuing his companion was to try and reach him with the boat and extend an oar for him to grasp. As he rowed desperately, he saw the other player go under and then emerge holding up a white cardboard sign with the number "22" on it. Moments later the friend disappeared again and then re-emerged with the sign still in his hands, but now displaying the number "45." Clark rowed as hard as he could but was unable to bridge the distance between himself and his fellow ballplayer. The next time he saw the placard rise above the surface of the lake, it again showed the number "22." Suddenly, the waters were calm again but his friend was nowhere to be seen. It was his crying out for him that jolted Clark out of his sleep. The fear that engulfed him as he recalled the dream sprang from realizing that his own uniform number was "22."

The final two games of the series were played on the weekend, with one o'clock starting times. On Saturday, Clark went to the park early to see the team trainer. He explained the sensations he had felt in the course of the two plays that cost the Red Sox both games.

"Can it be accounted for by some physical disability?" he asked.

The trainer put him through a series of arm and shoulder exercises, none of which gave Clark any discomfort or caused any disruption in his motion.

"You're perfectly fit," he was told. "I can't find anything wrong." What went unsaid, with the look the trainer gave him while shrugging his shoulders, was that Clark had no excuse for the errors he committed.

Dusty Harmon, the Red Sox manager, was waiting for him in the dugout when he went out to warm-up. "I think you can use a rest, Darrin. Take a seat today and we'll see about tomorrow."

Clark just nodded in response. As Harmon climbed the three steps to the field, Clark winced as his eyes registered the "45" on the back of the manager's uniform. Did the "45" intend to sink the "22"? he wondered. Was his career in jeopardy? Was that the dream's message?

He sat on the bench for eight and a half innings. In the bottom of the ninth, with his team again trailing by three runs, he was sent up as a pinch hitter. There were two outs and runners on first and second. Clark watched two outside curveballs go by and then drove the next pitch high off the left field wall above the scoreboard. The carom evaded the center fielder long enough to allow both runners to score.

As Clark took the turn at first base on the way to an easy double, he suddenly felt something hit against the instep of his right foot. It was as if he'd been tripped. He lost his balance and sprawled face down on the base path. He felt the dust and dirt rush into his mouth and cause him to choke. By the time he recovered and got to his feet, the first base coach was shouting at him to "come back, come back." Clark quickly retreated to the base. As he brushed himself off and shook his head in disgust, he realized that the coach was glaring at him. He met the gaze for a few seconds and didn't like what he saw.

The next batter singled into right center field, moving Clark to third. The team's radio announcer informed his frustrated listeners around New England that Clark would have easily scored the tying run had he not failed to reach second earlier. He also took the opportunity to recall other sad occasions in Red Sox history when a tripping base runner had cost the team victory in important games. Moments later, the second pinch hitter of the inning popped out to end the contest.

This time the reporters swarmed around Clark's locker as soon as they were allowed into the clubhouse. Red Sox fans were too high-strung and demanding to let three straight blunders of this magnitude sneak by without an explanation. The media covering the game for their respective newspapers and TV stations were all over him for answers. Clark tried getting away with a repeated "no comment" to the first flurry of questions, but it did no good. They continued to surround him, their pens and tape recorders at the ready. As he listened to their questions, Clark sensed the implication that he was either choking as the race for the playoffs came down to the last thirty-five games, or that he had some physical ailment he was concealing from management.

His frustration won out and he turned his chair around to face them. "Listen," he said, jerking his head from side to side to include them all in his answer, "I can't explain the screwups I've had in these last three games. On both of those throws, something seemed to just grab hold of my arm and keep me from making the play. Then, rounding first this afternoon, I'd swear someone stuck out his foot and tripped me. Don't tell me no one was near me because I know that. That's what makes this so weird. I've never fallen down running the bases before . . . ever! I'm perfectly okay physically—believe me, I checked—so there's no excuse for any of those plays. Right now that's all I can say about it because I can't figure it out. I don't want to sound like the pressure's getting to me, because it's not, but some strange things have been happening. It's like a science fiction story and I'm in the middle of it."

Clark looked around at everyone standing there, getting his words on their tapes and in their notebooks. He wondered if he shouldn't have said what he did, realizing how bizarre it must have sounded. He took a deep breath and let it out slowly. "That's it guys. I just feel terrible for what this has cost my teammates."

The questions kept coming, but the interview was over as far as he was concerned. He turned his chair back to his locker, stripped off his uniform, and headed for the trainer's room without saying another word. The members of the fourth estate had vacated the clubhouse long before he showered, dressed, and left himself.

The Sunday sports pages played up Clark's "confession" in dramatic fashion. Characterizations of his present state of mind ran the gamut from the ridiculous to the absurd. If any respect was due him for the six years he'd already been with the Red Sox, consistently contributing to the team's success, no one writing about him that day saw fit to give it. The Globe cartoonist, in three panels, drew him holding his bat at the plate as if he were playing cricket, running to first base backwards, and getting ready to catch a popup near second with his bare hands. "What Next?" the caption read.

The noise in the clubhouse switched abruptly to low whispering when Clark entered to get ready for that afternoon's game. He'd seen what had been written about him and wasn't surprised at the reception. It was best to just go about his business, he decided, and let things run their course. He put on his uniform, went out onto the field, and spent the next forty minutes stretching and running near the left field wall. When he returned to the dugout, Clark looked at the lineup card and saw that utility-man Mike Rooney was penciled in again at second base.

The game was a laugher for the Sox as they scored six runs in the first inning on the way to a 12-2 victory. Clark sat in the far corner of the dugout all afternoon. He got up only to give fisted high fives to three teammates who hit home runs and to keep his cup filled with Gatorade.

That night he had another bad dream. He saw himself driving alone through a cemetery during spring. He was admiring the manicured patches of late-blooming tulips as well as the lilac bushes that were just beginning to show their varied shades of purple. At a three-way intersection, Clark came upon a funeral cortege that consisted only of a hearse and a single chauffeur-driven limousine behind it. He decided to follow it, and then walked to the burial plot at a discreet distance behind the five people who emerged from the parked limo.

No member of the clergy was present. The cemetery employees put the coffin in place above the hole that had been dug for it. One of the men who had wheeled it from the hearse to its final resting place faced those in attendance and quickly read a few prayers from a small black book. Then, just before the deceased was lowered into the ground, a woman holding a shopping bag approached. She took a white baseball uniform shirt out of the bag, unfolded it, and placed it over the end of the casket. Watching her intently, Clark first saw the "Red Sox" lettering on the front of the shirt, and then, as she laid it down, the number "22" on the back. He woke up in a sweat and spent the next hour worrying about what it meant before falling back asleep.

Monday was an off day for the team, with an optional practice scheduled for ten in the morning. The Yankees would be Boston's next opponent, on Tuesday, Wednesday, and Thursday night. Clark was worn out from both the stress of the past few days and the lack of sleep, but felt certain that he'd be expected to show up for infield work.

Only one other player and two coaches were in the clubhouse when he arrived. Clark found an envelope sitting on the shelf of his locker. It had his name on it, no return address, and no postage stamp. He assumed that it had been delivered to the team's offices that morning and brought to his locker by one of the clerical staff. The handwritten letter inside was addressed to "Dear Mr. Clark."

"I think I can help you," it read. "Someone in the other world is trying to send you a message. I've seen it happen many times. Please take this seriously and call me at 617-391-1813." It was signed, "Mr. Espirito."

"Another fan letter, Clark?" one of the coaches asked, making no effort to hide the mockery in his voice.

He didn't let it upset him. They were frustrated too, he realized.

"Yeah," he answered, "some guy who saw that dive I took Saturday said I'd make a great goalie. He wants me to call the soccer team for a tryout."

The others laughed. Clark got into his uniform and laced up his spikes. He headed for the door to the tunnel leading to the field but stopped before reaching it. He returned to his locker and dug all the change out of his pants pocket. Taking the letter he'd received, he dialed the number from the pay telephone in the corner of the room. The phone was answered after just one ring.

"Hello," said a low, heavy voice, "this is Mr. Espirito. Is that you, Mr. Clark?"

"Yes, but how did—"

The voice cut him off. "I'm glad you called. There is a troubled soul on the other side that needs your help. Tell me, have you had any unusual dreams lately?"

"Yes," Clark said, "that's part of what's been happening."

"You've got to let me know what they were."

Clark already trusted the person on the other end of the line. "I'll be glad to. Can we meet this afternoon, maybe somewhere in Kenmore Square?"

"No, I mean tell them to me right now. It's important for you to do so."

Clark looked around at the handful of players and coaches in the clubhouse. He turned his back to them and spoke in just above a whisper. "I'm sort of in a public place, but I'll talk softly. Can you hear me okay?"

"Yes, Mr. Clark, perfectly. Let me hear what you dreamt."

As soon as he began to detail the first dream, the recorded voice of an operator broke in and asked for more money. He had three quarters and a nickel left, all of which he quickly deposited. He returned to the first dream, finished describing it, and, at Espirito's urging, went on to the second one.

When he was through, there was just a short pause before Espirito spoke. "Find out who wore the number "22" for the Red Sox before you, Mr. Clark. I feel certain the answer lies there. But don't wait. Whoever is calling out to you wants your help right away and will continue to hurt your play on the baseball field until you give it. Goodbye."

Clark heard the click and hung up the receiver. It suddenly occurred to him that he might be the butt of a prank being played by some of his teammates. He had to consider the unstamped envelope with its mysterious message, the strange voice on the telephone, as if someone was purposely disguising his own, and this Mr. Espirito knowing immediately who it was that called.

By the time he returned to his locker, the clubhouse was empty. He decided to do as he'd been told, even if it meant being further embarrassed by falling harder for the same joke. Clark realized that he'd be creating a stir by not going out for practice after the coaches had seen him in uniform, but changed back into his street clothes nevertheless. A few minutes later he was upstairs, in the team's offices. He found Bob O'Brien, the assistant general manager, in the reception area.

"Bob," he inquired, the words spilling out eagerly, "do we have a book or anything that shows who wore a particular number for the team over the years?"

"I'm pretty sure we do. What are you looking for?"

"I want to see who else wore my number."

O'Brien had other matters on his schedule that morning. This was trivial, something that could wait, he concluded. "Okay, but give me a while to find it. I should have it by the time your practice is over."

"I'm not working out today, Bob," Clark answered. He suddenly felt as if there were beads of sweat on his forehead. He took out his handkerchief and wiped his brow. "I'd appreciate it if you'd look for it right now. It's important."

O'Brien was irritated. He was ready to lecture the player about keeping things in perspective. But the serious look on Clark's face and the way he'd emphasized the word "important" convinced him to heed the request.

"Okay, make yourself comfortable," he said. "I'll be as quick as I can. There are a bunch of files I'll have to go through."

O'Brien returned about twenty minutes later. He was carrying two folders, one manila and one colored dark green. The latter was very full and had several wide elastics around it to keep it together. Clark got up to meet him.

"Here's the stuff," O'Brien said. "The small file tells you who wore all the numbers, and the big one is full of biographies of the players. Some of the bios are more complete than others. I thought you might want to refer to them after you checked out your number."

Clark took the folders and thanked him. O'Brien pointed to the conference room across the hall. "You can look them over in there—no one will be using it—and then just leave them on my desk if I'm not here when you're through."

"Thanks, Bob," Clark repeated. Moments later he closed the conference room door behind him.

There were two full pages of players who had worn the number "22" for the team, starting in 1930 when numbers were put on uniforms for the first time. Clark went to the end of the list, where his name appeared with the notation "1996– " next to it. Before him came Len Carlsen who had it for three years, 1993–1995, and Terry Ruger for the '91–'92 seasons. He knew them both. They had been flashes in the pan, power hitters in the minor leagues who turned into singles hitters when they were brought up. Their defensive play, at third base and right field, respectively, didn't make up for their lack of punch at the plate. Each had been let go by the Red Sox as part of a trade and neither survived very long in the big leagues after leaving Boston.

Working backwards, Clark found that the last Red Sox second baseman to have the uniform number "22" was Paul LaRoque. He had played with the team for just one year, in 1945. As soon as he mumbled the date out loud, Clarke remembered the sign with the number "45" on it from his first dream. He felt a shiver inside and then a heightened tension throughout his body. Something convinced him that he'd made the connection he was looking for.

In the other folder, under "L," Clark found a short biography of LaRoque. He was a homegrown product, born in Medford, just outside Boston, in 1923. His parents, Marie and Charles LaRoque, were French immigrants who had no other children. His mother was widowed when Paul was seven years old and died herself seven years later. Neither the ages of his parents nor the cause of their deaths were mentioned.

LaRoque played Park League baseball in Boston for three years and was signed to a professional contract by the Red Sox in 1941, shortly before his nineteenth birthday. Nothing in the biography indicated with whom LaRoque lived in the years immediately following his mother's death. He spent three minor league seasons in different locations, quickly moving up the baseball ladder when both his defensive skills and his batting average improved consistently. He was brought to the team's temporary spring training facility in Atlantic City, New Jersey in 1945 when its roster of veteran players was depleted by their earlier enlistments in the armed forces during World War Two.

LaRoque was the best second baseman in camp and won the job. He had excellent statistics that season, batting .317 with eleven home runs, while the team finished next to last in the eight-team pennant race. The club's regular players returned in 1946, following the end of the war, but LaRoque had enough talent to remain with the Red Sox as a spare infielder and pinch hitter. Then, on April first of that year, the day before the team was scheduled to break camp in Florida and head north by train for the opening of the new season, LaRoque drowned. It happened at a local beach when he tried to help a lifeguard save three young boys who had been carried out over their heads by a fast receding tide. He was the only victim of the unfortunate incident.

Since there was no living relative known to the team, they arranged the funeral. LaRoque was laid to rest in a plot close to the one containing his mother and father in Medford's Oak Grove Cemetery. At the funeral, the Red Sox honored his memory by having the wife of manager Joe Cronin place LaRoque's uniform shirt on the casket before he was buried.

Clark closed the folder and sat for several minutes staring at the wall in front of him. It was difficult for him to believe how close his dreams had come to the reality of LaRoque's life. If he had entertained any doubt about Espirito's message before, he couldn't any longer. Now there was no denying that LaRoque had been trying to contact him and had been affecting his play in the field to make Clark take notice. He was reaching out to the closest next of kin he probably had, another second baseman with the Red Sox who wore the number "22." Clark was pleasantly amused by the fact that his being African-American didn't matter to the dead player. But what did LaRoque want of him, he wondered. What could be troubling his spirit more than fifty years after his untimely death?

Clark returned the folders to O'Brien's office and left the building through the players' exit. He decided to visit the cemetery in Medford and get as close to LaRoque as he could. He withdrew some money from an ATM machine across the street and tried to telephone Espirito. After repeatedly getting a busy signal for several minutes, he gave up. Then, instead of driving to an area with which he was totally unfamiliar, he hailed a cab.

Clark told the taxi driver to wait for him when they entered the cemetery grounds and pulled up in front of the administration office. Inside, he learned the location of LaRoque's grave and directed the driver to the road from which it could be approached. He found it easily, in the sixth row of headstones, and bent down in front of the brown granite marker. Clark waited for something to happen, for LaRoque's spirit to communicate with him and let him know what it wanted.

After several minutes he got up and walked around the gravesite slowly, observing it from different angles. On the back of the headstone were carved the words, "Son of Marie and Charles," as if his lonely presence in the midst of others who did not have the LaRoque surname had to be explained or validated.

Suddenly, without his willing it, Clark found all his thoughts focusing on LaRoque's parents. He pictured them first as happy young immigrants in a new country, ready to work hard and build a life for themselves. He witnessed their joy in the birth of young Paul and saw father and son at a ball game in Fenway Park when the boy was about five or six years old. Charles's death, he could now see, came without warning down at the harbor. A thousand pounds of bagged coffee beans being mechanically lifted from ship to dock broke loose and fell on him as he worked in one of the holds of the boat that had brought it to Boston. Clark had subscribed Marie's death to a broken heart when he read LaRoque's biography and learned that she had never remarried. His vision now told him that she was stricken with a cancer that took her life only months after it was diagnosed. The last picture he saw in his mind's eye was that of the teenage Paul kneeling and weeping in front of his parents' grave.

Clark realized that LaRoque was trying to communicate some message about his father and mother. He remembered reading that he was buried close to his parents, and began to look around for their monument. As he walked up and down the rows in that section of the cemetery, he saw that a number of headstones had been pushed off their foundations and were lying flat on the ground. Clark assumed they had been vandalized by some young people who never considered the emotional havoc they might be creating. He avoided those stones in his search for the LaRoques, but was unable to locate them.

The sound of the cab's horn reminded him that he had already been there fifteen minutes longer than the estimate he'd given the driver. He was about fifty feet away from Paul LaRoque's grave when he turned around and made his way back toward it. A sudden noise alerted him to a squirrel that was sitting on one of the downed headstones, obviously enjoying its lunch. It remained there, unflappable, until he approached within six feet of it, and then hurried away. Clark couldn't help looking down at the spot it had vacated and found himself reading the names and dates of birth and death of Charles and Marie LaRoque. Charles had lived only twenty-eight years, seven fewer than his wife.

At that moment Clark realized what was disturbing the spirit of Paul LaRoque. He returned to his gravesite, kneeled down close to the stone, and said, "Don't worry, Paul, I'll have their headstone fixed as soon as possible."

The taxi stopped at the office again on the way out. The manager confirmed that vandalism was responsible for the overturned monuments. "There's no respect for the dead anymore," he said.

"Or for their spirits either," Clark thought to himself. He arranged for the LaRoques' headstones to be restored to their foundation the next day and paid the total cost of the work in advance.

It was three thirty in the afternoon when Clark got out of the cab at Fenway Park. He tipped the driver generously, signed an autograph for him, and headed for the team parking lot. In his car, he used his cell phone to try reaching Espirito. The line was busy again for a few minutes, but then someone finally picked up.

"Hello," the female voice said, "Medford Police, Officer D'Allesandro. This call is being recorded."

"I'm sorry," Clark answered, nonplussed at first. "I meant to call 391-1813."

"That's what you got," she said. "Area code 617. Did you want the police?"

"No, I don't," he said. "I'm a little confused. When I called this same number earlier today, it wasn't the police. I spoke to someone else. I'm looking right at the number on the note he sent me and that's what I dialed this morning."

Officer D'Allesandro was patient with him. "Whom did you speak to this morning?" she asked.

"It was a Mr. Espirito."

"Well, there's no one here in the station by that name or anything close to it, and no one answers this line except the officer on duty. I'm afraid I can't help you."

Clark tried one more time. "And just to be sure I heard you right, the number is 617-391-1813."

"That's been our number for my five years on the force and probably a long time before that."

"Okay," he said, "thanks anyway."

"You're welcome, sir. Have a good one."

By the time he arrived at his apartment, Clark had persuaded himself to forget about everything that had happened that day. He cooked dinner, took a hot bath while listening to his favorite music station on the radio, and went to bed. He slept like a baby.

During batting practice before the first game with the Yankees, Mike Rooney got hit on the leg by a line drive and had to be scratched from the starting lineup. Reluctantly, Dusty Harmon inserted Clark in his place. Three hours later Clark was the hero of Boston's victory over New York, going four for four with two doubles, driving in three runs, and scoring three more himself. It was the beginning of the most fantastic month he ever had in his major league career.

On the afternoon of the opening game of the World Series, with the Red Sox hosting the Chicago Cubs, Clark returned to the clubhouse after batting practice and found an envelope in his locker addressed to him. It had no return address or postage stamp. The note inside was short and sweet. He recognized the handwriting at once.

"Good luck in the Series," it read. "Your friends in Medford will be rooting for you." Mr. Espirito's signature followed, with a "P.S." below it. "By the way, do you know anyone who has two tickets for Game Seven?"

BOBBY AND ME

"If people don't want to come out to the ballpark, how are you going to stop them?"

—Yogi Berra

LISTEN, I'M GONNA say this first thing to all you writers just so everyone here knows how I feel. And this puts it on the record too, in case I ever start giving myself too much credit later on for where I am today.

Here it is in a nutshell. I don't know how many times in my life I told Bobby Sadovitz he was out of his mind for getting himself involved in one thing or another—those business deals of his—but every time he put those big bucks on the line, he came out of it smelling like roses. Even when he knew it was a hell of a risk, things just seemed to fall into place. And instead of telling me to get lost or grow a pair of balls, which he could've done a few times, he ignored whatever I said and took me along with him to bigger and better things. When I stop and think about it, I've had a lot of fun in this life. Most of it, thanks to Bobby, is on account of something I said on a baseball field one Sunday morning about thirty-three years ago.

Okay, okay, don't all shout at once. I guess that means I've got to tell you the story, so let's get on with it.

Bobby and me both grew up in Dorchester. For you out-of-town scribes, that's a suburb of Boston, maybe ten miles on a straight line from Fenway Park. He lived in the Jewish section, while our house was a few miles away in a part of town that was mostly Irish and a little Italian. When I say "house," don't get me wrong. I'm talking about what's called a three-decker, with a different family on every floor. Everyone paid rent, except sometimes the landlord had one of the apartments for himself. There was one after another of these three-deckers on every street, with about ten feet of sick-looking grass or dirt between each one. Just enough space to park a car if you couldn't find a place on the street. They all had a front porch you could go out on and see what was happening in both directions. And there was a porch in back, too, where you could hang laundry out to dry or put a rug over the clothesline and beat the dust and dirt out of it. The fun began whenever an upstairs neighbor started whacking a rug right after someone else hung all their underwear out on a line.

Bobby and me went to different high schools. Most of the Jewish kids went to Dorchester South, and everyone said that's where you ought to be if you had any brains and were thinking about going to college. Dorchester North was home for the jocks and the kids who couldn't wait to take woodworking or get into the auto repair shop.

I mean it was set up so that anyone in Dorchester could go to either place, but almost everyone went to the one closest to where they lived because there was no such thing back in the fifties as school buses going from one side of town to another. If your old man left for work at six in the morning, that was it as far as having any wheels to take you some-place. There were no two-car families then either, not where we lived, so your mother couldn't drive you to school later on in the morning. I had some buddies whose folks had no car at all. Their old man used to have to get out there every day and wait for the trolley—we called it the streetcar—to come and take them near where they worked, or get off at one of the stations where they could transfer to the train into Boston if they had a job downtown.

The streetcar went by half a block from where I lived. When it was freezing cold in the winter, I felt sorry for those guys having to stand out there waiting for it to show up. They'd be hunched way over, with their shoulders pushing right up at their heads and their hands deep in their coat or pants pockets. You could see them beating time with their feet on the sidewalk to try to keep them warm. There was no such thing as a schedule to give you some idea when the next car was supposed to be there. The jokers in the MTA office—that stood for Massachusetts Transit Authority—would tell you a car would be by every fifteen minutes even if you were calling to let them know nothing had shown up for an hour. They said they'd check out the reason for the delay and call you back, but they never did, and the cars came whenever they got there and that was it.

The worst times were when you'd wait out there a half hour or so in the freezing cold, feeling sure you were going to wet your pants any minute. Then two trolleys would show up, one right behind the other, and both of them would be half empty. You could try getting the driver to tell you what the hell took so long by making some joke about it while you threw your money in the box. Like I said, you could try, but they'd just mumble something about trouble on the line and tell you to go sit down. Every one of those guys owed their jobs to a favor some local politician did for them, so I guess they didn't figure they had to be friendly to the passengers or answer any question they got asked.

My father's first cousin sometimes worked the line near our house and he wasn't any different. I never said hello or anything else to him when I got on in case he got into an argument with one of the passengers during the ride. In those days the drivers were allowed to break a dollar bill for you if you didn't have the right change, and everyone said that the "T"—that was the short name for the system—was lucky if the conductors treated them like equal partners and turned in half the money they collected.

But I'm getting off the subject here. I tend to ramble a little when I get into something, as you Boston guys will probably find out during the season. I always say that learning a little more about one thing or another won't kill you. That's especially so for you younger generation people who never saw these things yourselves. You're better off just letting me finish whatever I'm saying than interrupting my train of thought.

I didn't mean for you to think that Bobby and me knew each other growing up. If you didn't go to the same high school or hang out at the same places, there was almost no chance for that to happen. Bobby and his gang played basketball at a place called the Hecht House, which was where the Jewish kids went for their dances and stuff like that. They got to meet girls from the neighborhood there who they didn't know from school. By the way, back then a "gang" was just a bunch of guys who lived near each other and played ball together all the time. It was a word you could use without making people worry about what kind of trouble you were going to cause.

Where I lived, we went to the YMCA to play ball and to church for socials. It was always tougher for us to get on the basketball court at the "Y" because everyone from all over Dorchester wanted to use it, even the guys in their forties and fifties with their two-handed set shots. But it was a lot better place to play in than the Hecht House. I got into some games over there after I got to know Bobby a little better, and you could kill yourself driving to the basket too hard because there wasn't more than a couple of feet from either end of the court to the brick wall of the building. I could never figure out why they didn't put some thick mats up against those walls—at least right behind the baskets—but they sure as hell didn't. Not in my time, anyway.

We had our bowling alley and they had theirs, although we were still setting up pins by hand a couple of years after the place they went to started using automatic pinsetters. That didn't bother me, though, because working the alleys was an easy way to pick up a few extra bucks. And in those days there were movie theatres all over the place, so you didn't have to go into some other neighborhood to catch a double feature or keep up with whatever serial they were showing on Saturday.

I can tell by those looks you're giving me that some of you never heard of a serial. Just another one of the finer things in life you missed out on. A serial was an adventure story that they broke down into about ten parts. They used to call them "cliffhangers," and you got to see the next chapter every Saturday matinee until it was over. At the end of each one, the hero was going over a cliff in his car or was tied up in a building that was about to explode, something like that. You knew he wouldn't get killed, but you had to go back the next week to find out how he got out of it and see which one of your friends had guessed right. I'm talking about the days when all it cost to get into the movies was twenty-one cents.

My favorite serial was about Dr. Fu Manchu. He was a nasty character, a real villain with this mean-looking mustache. Whenever some cop or private eye got into his office trying to solve a murder or something, he pressed a button under his desk and the floor opened up where the poor guy was standing. You knew that if they weren't dead, they'd be on a slow boat to China when they woke up.

Anyway, about the only time I ever got into that part of Dorchester where Bobby lived was to play baseball on Sunday mornings. The games usually started in May and kept going right through most of October. You just played every week until not enough guys showed up to field two teams.

There was this real tremendous playground over there, called Franklin Field. You could probably have eight ball games going at one time if no one else came down to play soccer or cricket or touch football. There was one diamond that was laid out beautifully at the far end of the field with a grandstand on the first base side that could hold a few hundred people. It was built out of concrete and had long wooden benches. I never saw more than thirty or forty people in the stands there at one time, except for the Fourth of July when it was jammed because they were the best seats for the fireworks show. For us, it was the closest thing to a big league field that we had.

A couple of guys in tan uniforms with a City of Boston patch on the shoulder mowed the infield grass on that diamond every week and then did about another 200 feet into the outfield. There were no fences, but some of the players on the park league teams that used that field hit balls you knew were legitimate home runs when they went fifty feet or more on the fly past the line where the maintenance crew quit mowing. They fixed up the batter's box with chalk, just like you'd see at Fenway. And they had white lines going from home down to the bases, but they didn't bother with a coach's box on either side.

There were four more diamonds in the middle of Franklin Field, with a big wire backstop separating each two fields, home plate to home plate if you know what I mean. The teams that played soccer went to one part of the field that was all grass. Some of us used to watch it for a while but we never got interested in it. It was just boring. There was no action and no scoring, compared to baseball. On some Sundays the black guys who came from the Caribbean islands showed up for a game of cricket, dressed in white, head to toe. And there were always two or three softball games going on wherever there was a little room left. They just walked off the distance between bases and threw someone's shirt or jacket there to mark each one.

Each of the diamonds had a regular bunch of guys who showed up to play every Sunday morning. By eight o'clock there'd be batting practice going on at all the fields, and the game I played in always got started as soon as everyone there had taken at least three cuts. Most of the guys were in their late twenties or early thirties, but a few were a lot older. Two of them with gray hair were the managers every week. They're the ones who chose sides. One always wore a Boston Braves hat, even after the team moved to Milwaukee. Mr. Braves was usually in a hurry to get the game started. He'd flip a bat to the other guy—his name was Pete and he wore a short sleeve sweatshirt every Sunday that said "Norwell" on it. From the spot where Pete caught it, they took turns making a fist around the bat and working their way down the handle until there wasn't any room left. The guy who squeezed in the last fist got first pick, and everyone pretty much knew who the first seven guys on each team would be.

Now the time I'm talking about is the end of my junior year at North. School still had a few weeks to go, but the baseball team had already finished up its schedule. I'd done real well in the league we were in and there were a few good stories about me in the local paper after some of the games. The guys on the team who got letters and were coming back the next year elected me captain, and my picture was on the front page of the Dorchester paper. So a lot of the regulars I played with on Sunday knew something about me. Besides, I think I'd impressed a few of them the summer before that when I started showing up in July and got into a few of the games.

Most of the time I was somewhere between the twelfth and fourteenth player to get picked each week. It usually depended on how I'd done the game before. Mr. Braves would play me at first if I was on his team because he knew that was my position at school. But Pete was his own first baseman, so he'd stick me in left field or center, depending who else was on our side.

Like I said, the first fourteen guys or so were pretty much the same ones every week, and there'd usually be about seven to ten more there, hoping to get on one of the teams. After both sides were picked, the extras usually drifted off, but one or two always hung around in case someone had to leave early or two guys got in an argument over some play and one of them said, "Screw this," and took off. That happened a few times.

Anyhow, I began noticing Bobby at the games because he had the letter "B" painted in white on top of each of his spikes. He told me later that his mother made him do it. She didn't want to spend twenty bucks for a pair of spikes in the first place just for him to "waste your time playing with a ball,"—that's how he said it. She made sure he understood there wouldn't be a second pair if he lost those. Some of the guys kidded him about it, and it bothered him until he started wearing a matching Red Sox cap with the fancy "B" in front. That's when he stopped worrying about what his spikes looked like.

Bobby showed up every Sunday, but both Pete and Mr. Braves always looked right past him when they were choosing their teams. You couldn't blame either of them because he didn't look anything like a ballplayer. He was short and pudgy—like he was in training to get as fat as he is today—wore glasses and had a pasty baby face. He swung righty, and if he hit the ball at all in batting practice, it was usually either a weak grounder or a popup to the right side. He moved pretty slow, too. But he always stuck around while we were playing, and tried to get someone else who wasn't in the game to play catch with him down one of the foul lines. Once in a while, at the end of some 16–11 kind of game that dragged on all morning, he got in for the last inning or so when someone had to get home. When that happened, one or two guys always got moved around and Bobby was put in right field. In those days, the worst player on any team got sent out to right and then got crucified if he couldn't field like Willie Mays.

Okay, so this day I'm telling you about was the first time Bobby and I ever spoke to each other. We were standing about ten feet apart in the infield during batting practice—out at shortstop—when he asked me if I knew what college I was going to when I graduated North. I didn't know who he was or why the hell he was interested, but just being there on a baseball diamond together made it seem okay to answer.

"I haven't thought about it, but my family couldn't afford it anyway," I told him. "You go to North?" I asked.

"Are you kidding?" he shot back. "The eleventh commandment at my temple is, 'Thou shalt not go to Dorchester North.'"

Now that's the kind of answer that could get you pissed off at someone real fast, right? I mean you'd figure he's an asshole. But there was something about the way he said it, the same way he still is today after all those years. You could see that goofy smile on his fat face, with those two chipped teeth in front, and then he had a quick follow-up to show you he was just fooling around. "But if I ever have to get my car fixed in Dorchester, I'll never take it to someone who graduated from South."

When I kind of half smiled at that, he said, "I'm at South, part of the college-bound crowd, same year as you. I've seen you play in school games and here too, and you're good, in case you don't know it. You could get into some college in Boston on a baseball scholarship if you had half decent grades. Did you take the PSATs this year?"

For some reason I had, just on the wild chance that I might apply to one or two schools if I could get a big enough loan, and I told him. When he asked me my scores, I said I had a six-fifty in English and seven hundred in Math. That got him excited.

"Holy shit!" he kind of hollered, "You're a goddam genius. Your score would probably put you in the top fifteen percent at South. That means eighty-five percent of South is dumber than some goy."

He waited a few seconds and then asked me if I knew what a goy was. I'd heard the word before but I wasn't sure what it meant. So he explained it to me. Then he said there was probably some Jew in my family history who passed down all the brains. But before I could tell him to get lost, or something worse than that, he gave me the toothy smile again and said, "Just kidding, I'm just kidding."

The guy at the plate hit a grounder to my left and it took a tricky hop just as I put my glove down, but I reacted fast and fielded it cleanly. Whoever was throwing batting practice was already in the middle of his next pitch, so I just flipped the ball back over near the mound.

"Nice play," Bobby said. "You know, you could probably get accepted to play baseball any place you want. You've got talent and smarts. You don't need money or good looks." And there was that shit-eating grin again.

I felt real good about it when he said that. The guidance counselor at North had never said a word about college to me, and I knew that she already had a copy of my scores.

"What's your name?" I asked him.

"Bobby Sadovitz," he said. He came right over and shook hands with me although I never would have thought of doing it if he hadn't made the first move. "I live over there, across the field on Wales Street. It's that brown house on the corner." He pointed toward Talbot Avenue, a main drag that ran next to the field.

"You mean the one across from the gas station?"

"Yeah, we're on the middle floor."

"I'm on the middle floor too," I told him. Then I asked him if he knew where he was going to college.

"B.U." he said. "They have a large quota for fat, Jewish kids, even those with a straight "C" average who didn't crack twelve hundred on the exams."

Just then Mr. Braves started hollering for everyone to come in so we could choose sides and get started. Bobby looked around, and I could see he was counting how many guys were out there, figuring his chances. There must have been about two dozen. Mr. Braves and Pete were already on their third picks—Pete got first choice—by the time we got close to them. I was hoping Mr. Braves would get me on his side because I wanted to play the infield, but Pete took me sixth.

After they both had eight players, Pete looked around at who was left. Some of them began staring down at the ground or turning their heads every which way. I guess they knew how bad they were and seemed almost afraid to eyeball Pete and be picked to start the game. But Bobby had a real eager look on his face and he had both hands around the handle of a bat that he was resting on his shoulder.

I happened to be standing next to Pete just then, and all of a sudden he said to me, "What do you think, Jim? Help me out."

I looked at the hopefuls, pointed at Bobby, and told a fat lie. "I've seen him play in other games and he's a pretty good outfielder." I figured Pete was looking for someone to stick out in right field.

Pete gave him the once-over and looked like he wondered if I knew what I was talking about. But then he said, "Okay, we'll take the man with the 'B' on his spikes. What's your name, kid?"

"Bobby."

"You're number nine today, Bobby," Pete told him. "Play right field and hit last."

Bobby looked real serious when he shook his head to say okay. But as soon as Pete turned away, he gave me that big mouth grin of his, with one chin flopping on top of the other. I can still see it like it was yesterday.

I know what you're going to ask. The answer is that Bobby didn't get any hits in the game or do anything unusual in right field, but he did help us win. The guy up ahead of him got on base twice to start an inning, and Pete had Bobby bunt each time. Well, surprise, surprise, he really knew how to handle the bat to lay one down. He didn't drop his arms and show bunt until the pitch was on its way, and he held the bat just right to make nice, soft contact with the ball. Bobby moved the runner up both times and someone else brought him in.

Pete made a point of going over to him on the bench and telling him he'd done a good job. He put his arm around Bobby's shoulder the second time and said, "Nice bunt, kid. That's the way it's supposed to be done." So I figured Pete would remember what Bobby did and pick him again when he was looking for a ninth man. And I was right. That's how I first got involved with Bobby Sadovitz.

Now let me tell you quickly what happened after that because everyone will be out on the field in a few minutes and I've got a practice to run.

Bobby helped me get a baseball scholarship at B.U. He went through the whole application process with me, and I asked him to be my roommate. I could tell you a lot of wild stories about those days but we don't have time for that right now. I'll say this much. We became better friends all the time. We both liked living in the dorms and there was never any question about staying together from year to year. Bobby had some sort of moneymaking business going on all the time, it seems, to help pay his room and board. I worked with him on most of them to make a few bucks for myself. At one time or another we delivered pizza in the dorms, picked up dry cleaning, sold stationery out of our room and scalped theatre tickets. Bobby's dad had a friend in a downtown Boston agency who could get us a bunch of tickets any time there was a hot show around.

He also spent a lot of time playing cards for money, and he usually won. I didn't mind leaving our room whenever there was going to be a game there that might last all night. I'd just go sleep in one of the player's beds.

My biggest contribution to his life back then was helping him get dates. I was B.U.'s best baseball player my last three years there, and that got me a lot of attention. There were always girls hanging around the team, and I could usually get the one I was going out with to bring along her roommate for Bobby. It just so happens, by the way, that I fixed him up with Arlene, his wife. They got married a few years after we graduated.

The Cardinals signed me when I got out of school and I played in their system for three years before being traded to Cleveland. The Indians optioned me out a couple of times, but then I stayed with them for ten seasons, from '61 through '70, before finishing out my playing career with the Tigers. That's when I got lucky, getting myself a World Series ring for being the 25th guy on the club when they won it all. I knew I wanted to stay in baseball, and Detroit gave me the chance to coach in "A" ball. Eventually, I worked my way up to managing at the top level in their farm system.

Meanwhile, Bobby was doing all those things that made him as rich as he is today. He started as an accountant after he got his degree, and made his first bundle buying a lot of two-dollar stock when a company owned by one of his clients went public. High tech and computers were brand new stuff back then, and you had to have a real sense of vision about the future. I thought he was nuts at the time, that he was throwing money away, but he kept after me until I bought some of the stock too. I don't have to tell you how big PlanetSoft is today. After a couple of stock splits, Bobby sold all his shares at about fifty points higher than what he got in for. And needless to say, I made a small killing on it myself.

Bobby used most of his profits to buy a couple of radio stations in Boston, one AM and one FM outlet. I thought he'd gone off the deep end on that one because in those days most small stations lost money every year. I told him I wanted no part of it. But he hired new announcers and DJs, changed the formats around, and built two winners. Some of you know that he even started the first sports talk show in Boston on his AM station and did it himself for a while. It was Bobby's idea to have listeners call in and say what they liked or didn't like about all the local teams and players. Every caller felt that he could manage or coach the team better than whoever had the job.

A few years after he bought the stations, Bobby insisted on selling me a piece of what he owned at the same price it would have cost me if I'd gone in with him originally. He said he wanted me to learn all about how they worked and keep an eye on them for him during my off seasons. Later on, when he figured the time was right, he negotiated a deal with Boston Broadcasting and they took over both stations for about four times what he paid.

After that, Bobby got interested in real estate. He bought a decrepit shopping mall out in one of the suburbs, turned it around in no time with a couple of new anchor stores and some great ideas, and got rid of it right away for one hell of a price. I was against that one too, but he took me along for the ride.

Then, once he really got a feel for what real estate was all about, and just before prices for land started jumping every day in the late seventies,

Bobby bought the old racetrack out in Eastboro. It had been shut down for almost four years. Two hundred and sixty acres of land came with it. First, he fixed the place up, put in a new dining room along with some great food concessions in the grandstand, and got the track operating again.

When the crowds began filling up the place on a regular basis, a business group came to Bobby out of the blue. They wanted to build a new tennis stadium right next to the track because the location was halfway between Boston and Providence. They figured they could fill it for a sanctioned big-time tournament every year, and have a great indoor/outdoor facility with club memberships the rest of the time. He thought it was a sensational idea, so he gave them a piece of land in return for a percentage of the profits.

They got it done, and it worked out beautifully with the Greater New England Tennis Open. That's when Bobby had an architect draw up plans for a condo development on the property, along with a hotel, some office space, a movie theatre, and a few restaurants. The kind of money he was talking about raising for the project scared the hell out of me, but he put together a group of investors, including a little bit from yours truly, and the rest is history. In no time, Eastboro Park was getting awards for design and elegant living from all over the country.

Five years after it first opened, when everyone else figured that prices for condos would never stop going up, Bobby convinced the investor group to sell out to Madison General Life Insurance. The timing was absolutely perfect. He caught the market right at the peak. He became a multi-millionaire and I had more money in the bank than I knew what to do with.

So here we are today. Neither of us could have ever dreamed this would happen, not when we were playing baseball in Franklin Field on Sunday mornings. For Bobby, owning this baseball team isn't another investment, it's a dream come true. And for me, it's my chance to finally get back to the big leagues in style. Everyone knows there's no better job in baseball than being manager of the Boston Red Sox. So like I said before, I wouldn't be here today if it wasn't for that line of crap I gave Pete about Bobby Sadovitz a long time ago. That's the truth.

Well, here come my coaches on the field. It's time to get this show on the road. I've been waiting for the first day of spring training all winter and I'm raring to go. Now before you ask me who that fat guy is over there, wearing number 99 with the big double chin and the white "B" on his spikes, I'll tell you. He's just a dear old friend of mine who's going to be our unofficial bunting instructor.

A CORNER FOR LOVE

*"One percent of ballplayers are leaders of men. The other
ninety-nine percent are followers of women."*

—John McGraw

LOOKING BACK, PAULA McDonough realized that the biggest decision of
her life began taking shape on a Sunday afternoon in July when she
was six years old and held tightly to her father's hand as he led her up the
short ramp to the grandstand on the third base side of the field. That's
when she got her first look at the open expanse of Fenway Park, home
of the Boston Red Sox. She thought of it often in later years, especially
while hiking the mountain trails around the University of Vermont with
Pete. The endless variations of green in the trees and shrubs along the
path reminded her of how the lush Fenway grass, glittering in the sun-
shine, crept close to the high outfield wall, and of the "Green Monster,"
more subdued in color, that stretched from the left field foul line to
the center field bleachers. And she recalled how the color of the playing
field and the surrounding perimeters of the park were complemented by
thousands and thousands of semi-gloss green seats.

She had grown up in West Roxbury, the younger daughter of a construction worker and a nurse, who worked at whichever hospital would limit her schedule to the six hours a day her children were in school. Maureen, her older sister, was born with music in her soul, and never even flirted with the idea of participating in sports. Paul and Joan McDonough knew ahead of time that their second child would have to be their last. The immediate disappointment of not having a son—"He'll be a junior, of course," Paul had said, and his wife agreed—gave rise to the name with which Paula was christened. It also guaranteed her father's determination to see her develop whatever athletic ability she had, along with a love for baseball, the only game that mattered to him.

When Paula was fourteen, her father bought season tickets for all the Red Sox home games played on Saturday and Sunday, and renewed them each year. He had a special fondness for sitting almost up against the left field wall, in the last two seats of the second row of the grandstand. Only a foot away from the yellow foul pole, he could see every inch of Fenway Park from that corner. He loved being able to look down and offer his encouragement to the Sox left fielder.

They had seen Ted Williams play out the string in Boston, retiring at the end of the 1960 season. Paula would always remember the home run that he hit in the last at bat of his career on that dreary September afternoon. Her father had picked her up at school to join the meager crowd that bade "The Kid" adieu. They watched Carl Yastrzemski, his successor, mature as a player during the sixties. Yaz's teams usually got off to a fast start, but had the local sportswriters penning the inevitable "Wait 'til next year" by the middle of July.

Her father often told Paula that being at Fenway Park meant a lot more to him than just watching a ball game. "Sometimes, when I sit here, I just tune out the noise of the crowd and what's happening on the field, and think about who I am and where I'm going. For some reason, this is the best place in the world for me to come to grips with any decisions I've been trying to make."

As the nine innings of any game moved along, he found moments to inquire about how she was doing. Paula began looking forward to those weekend afternoons when the Red Sox played at home and she could seek his advice or let him know about some new development in her life.

Paula couldn't remember when she'd had the first meaningful discussion with her father about boys, only that it had been at the ballpark. He told her that they were an interesting and inescapable part of her growing up. "Some day your own Prince Charming is going to come along and make you very happy," he said.

In her junior year of high school, Paula went out with Terry Galvin. They liked each other from the start and dated regularly after that. He was the All-American redheaded boy with freckles who played both baseball and hockey at school and had a talent for performing comedy routines. Time passed, and as graduation approached, Terry spoke of becoming a pediatric surgeon. Paul McDonough liked Terry and was thrilled at seeing him escort his daughter to their senior prom. He wondered whether the strong attraction between the two of them would continue when they finished high school and went off to different colleges.

At the end of Paula's freshman year at the University of Vermont, her father helped her find work in the office trailer on a construction site where he was employed. Although they drove to and from the job together each day, their serious conversations were still saved for the weekend afternoons they shared in the Fenway Park grandstand. It was at one of those games that Paula let him know about the social life she'd had at college that year.

"I mean, I went out whenever I wanted, usually with a bunch of kids, but I couldn't really think of dating anyone seriously. Terry called a lot and wrote to me from Tulane, but he's too far away to visit, even on the big campus weekends. So I spent most Saturday nights in the library."

"How are things with him now that you're both home?" he asked.

"They're good, Dad," she said. "We still have fun together, but I feel as if I shouldn't see him as often as he wants me to. I think I ought to tell him that both of us have to be free to date other people at school."

He wanted to ask her if she loved Terry, but she was still too much his baby for him to feel comfortable with either the question or the answer she might give him. So he said that he agreed with her and that he was sure Terry would understand.

In the first week of her sophomore year, Paula met Pete Donnelly, a transfer student from Temple University, who lived just outside Philadelphia. She was drawn to him immediately. He was tall, with the dark blond hair and features of his Scandinavian mother. Pete showed no interest in the regular campus sports, preferring mountain climbing, sailing and skiing. He was very good at all three. He was also a voracious reader who loved to discuss books when he sat with Paula in a downtown Burlington coffee shop or when they drove to a nearby hiking trail in his new 1964 Karmann Ghia. They dated frequently and Paula often spoke of him in her collect calls home.

During the second semester of that year, Paula realized that her feelings for Terry and Pete were equally strong. She decided to make some adjustments in her life that would let her continue both relationships without having to commit to either. She stayed at school during spring break, knowing that Terry was returning to Boston. But she let Pete believe she was going home and encouraged him to join his friends who were spending the week in Ft. Lauderdale.

On the third Saturday in May, three days after she finished her final exams and left Vermont, Paula went to the ball game with her father. She listened to him point out the new players on the team and predict that the Red Sox pitching staff would again get them nowhere that year.

"I'd like to think we could finish as high as fourth, but realistically this is an eighth place ball club," he told her. "I really feel sorry for Pesky having to manage this bunch." He tapped her on the knee with his program. "So how about letting your old man know why you stayed up at school during the break last month. It kind of upset your mother that you weren't home for Easter."

Paula explained the problem, only after getting him to promise that he wouldn't discuss it with the rest of the family. She knew he'd feel honor bound not to come out and say that Paula told him this or that; but she didn't want him to give in to speculating out loud, asking her mother if she thought there was any chance Paula might be coming home less often just to avoid Terry. She also told her father that she was leaving in June to waitress at a resort hotel in the Catskills.

"I'll be back one week before classes start. We'll get to a couple more games if the Sox are at home, but I haven't given you the big news yet."

"I may not be ready for it," he said. "You just informed me that I've got to spend the whole summer out here with one of my brothers. Is the rest of it as bad?"

Paula laughed and took a deep breath before continuing. "I've decided to spend my junior year in London. I'll get to see another culture and I won't have to cope with this Terry/Pete thing. Maybe being away from both of them will help me decide which one I like most." She had intended to say "love," but something about the way her father looked at her made her switch words at the last moment. "And don't worry about the cost. It will be the same as being in Vermont and I'm saving money for air fare."

"No more collect calls?" he asked, smiling and raising his eyebrows mischievously for her.

"Less often, I promise."

"If you really mean that, we won't let you go."

"Thanks, Daddy." Her eyes misted over.

A loud crack of the bat drew their attention. They stopped talking long enough to stand and watch the ball hit by one of the Baltimore Orioles rise on a long high arc toward center field and land about twelve rows deep in the bleachers. "Well, if we don't lead the league in anything else, we'll be number one in gopher balls given up," he said.

Paul McDonough waited until the hitter circled the bases and was on his way back to the visitors' dugout. "Let me tell you something, Paula," he began, indicating by the wag of a forefinger that he was about to say something he considered important. "I sat in this ballpark in the summer of 1942, trying to make two decisions. The first was whether to join the Army, and the second was whether to ask your mother to marry me. We had two seats somewhere behind home plate when the game started, but the place was pretty empty so we moved over here, to be alone, sort of, and talk.

"I remember like it was yesterday, the Sox were six runs behind the Yankees when I made up my mind to enlist and to pop the question. Your mother said 'Yes' right away, even though she knew I wouldn't be around very long. Over the next two innings the Sox rallied for seven runs to win the game." He smiled and then chuckled. "Your mother figured they did it just for us. She always said they'd have lost if I didn't propose. Somehow I've got the feeling that after you're through running away from these guys, no matter how long it takes, you'll be sitting right here yourself when you decide what to do."

It took three years for Paula to learn that her father was right, that running from life didn't help. She corresponded regularly with both Pete and Terry from England, and missed both of them very much. She spent some time at home with Terry the summer before her senior year, but was relieved that he had to devote a large part of every week to studying for the medical school boards. Back in Vermont, Paula resumed dating Pete, but forced herself to do it on a limited basis. There were times when each of her boyfriends began to talk about getting married after college, but she always found a way to change the subject before it got too serious.

Paula graduated with a degree in psychology and decided to try advertising as a career. Her search ended with a job in a small office in Boston. Pete had urged her to go to Philadelphia. He suggested that his father could help her get a position in a top agency there, but she told him that she wanted to be close to her family, at least for a while. Terry had been accepted at Tufts Medical School, just outside Boston, but she knew he'd be far too busy with his studies to see her more than occasionally. Paula felt the anguish of wanting to spend most of her time with both of them, yet afraid to be with either one very long.

The baseball season of 1966 was a dismal one in Boston. The team finished in ninth place, but Paula and her father still managed to take in a number of weekend games together. As they watched the Red Sox's inept performances, there was no talk about Terry or Pete unless Paula brought it up herself, reaching out for his support.

A week before Thanksgiving, Paul McDonough fell off some wet scaffolding and seriously injured his back. The operation on his spine was successful, but he learned that it would be almost a full year before he'd be able to maneuver well enough to return to work. When the renewal application for his season tickets arrived in January, he told Paula that he was giving them up unless she wanted the seats herself.

"This '67 team probably won't be any better than last year," he said. "My guess is that we can get the same tickets the year after once I'm healed and ready to go back." Paula agreed.

As it turned out, the Red Sox of that year played to the tune of the "Impossible Dream." Paula, who was sharing an apartment in Boston, watched some of the games with her father in his den at home, but didn't purchase any tickets herself. Terry called a few times during the summer, inviting her to go with him, but it was usually at the last minute, after she had already committed to doing something else.

With two games left to play in the incredible season, the Red Sox trailed the Minnesota Twins by one game in the race for the American League pennant. As if by fate, the schedule had the two teams playing each other in Saturday and Sunday games at Fenway Park.

Pete had made plans earlier to be in Boston that weekend and to spend Saturday with Paula. He called from the airport on Friday night, just after arriving.

"Hey, I can get tickets to the game tomorrow if you want to go."

"Are you kidding? That's fantastic!" she said. Later on, Paula fell asleep wondering if her father's prediction was about to come true.

Their seats were in the fifth row of boxes behind the Red Sox dugout. Paula cheered from the start as the team took a 3–2 lead behind Jose Santiago. In the seventh inning she joined the screaming crowd in a long, standing ovation for Yastrzemski when he hit a three-run homer to put the game on ice. She and Pete kissed when the final out was made, but only to celebrate the Red Sox victory. Fenway Park had come up empty for her.

That night, however, over dinner at the Ritz-Carlton, Pete asked Paula to marry him. The setting was romantic, and she was convinced earlier in the day that she would accept his proposal, if it came. But suddenly, without knowing why, she searched for the right words to put him off a while longer. He let her do it, still holding her hand in his, but insisted on her making a decision before he returned to Philadelphia the next afternoon.

The telephone rang at nine thirty on Sunday morning. Paula had slept very little that night, tossing and turning over what she would tell Pete when they spoke. Still undecided, she let the answering machine take the call, but picked up the receiver as soon as she heard Terry's voice. He had two tickets for the final game and wanted to meet her for brunch in an hour. Could she go? "Of course," she told him, and decided that she would call Pete at home later in the evening.

Paula couldn't believe it when Terry entered the second row of Section 33 in front of her and led her to the same two seats she and her father had shared for years. He saw the look on her face and smiled.

"Maybe your dad never told you that he invited me to some games when you weren't around, especially that summer you worked in the Catskills. I love these seats. When you told me that he turned in his season tickets, I asked for these whenever I came out here. They were always available. You missed out the first few times."

They talked only about baseball as the Red Sox fell behind 2–0 and the crowd's tension grew. In the fifth inning, Terry excused himself and said he'd be back as soon as he could. He asked Paula to keep score for him while he was gone. When he returned and sat down again, the Twins were already batting in the sixth. He told Paula that he wanted her to listen to him for a minute.

"I've made two decisions here today," he began. "The first was to be sure I could spend a Saturday or Sunday in these seats anytime I wanted. So I just went to the ticket office and gave them a deposit for next year's weekend games. The second is that I want to be certain my son or daughter can sit right here and learn all about baseball from either you or your father when I can't be here myself." He stopped talking and looked into her eyes for several moments. "Yes, that means just what you're thinking, Paula. I've been in love with you since our first date. Will you marry me?"

The tears didn't wait for her answer, and just as quickly Paula knew that she was finally through running away. "Yes," she whispered, taking the hand he held out to her, and leaned over to share his kiss.

Pitcher Jim Lonborg led off the last of the sixth with a bunt single that surprised the Twins and started a loud rhythmic applause from the stands. The visiting team seemed to unravel. Yaz came through with another key hit in the five run uprising, and the Red Sox went on to win the pennant. Paula knew they had done it for Terry and her.

LITTLE LEAGUE HOME RUN

"I don't want to play golf. When I hit a ball, I want someone else to go chase it."

—Rogers Hornsby

WHEN SHAWN TRACEY was called in from the Giants' bullpen to stop the Phillies' rally in the last half of the eighth inning, Andy Turner knew the depths of depression as he sat in the home team's dugout, watching the action on the field. The afternoon shadows had already worked their way past the pitcher's mound toward the first base side of the park. The Saturday crowd had been shouting its support and waving white handkerchiefs while the Phillies scored twice and loaded the bases with the tying runs. Now they sat back dejectedly when the left-handed Tracey threw a third strike past Rusty Wilson, the team's catcher, to end the threat.

"Atta boy, Shawn, you old bastard." Turner whispered it to himself as the veteran Giants' pitcher stared in at home plate for a few moments, savoring his accomplishment, before walking slowly to his own team's dugout. It was impossible for Turner not to think back to the days when the two of them were teammates. He recalled how many times he had seen that same look of satisfaction on Tracey's face—from his own crouching position behind the plate—as another strikeout pitch tore into his mitt. And how they used to go back to the bench at the end of the inning and high five each other for making it happen.

They had been the best battery in the league for seven years, leading the Atlanta Braves to two pennants and one world championship. Tracey had averaged just under twenty wins a season in that time, but reached a high of twenty-six the same glorious summer in which Turner was voted the Most Valuable Player in the National League. He had earned the honor by catching 148 games, hitting 37 homers and knocking in 109 runs.

Now, six years after Atlanta traded him to the Dodgers, and four seasons since the Phillies signed him away from LA as a free agent, Turner spent most of his time on the bench. His left knee had been through two operations, the second one worse than the first, and his catching days were over. It was painful for him to squat behind the plate and there was no way he could come out of his crouch fast enough to cut down a runner stealing second.

Chris Conlon was still looking for his first pennant in his fifth year of managing the Phillies. Once in a while he sent Turner to the bullpen to warm up the relief pitchers if he'd already had to put his backup catcher in the game. And occasionally he had him take over first base when True Dempsey, another long-time veteran, was rested in the late innings. Turner was carried on the roster as a catcher, but was really there to pinch hit when Conlon needed the long ball.

At thirty-seven, Andy Turner wasn't kidding himself about how much baseball he had left in him. Sixteen years was a long time in the big leagues, and no one kept you around if you couldn't contribute. Still, despite the downward spiral in his batting average and other power numbers since the doctors first cut into his knee, he could deliver in the clutch. And he was a team-oriented player who willingly shared his experience with the young pitchers and catchers on the Phillies' staff.

It didn't hurt at all that Conlon had been the pitching coach on the Braves for three years before leaving for his first major league managing job. During that time, he and Turner were very close. The Atlanta success story in those years had boosted Conlon's reputation as a coach and put him on several other teams' short lists for managerial openings. Conlon knew that Turner's ability to make the right call in tight situations was the reason behind much of the pitching staff's success, and he pushed hard to bring him to the Phillies when Turner refused to sign a new contract in LA.

Other than the problem with his knee, Turner was in excellent shape. He carried 190 pounds on his six foot, two-inch frame, and none of it was flab. He took three weeks off at the end of every season to totally unwind, then began a daily regimen of running and swimming that brought him into spring training rejuvenated and ready to play.

He was a handsome man who took pride in the "sexy" label he had always carried. During the season, Turner let his full mane of straight black hair grow several inches below the back of his baseball cap. His features were marred only by an inch long scar on his temple, above his right eye, the result of a violent collision at home plate during his days with the Braves. In a way he never understood and which the television cameras didn't catch, a base runner's spike had somehow made contact with his head. Turner's brown eyes had a sparkle that heralded his good nature and complemented the ready smile that attracted both players and sportswriters alike.

This season had been his worst. He felt as strong as ever, and was ready for his role in the 162 game grind when opening day came around. But his bat had not been producing enough of the hits Conlon expected from him. Now, in the middle of July, one week after the All-Star break, Turner was batting .241 and had produced just four home runs and six doubles. He watched hours of videotape from other games in which he delivered big hits, trying to see whether he was doing anything differently in the batter's box. He took extra batting practice after a number of games, getting Conlon or one of the coaches to throw ball after ball to him while watching his arms, the movement of his feet, and his swing.

On a couple of occasions his hitting improved for a while, and he thought each time that he was on the road back to respectability. But the bubble kept bursting. One of his home runs had been a dramatic grand slam in the ninth inning to win the game. But the "new beginning," as he thought of it then, didn't last. He had nothing to show for his last seven trips to the plate as a pinch hitter. His frustration was at a level he'd never had to face before.

"Your old partner can still turn it on, Andy, huh?"

Turner hadn't seen Conlon sit down next to him on the bench. The manager hardly ever strayed from his end of the dugout, closest to home plate. Rather, he barked out his directions or called a player over to him when he had something to say.

Turner took off his cap and wiped the sweat from his head with his bare forearm. "Yeh, skip, not too bad for another one of us dinosaurs," he said, and winked at Conlon.

"How'd you like to grab a bat when we're up?" Conlon asked, and continued speaking without waiting for an answer. "I know you haven't seen him for a while, since he's been over in the other league the last few years, but maybe for old time's sake, huh?"

Turner understood what was going on. Conlon didn't want to embarrass him with an at bat against Tracey if Turner didn't think he could hit his old battery-mate. If Tracey's curve ball and slider looked too good from what he had seen of it in the eighth inning, forget it. They were down by three runs, so if the guys due up first couldn't get a rally started, Conlon could use someone else to pinch-hit from the right side. That's why he came over and asked instead of just hollering down the bench for Turner to get loose. Andy appreciated the gesture, and suspected that Conlon was the rare manager who would think of it.

"I'm ready anytime," he answered. "Can't bust one out of here if I'm sitting on my duff."

Conlon made a fist with his left hand and jabbed it playfully into Turner's right side. "Let's see what happens," he said, then got up and walked back toward his end of the dugout. Turner watched him, seeing the large perspiration stains that had formed on the back and around the armpits of his manager's shirt. He couldn't help noticing all the extra weight that the fifty-year-old Conlon was carrying on his belt line and in the seat of his pants.

The Giants went down in order. Tracey returned to the mound in the last of the ninth and struck out the first batter he faced, a pinch hitter for the pitcher. The Phillies' leadoff man caught the third baseman playing too deep. He bunted the ball in that direction and reached first without a throw. Tracey was visibly irritated by the lapse. He let his temper get the best of him, walking the next batter on five pitches.

Conlon's number-three hitter was the left-handed Ernie Rizzo. He had a batting average just over .230 against southpaw pitchers, but was the team's second leading home run hitter. He would represent the potential tying run at the plate. Rizzo wasn't someone the manager could hit for without inviting a lot of criticism from the press if the move didn't pay off. Allowed to swing, he got into a quick, two strike hole, but fought off a couple of nasty pitches from Tracey before reaching for a curve and dunking it into short left center field. A run scored, making it 7–5, and the Phillies had a man on first and second with one out.

The fans picked up the tempo of their rhythmic applause. They put their handkerchiefs back in play again as Kyle Rhodes, the cleanup hitter, moved to the plate. The team's play-by-play radio announcer was suddenly much more animated than he had been before Rizzo's hit. He informed his listeners for the third time that day that Rhodes was in the midst of a recent hot streak. He had batted .432 and driven in 13 runs over the course of his last ten games. Six of those came on balls that had reached the bleachers.

Rhodes was a powerfully built right-handed hitter, very compact at three inches under six feet. His reputation around the league rested on the incredible distances some of his home runs had traveled. It was said that if anyone was ever going to hit a ball out of a certain park where it had never been done, Rhodes was the best candidate to pull it off. He had a straightaway stance and looked menacing from the pitcher's mound as he stood with his feet close together, his knees bent far forward, and his arms and bat high in the air. He was often compared to a tightly coiled spring waiting to be released.

Tracey came inside on the first pitch to Rhodes with a fastball, intending to move the muscular center fielder off the plate, but the ball was close enough to being a strike to get him to swing. The crowd rose at the crack of the bat as the ball took off on a long, high arc down the left field line. There was no doubt it had enough distance to clear the wall, 360 feet away. Rhodes stood at home, watching the drive begin to hook toward the foul pole. He tried to will it fair with a pushing motion of his hands toward first base. Conlon and the players on the Phillies' bench left their seats and scampered up the first two steps of the dugout to get a better view of the ball as it flew out of the park. The home plate umpire yanked off his mask, and the umpire at third ran toward the outfield, attempting to straddle the foul line as he watched the ball begin to disappear. The hooking increased dramatically as the ball continued its flight. There was no argument from Conlon when both umpires signaled that it had gone foul before it reached the 50-foot high yellow pole in the left field corner of the park.

Rhodes returned to the batter's box, determined to continue his recent heroics with another clutch hit. Tracey appeared unruffled by the fact that the pitch had almost cost him, and his team, the game. In the Phillies' dugout, Turner knew that Tracey had already decided what he would throw Rhodes on every pitch. The mistake he had almost made would not change his plan. Tracey got a second strike on a perfect slider that caught the outside edge of the plate. Then, after wasting two high fastballs, he threw another slider that had Rhodes lunging at it as it crossed the plate below his knees.

Silence infected the grandstands in a heartbeat. The loud handclapping that had been going on from the time Rhodes strode to the plate came to a sudden halt. It was as if everyone realized at the same moment that the team's last best chance to win the game had slipped away.

Conlon didn't return to his seat after leaving it to watch the long Rhodes foul. He looked down the bench at Turner and saw that his veteran player was bent over, doing some stretching exercises. When Tracey made Rhodes his third strikeout victim, Conlon called out to Murray as the left-handed hitting third baseman began moving away from the on-deck circle toward the plate. He motioned him back to the dugout, waiting until Murray got there before letting everyone know his decision.

"Turner, you're the hitter," he hollered, first pointing a finger at him and then giving him the thumbs up sign as he raised his arm in the air.

Turner made his way toward the bat rack. He decided to swing a thirty-five-inch bat instead of the one-inch shorter model he usually used. He sensed that Tracey would not be overpowering him and that he might be able to get a little more wood on a curveball or slider. He picked out one that felt good to him and started out of the dugout.

The public-address announcer informed the fans that Turner had entered the game to bat for Murray. The onetime MVP was aware of a smattering of applause as he pushed the metal donut up the handle of the bat and began taking some practice swings to get loose. He knew that the crowd was trying to encourage him. He was also well aware that their enthusiasm for his presence at this crucial juncture of the game was diminished by the sight of his season's statistics being flashed across the giant scoreboard in center field.

Tracey had stopped to exchange a little small talk with Turner in the outfield as the players were doing some warm-up sprints before the game. Now he stood on the mound with his back to the plate. Turner wondered whether the pitcher was thinking back to the last time they faced each other. He was with the Dodgers then and Tracey was in his last year with the Braves, before going to Detroit; but he had become the number-four pitcher in Atlanta's starting rotation, winning only about the same number of games he lost. Turner went two for three against him that day, striking out once. But his second hit was a two-run homer in the seventh inning that knocked Tracey out of the game and provided the winning margin. He'd remembered that Tracey had a way of tipping off his changeup every so often if you were very familiar with his delivery and were watching him closely. The home run had come on that pitch.

"Let's go, Turner," he heard Dee Bentley, the home plate umpire, holler.

Turner realized that he had been completely absorbed in thinking about his last game against Tracey, even as he stood there trying to loosen the muscles in his back and shoulders by swinging the bat in a circle high above his head. He let the donut drop back onto the ground in the on-deck circle. The patch of grass was painted fire engine red, with the Phillies' logo inside in white. Tracey eyed him intently as Turner dug a little hole with his spikes at the plate and then planted his back foot in the position he needed for his mostly open stance.

"I still owe you for the last time, Andy," Tracey said, speaking just loud enough for his old friend to hear.

Turner smiled. He'd been right about what Tracey was thinking. "I don't remember, Shawn. What happened?"

"Bullshit," the pitcher said, putting his left foot on the rubber and looking in for the sign.

Turner waved his bat a couple of times and began concentrating on Tracey's pitching hand. As soon as the ball was on its way, he picked up the spin and knew it was a curve. He watched it break inside and didn't swing, certain that it missed the strike zone.

"Stee-rike," Bentley called, turning to the right and pumping his fist.

"Inside, ump," Turner said, disagreeing, without protesting too strongly or turning around.

"You hit 'em, I call 'em, Turner. That's the system."

He stepped out of the batter's box momentarily, and then got back in.

"Inside corner," Bentley added, apparently deciding that his first answer had been too harsh for Turner's mild complaint. "Just nicked it."

Tracey was ready. He stretched, bobbed his head back and forth as the runners took their short leads, and pitched again. The ball came in hard, rising a little as it cut across the outside edge of the plate. Turner wasn't expecting a fastball, not on that count, and knew right away that he had probably let the best pitch he'd see from Tracey go by. He had nothing to say when Bentley repeated his strike call, and had no trouble hearing the fan with the raspy voice shouting at him from behind the Giants' dugout to take the bat off his shoulder and swing.

Turner walked a short distance away from the plate. He needed some time to think about the situation, to try and figure out what Tracey would do with a two-strike pitch. He could waste the next couple, trying to get his old friend to bite on a curve or slider outside the strike zone. Or he might show him a fastball inside to try and set up a curve breaking over the outside corner. Turner also knew that he had to stay alert for the changeup because Tracey usually saved it until he already had two strikes in the count. He decided that he'd better protect the outside of the plate.

When he got back in the batter's box, he saw that Tracey was smiling at him. "No changeup this trip, Andy," he said, as he set himself and got ready to pitch. "No changeup home runs today."

The taunting sound in Tracey's voice disrupted him and took away his concentration. Turner asked the umpire for time and stepped out again. The Shawn Tracey he had known all those years with the Braves never spoke to a hitter that way, never challenged him or teased him about what pitch was or wasn't coming next. He suddenly realized how much this personal duel meant to his former teammate. He understood, as only a player nearing the end of his career could, that Tracey still felt the sting of the home run Turner had hit to beat him four years earlier. Perhaps the pitcher felt this would be his last chance to even the score. Turner decided that the only thing he could count on was that Tracey would be true to his word and not let him see a changeup; that he wouldn't risk getting beat on the same pitch again.

Turner banged the dirt out of his spikes with the end of the bat and stepped in. Tracey tried to tempt him to go after a curveball that didn't have enough break on it and stayed outside the plate. Before the next pitch, he fired the ball over to first base twice. The throws forced Rizzo to dive back each time and served notice that he'd better not get too far off the bag.

Ball two looked like a fastball for an instant, but Turner picked up the spin of a slider and watched it drop down below his knees. With the count now even, Tracey didn't want the pace to slow down, to give Turner more time to think. He looked in for the next sign right away, shook it off twice before nodding agreement, and went into his stretch.

Turner readied himself in the batter's box and concentrated on Tracey's movements. He tried to figure out what pitch he'd be calling for in this situation if he were behind the plate, sending out the signs to Tracey as he did for so many years. As the pitcher's right leg came toward the plate, Turner caught the look of affected strain on Tracey's face and the slight jerking motion of his head. They were the telltale signs he had become totally familiar with in the past when he crouched behind home, waiting for Tracey to pull the string and throw the changeup he had called for. The hitter, poised to swing at a fastball that would reach him in less than a second from its moment of release, would be way out in front of the pitch, completely fooled.

Turner couldn't believe what Tracey was doing. He tried to adjust immediately, to start looking for the spin on the slow curve so he could time his swing and step into the pitch with as much power as possible. He wanted to be able to hit the changeup out of the park again.

The pitch was on him, a blazing fastball on the outside part of the plate, before he realized he'd been fooled. Tracey had pulled out all the stops, knowing how Turner would react, and had set him up with the phony look on his face and the jerking head movement. He must have practiced it over the years, Turner thought later, just waiting for the next time the two of them faced each other.

Turner swung at the last instant and barely got a piece of the ball, hitting it hard on the ground a few feet to the right of the first baseman. He cursed out loud as he dropped the bat and started down the line. Head lowered, he realized that he had failed to come through again when it counted. Moments later, when the sound of the crowd told him something had happened, he looked up to see that the ball had gotten through to the outfield. He found out afterwards, watching a replay in the clubhouse, that the first baseman had played the ball nonchalantly and wasn't in a position to block it with his body when it took an unexpected bounce over his glove.

Turner watched the play unfold as he ran to first. The right fielder had to go a long way toward the foul line to retrieve the ball. The runner on second base would score easily. With two outs, the runner on first who represented the tying run might try to follow him in if there was any chance he could make it. That meant the throw from the right fielder would come in to the plate. Anticipating that, the first base coach was waving his arms at Turner, shouting at him to make the turn at first and keep on going. He figured that even if the throw home was cut off, Turner would have time to reach second safely. He'd be in scoring position with the winning run.

Moving as fast as he could, Turner saw Rizzo make the turn at third and then get held up by the Phillies' coach who was more than halfway down the line himself. On his way to second, Turner made the kind of mental error a manager might expect from a rookie, looking over his left shoulder to see where the ball was and whether there would be any play on him at that base. At that instant, he tripped and fell to the ground, closing his eyes as he landed on his shoulder.

Turner felt an immediate jab of pain from his left wrist, which had tried to cushion the impact. Hearing the shortstop calling for the ball, he got up and began staggering the twenty feet from there to the base. As he got close, he made a diving, headfirst slide toward second, his arms outstretched. Lying prone, he saw the shortstop's feet leave the ground, going high in the air. Another roar from the fans rang in his ears as his hand touched the base, and he realized at once that the throw must have gone into center field.

Turner knew the error would tie the game and he heard the frantic cry from the coach at third urging him to "Go, Andy, go, go." Some of the dirt stirred up by his desperate slide had gotten in his eyes, forcing him to keep them closed for a second or two. But he struggled to his feet and started the third ninety-foot leg of his incredible journey. This time his destination seemed miles away, and he sensed that despite the rapid movement he tried to get from his arms and legs, he was making very slow progress.

The coach at third was close to the foul line, waving his hands down toward the ground, giving Turner the sign to slide. Again, sucking in all the air he could, he hurled his body toward the base, head first. He wasn't quite sure what happened when he felt a small blow on the back of his batting helmet. The umpire's hoarse call, "He's safe," was followed almost immediately by a loud eruption from the stands. Still lying in the dirt, Turner could see that the ball had eluded the third baseman and rolled into the Phillies' dugout. He learned later that the throw had hit him on the head during his slide and changed direction.

"Runner scores," he heard the umpire shout. The coach was on his hands and knees next to Turner's head, telling him what a great slide it was, and saying, while he laughed, "Get up, Andy, you're the winning run."

Turner picked himself up again, and without brushing any of the dirt off his uniform, trotted down the line. Most of his teammates were waiting for him, and the high fives began even before he stepped on the plate. As he turned toward the Phillies' dugout, Turner saw Tracey, who had come off the mound earlier to back up the catcher. He stopped and smiled at him.

"You faked the shit out of me, Shawn. It was one hell of a pitch."

The compliment didn't change the look of chagrin on Tracey's face. "Goddamm little league home run," he said, spitting out each word deliberately, and began walking off in the other direction.

Turner enjoyed being the center of attention in the clubhouse. It had been a while since the other players had a reason to come by his locker. "Nice going, old man," they said, and joked about his adventure on the field. The writers covering the team saw a great column in what had happened, especially in view of Turner's close relationship in the past with Tracey. They stood around prodding him for as many quotes as they could get. Turner got laughs out of everyone in describing his many thoughts during the grueling ordeal that started and ended at home.

When they had gone off to write their stories, Turner undressed and took a shower. The hot water stung at first but then began to relax him as he let it pound on his back and shoulders. He was alone in the shower room. He couldn't help smiling as he again played out in detail his odyssey on the base paths. He had gone up to the plate hoping to become a hero with one swing of the bat, but instead had set in motion a series of the most unlikely events. It was an important "W" for the Phillies. He had scored the winning run, but in his heart he knew that he had really failed to deliver.

As Turner was dressing in the almost empty clubhouse, Tim Hammonds, the first base coach, walked over to his locker. In his playing days, Hammonds had led the league in stolen bases for six consecutive seasons. Everyone knew that he would have challenged the all-time record had he not torn a cartilage when he slipped, chasing a fly ball in a very wet outfield.

"Nice goin', Andrew, some base runnin'. Couldn't a done it no better myself." He showed two gold upper teeth in front when he smiled. "Chris says stop by a minute before you leave, okay? See you tomorrow, old man, but you rest up good tonight, you hear? You gonna be our pinch runner tomorrow if we need one." He laughed at his joke and headed toward the corridor that led to the players' parking lot.

The door to Conlon's office was open and he was riding the stationary bicycle when Turner went in. "One more minute," the manager said, raising his forefinger, and continued peddling at a speed Turner couldn't see doing him much good. Conlon wore no shirt, but still had on his uniform pants. He had changed from spikes into a pair of sneakers that remained unlaced.

Turner sat down on a chair in front of the desk and noticed about a half dozen cigarette butts in the ashtray. There were also four baseballs in a box that normally held a dozen. He wondered whether anyone had asked Conlon to get Turner's autograph on them.

Conlon finished exercising and moved to the black vinyl executive chair behind his desk. "That was one hell of a run," he said, smiling at Turner. He immediately reached for a cigarette from the pack of Marlboros he took out of the top drawer. "I was hoping you wouldn't have a heart attack before you got to third. I almost had one of my own when you fell down on the way to second." Turner laughed. "You don't get to see three errors on one play too often," Conlon continued. "That kind of stuff is what makes managers grow old fast." He flicked his Zippo lighter, took a heavy drag on the cigarette, and stared at Turner for several seconds before going on. "The front office calls the shots here, Andy. I don't have to tell you that. I may disagree, but the owner's going to listen to Dan, not me. He's been the general manager here forever and what he says carries the most weight."

Conlon allowed his head to rest briefly on the back of the chair, and then sat forward again. "Dan's been trying to trade you to one of the clubs that looks like it'll be making a run for the pennant, but he couldn't get anyone to go for a deal. He was looking to pick up one or two prospects in Triple A, or even Double A. Now he wants to start taking a look at some of our own kids. Wants to get an idea whether any of them will be able to help the club next year. That means making some room on the roster."

Turner took a deep breath. The concern he felt as soon as Conlon mentioned the front office gave way to a throbbing in his chest. Conlon's speech wasn't over, but Turner already knew his place on the bottom line. He told himself that he had to control his emotions, to make it as easy as he could on his old friend who had kept him on the team longer than he probably deserved. He could see that Conlon was having an obviously difficult time breaking the news.

"I'm too old to be sent down, Chris, so I guess that means the club's going to let me go, right?"

Conlon dragged on the cigarette again, turned his head to the side before exhaling a cloud of smoke, and then pressed the cigarette against the inside of the ashtray several times to extinguish it. He dropped the butt in the tray and ignored the smoke that kept rising from the few shreds of tobacco that were still glowing.

"You're released as of right now," he said. "Dan made the decision before the game. I think you got a chance to catch on with someone now that they don't have to lose a player to get you. A few clubs can use someone with power down the stretch. That's why I wanted you to hit against Tracey in the ninth. I was praying you'd catch hold of one and win the game for us. Then you'd be getting a bunch of phone calls. But hell, Andy, some of these GM's are so dumb they may read about the game and figure you got an inside the park job. They'll think you got power and speed." He laughed, nervously, and Turner joined him.

"You're right," Turner said. He got up and offered Conlon his hand. "I appreciate your giving me the chance today, Chris. Maybe some other club will be interested, maybe not. If it's not the end of the line, it's pretty close, anyway. I've put in my time and maybe it's just the right note to go out on. This way, if anybody ever asks me what I did in my last at bat in the big leagues, I can tell them I whacked the ball off my old buddy, Shawn Tracey, and touched all the bases. Hell, with what I had to go through out there, I'll even be able to say it with a straight face."

They laughed, shook hands and wished each other good luck. As Turner walked to the door, he remembered the look on Tracey's face at the end of the game. He turned back to Conlon. "And if I'm lucky," he said, "no one will remember that it was just a little league home run."

ALL IN THE FAMILY

"Family is everything. It is even more important than baseball."

—Luis Tiant

I T WAS JUST after 1:00 a.m. when the bus carrying the Scranton Miners pulled into the large yard across from the team's stadium. Half the lot was taken up by a fleet of Town Taxis that rented the space for a twelve-hour period each day. The bus slowed easily at first, but gave a final lurch as it parked close to the high wire fence in a rear corner of the yard. The team had played and lost a night game in Harrisburg, swept in the three-game series by the Hurricanes, and returned to Scranton with box suppers and no stops along the way.

Jimmy Diamond was awake for the last hour of the trip, staring mindlessly out the window at the traffic moving in the opposite direction. He couldn't stop replaying the game in his head, berating himself for the error he made at shortstop that turned the game around and led to the team's defeat. His misplay was followed by a walk and two consecutive doubles into the same gap between the center and left fielders. The second one, hitting off the wall on one bounce, forced Hoby Barton, the manager, to make his slow walk to the mound and remove

Whitey Nordstrom, his pitcher, from the game. In the dugout, when the Hurricanes' six-run burst had ended, Diamond went over to Nordstrom who had a towel around his neck and a scowl on his face.

"Sorry, Whitey, all my fault."

"Yeah, I shoulda been outta the inning on that ball."

"You're right. I fucked up. Sorry."

Nordstrom looked away without answering and spit on the dugout floor. Diamond turned, walked toward the other end of the shabby enclosure, and sat down next to Don Tomasetti, the catcher and team captain.

"I saw you talking to Whitey," Tomasetti said, while removing his shin guards in anticipation of batting third in the new inning. "Didn't let you off the hook, did he?"

"That's okay. He's got a right to be pissed. He deserved a 'W' tonight and I took it away from him."

"You should have heard what he said when Hoby came out to get him. You weren't his candidate for the Hall of Fame right then. But if he wants to make it into the rotation, what he showed after your error didn't help him."

"It didn't help me either," Diamond said. "A couple more like that and Hoby will have someone else out at shortstop."

When the bus jerked to a stop, Diamond got up quickly and put on the jacket he pulled down from the rack above his seat. He made his way outside and over to the baggage compartment where the driver had begun unloading duffel bags onto the ground. In a phone call the night before, Diamond's wife informed him that she wouldn't be picking him up when the team returned to Scranton. Now he was anxious to find his bag and ask Luis Cavalho, who lived in his direction, for a ride home. He had gone to the back of the bus earlier to speak to Cavalho, but the center fielder was asleep, curled up across two seats. As Diamond watched the bags being pulled out, looking for the one with the large red plastic tag tied to the top, Jack Wheeler, the pitcher who was knocked out of the first game of the series without completing four innings, walked past him and over to the driver.

"Hey, fat man," Wheeler hollered, stepping up to where the driver was leaning in and reaching for another bag. "Fat man, I want to talk to you."

The driver pulled the duffel bag out, set it down behind the ones that were already on the ground, and turned toward Wheeler. Recognizing him, he asked, "Were you speaking to me, Mr. Wheeler?"

"Yeah, you heard right. What's your name, anyway?"

"I'm Kevin. Is there a problem?"

"You're goddam right there's a problem. This is the third time we come back from a road trip and the third time you jerked this fuckin' bus to a stop and made me about bust my head on the seat in front. You better fuckin' understand next time you do that again I'm going to jerk you around from one end of this lot to the other."

The driver took a step back toward the baggage compartment. "I'm sorry, Mr. Wheeler. I do that so everyone will wake up and know we're here. Most of the players who are sleeping don't like someone shaking them or hollering at them when the bus stops. You're the first person who's complained about it."

Wheeler was known for being a hothead and had few friends on the team. He'd been called up the year before, in September, to pitch a few games in the big leagues and seemed to think that gave him the right to sound off at anyone whenever he pleased.

"I may be the first, but I'll be the last one too, as far as you go, if it happens again. When I'm through with you, you won't want to drive no buses no more."

Diamond stepped in before the driver had a chance to answer. "Okay, Jack, you made your point. Hoby drove back in the van with the coaches, so Kevin can't ask any of them what to do. The next time he sees them, when we do the Columbus trip in a couple of weeks, he'll tell them what you said."

Wheeler looked around and saw that a number of the players were waiting for the driver to empty out the baggage compartment. He glared at Diamond and started walking past him toward the bags that were already on the ground. "Good game tonight, Jimmy," he said, a smirk on his face.

Diamond's bag was the next one pulled out. He grabbed it by the handle, stepped back and spotted Cavalho getting off the bus. He waited until Cavalho got closer before asking him if he could bum a ride home.

"Sure, man, I'll take you to your place, and no charge if you buy me a drink."

"It's after one o'clock, Luis. There's no bars open now."

"Don't you worry about that. I know where to go. You with me?"

Diamond didn't want to go looking for a cab and spend twenty-five dollars to get home. "Yeah, I'll go," he said, "but just one beer, right?"

"That's it," Cavalho answered. "One beer to help me forget going 0 for four again. I need my medicine."

"But you going for the collar wasn't as bad as my error." Diamond saw that the driver was closing the door to the baggage compartment. "Find your duffel and let's go."

The bar had no sign outside identifying it as a drinking establishment, and heavy green shades that were hung in the windows on both sides of the door kept passersby from looking in. Diamond recognized the neighborhood as one in which mostly Latinos now lived.

"I don't know what time they close this place, or if they ever do," Cavalho said. "I've been here at three in the morning and the owner was still behind the bar. The cops know this place is here, but they'll stop in for a drink themselves while they're working, and probably it's on the house."

Diamond counted seven booths in the bar as Cavalho led him to the one furthest from the door. A young couple occupied one of the booths and three dark-skinned men, well-dressed in jackets and ties, were in another.

"The guy across from the other two is on the City Council," Cavalho said. "I've seen him here a few times. The other two are probably looking for a favor. I'll bet a few bucks changes hands before they leave here tonight."

A tall, well-built man came to take their order. He wore a Phillies T-shirt, a beaded necklace and white sneakers. A nod of his head indicated that he recognized Luis. "How you doin'?" he asked.

"Okay," Cavalho replied. "This is my buddy, Jimmy. We'll have a couple beers."

"Glad to know you, Jimmy. You're his buddy, you're welcome any time. Be right back with the drinks."

"He's the owner," Cavalho said. "His name's Rafael, but everyone calls him Rick. You can only pay cash here, but I heard Rick will loan you money if he trusts you and you're sure you can get it back to him in two weeks. If you don't, I don't know what happens after that." He smiled, and Diamond smiled back.

"How old are you now, Luis?"

"Twenty-six, man. I'll be twenty-seven in September."

"And this is your third year in Scranton and you've never been called up to play in Philadelphia. What's your future in baseball at your age? I mean why do you stay in it if it looks like you'll never get to the big leagues?"

Cavalho reached over to his jacket on the seat and took out a pack of cigarettes. He lit one for himself and returned the pack to his jacket without offering a cigarette to Diamond.

"I stay in it, Jimmy, because baseball's all I've ever done since I was a kid, maybe eight years old. Getting to the majors has been my dream forever. Whoever's seen me play knows I'm a better center fielder than Johnson, and he's been the Phillies starter for two years. The difference between us is that he can hit .280 off big league pitchers and I hit .245 down here in Triple-A. They probably figure I'd drop another twenty points on my average if they called me up. But I ain't given up yet on becoming a better hitter, more consistent and even reaching the fences once in a while. The coaches are working with me on it and one of these days everything's gonna fall into place. I know it. Then I'll tell the Phillies to either call me up or trade me to some other club that will."

While Cavalho spoke, Rick brought their beers to the table and Diamond gave him a ten dollar bill. "Keep the change," he said.

Rick nodded, winked at Diamond and left.

"So how long do you keep that dream, Luis? Is there a cutoff date? When do you start the rest of your life if you never become a hitter?"

"I don't know, man. I ain't asked myself that yet. That's a negative and I want to think only positive. I want to see me picking up my duffel bag with a big smile on my face and going up to play in Philadelphia, not tears in my eyes because the club just released me. I want that dream to keep going."

"But what if you had to go back to the Dominican? What would you do there?"

"Not the Dominican, Jimmy. I'm from Puerto Rico."

"I'm sorry, I thought . . ."

"That's okay. But what I'd do there, I don't know. One brother-in-law's in construction and the other one's got a restaurant inside a casino. Maybe go to work for one of them." Cavalho put out his cigarette. "What about you, Jimmy, how long you gonna be here? How much you love the game?"

"If you're done with your beer, I'll tell you in the car. I don't want my wife worrying about me."

"I'm all set. Let me just finish what's in the bottle. Don't want to let a good beer go to waste."

"So let's hear it," Cavalho said as soon as they started moving.

"I'm the same as you, Luis, playing ball all my life. My Dad gave me a bat with my own name on it—'Jimmy Diamond model' it said—when I was in second grade, seven years old. I used to swing that bat an hour at a time, and kept swinging as I got older and used heavier ones. I got to be one hell of a hitter. Believe it or not I batted close to .500 in both my junior and senior years in high school. No shit. Not a lot of long balls, but I was on base and knocking in runs all the time. I was offered a couple of scholarships to play in college, but I took a bonus instead and got sent to Single-A down in Clearwater. That's where I met my wife. She was from Texas and studying nursing at a college there. I had a good year, especially the end of the season, so the Phillies moved me up to Reading. A couple of the coaches there spent time in the big leagues and taught me stuff about playing shortstop I never knew. It didn't hurt that both of them knew my Dad, and one had been on the same team with him for a few years."

Cavalho stopped the car at a traffic light and looked over at Diamond. "What do you mean?" he asked. "Who was your old man?"

Diamond smiled as he began to answer. "He played in the majors for eleven years. His first nine were with Cincinnati and the last two with Detroit. He was a good corner outfielder, but not fast enough for center. He always batted between .270 and .290 but he could hit for power. In his best year he had thirty-seven home runs. They loved him in Cincy, but when he hurt his hip and couldn't play every day, the Reds traded him to Detroit. The Tigers figured he could help the team as a lefty pinch hitter. They offered him a new contract after two years, but he'd had enough, he said, and there was a business thing at home doing something he liked, so he retired. He was there to watch me and teach me stuff when I was in junior high and high school."

"You're one lucky son of a bitch," Cavalho said.

"Anyway," Diamond continued, "I went back to Reading for a second year, but only stayed there a couple of months. My hitting and fielding were good and steady, and the Club figured I was ready to play here. When they told me I was going to Scranton, Heather and I decided to get married right away. The front office gave me five days to report here so we could have a short honeymoon."

"So you're pretty sure you'll get a chance to play in Philly, huh?"

"If I stay healthy, Luis, it ought to be a sure thing. Joey Kendall's a free agent when the season's over and the Philadelphia papers say the team won't pay him what he thinks he's worth to stay there. I've heard from some people close to the ballclub that they'll call me up in September and let me play in enough games to show what I can do. They don't expect to make the playoffs this year so the fans won't care if I'm in the lineup. I'll be in the right place at the right time, and hopefully I won't blow it."

They were approaching the apartment complex where Diamond lived, and Cavalho slowed down. "What about when you're all done," he asked, "what will you do then? Go work with your old man?"

"No way, Luis. I'm making baseball my life. When I'm through playing, I'll ask the club I'm with to let me coach in the minors. And I'll do that for as long as it takes to move up and manage in the big leagues. That's the job I want until I retire. My big dream is to have my own kid on the team I manage. He'd be the shortstop, of course, because that's what I'd teach him to play as soon as he was old enough to have a mitt. And maybe he'd even be the reason we get to play in the World Series and win it. Some dream, huh? You know, Luis, you ought to think about being a coach, too. No one's as good as you at stealing bases, and you could teach that. The same for knowing how to play center field. You could do those things and coach one of the bases during the games. I'm sure the money's better than doing construction in Puerto Rico, and you'd be doing what you love to do. Think about it."

"Yeah, I'll think about it. And when you're a big league manager, you get me on your team, okay?" Luis gave him a big smile.

Diamond pointed to the next apartment building on the street. "That's the one, Luis. Stop there. The most beautiful girl in the world is waiting for me on the third floor." He got out and pulled his duffel bag from the back seat. "Thanks for the ride," he said. "I'll see you at the ballpark in the morning."

"Okay, mister Philadelphia shortstop, I'll be there. And don't forget what you got to do when you're a manager."

Diamond tried to be as quiet as he could when he turned the key in the lock and then opened and closed the door to his apartment. He leaned his bag up against the wall and turned on the Tiffany-styled lamp that hung from the ceiling over the kitchen table. Looking down the short hallway, he saw that the bedroom door was closed. That meant, he knew, that Heather didn't want to be awakened by any noise he might inadvertently make when he got home.

Diamond took off the windbreaker he was wearing and threw it on a kitchen chair. He noticed the envelope sitting next to a pile of *Scranton Times* newspapers on the table and recognized it as stationery Heather used whenever she wrote to someone in her family. A sudden urge to urinate took him to the bathroom where he also washed his hands and face and brushed his teeth.

Returning to the kitchen, he sat down and reached for the *Times* on top of the pile. He turned to the sports section, anxious to see how the previous day's game against the Hurricanes was reported. He knew that Paul Gilroy, the *Times* columnist who covered the Miners, was trying to make a name for himself, and often went overboard in describing the team's play, especially when it was bad. Two costly errors and the failure to hit with men on base had resulted in a 4–1 loss for the Miners, wasting an otherwise excellent pitching performance by Ward Masterson. Both errors were committed by Danny Davis, the second baseman, who dropped a throw on a double play ball, and later let a ground ball skip under his glove, allowing two runs to score when the inning should have been over. Gilroy used the occasion to compare Davis's statistics to those of the other second basemen in the league, pointing out that Davis had committed the most errors and had the second lowest batting average of those in the group who played regularly. Diamond knew that the attack would put pressure on Hoby Bailey to sit Davis down in favor of one of the other infielders, and began to worry that Gilroy would attempt to embarrass him also for the error that allowed the Hurricanes to sweep the series.

After quickly perusing the rest of the sports page, Diamond reached for the envelope. He saw that nothing was written on the front of it and that it was unsealed. His first thought was that Heather intended to use it for a letter to her family or a close friend but hadn't gotten around to writing it. She probably tired suddenly, he surmised, and closed the bedroom door before going to sleep. She may even have written the letter in the bedroom, he thought, and brought the envelope into the kitchen where she kept her address book. When he saw that a piece of Heather's stationery was inside, he removed it and was surprised to find the words "Dear Jimmy" at the top of the page. It read:

> *"I'm guessing that before you begin reading this letter, you'll have taken a beer out of the refrigerator and maybe made yourself a sandwich if you didn't like what they gave you to eat on the bus. You may even want to read some of the sports news in the papers I saved for you on the table."*

Diamond smiled. For some reason the words reminded him of the love letters that passed between Heather and himself before they got married.

> *"And if you haven't yet gone into the bedroom and seen that I'm not there, this is where the hard part of my letter starts."*

As soon as he read the last sentence, Diamond felt a sharp contraction in his stomach and a sense of panic an instant later. Still holding the letter, he ran to the bedroom and saw that Heather wasn't there. The bed was made and the closet door was open. He looked inside and saw that some of his wife's clothes were gone, what apparently she could fit into the one suitcase that was missing.

Heather had left him, he realized, still in a state of panic, but why? He was devastated, unable to comprehend and unwilling to accept what was happening. "Why?" he cried out. "Why, for Christ sakes? What did I do? What the fuck is wrong?" He returned to the kitchen and remained standing as he continued reading the letter.

> *"This isn't your fault, Jimmy, so don't blame yourself for what I'm doing. I love you very much, and always will, but I realize that I'll never be happy as a ballplayer's wife. I've had last season and this season to go through it, and it keeps getting worse. You're home one week and gone the next for more than half the year. I've tried to get used to being alone when you're not here, but I can't do it. And it's not as if it's something you have to do for just a short time. It will always be like this, for as long as you'll be playing baseball, and that could be for the next fifteen or twenty years. That means I'd have to get along without you for so much of the time. When you're away, there'd be no one to help me with our children, and they wouldn't have a father to play with them and do all those things a father does. I guess that's in my mind a lot now because I just found out last week, when you left for those games in Allentown and Harrisburg, that I'm pregnant."*

Diamond didn't know how to react to the news. His head was still reeling from the fact that Heather was gone, that she had walked out on him without even discussing what was in her letter. He felt cheated to have to learn this way, without any joy in the moment, that he was going to be a father. How could she leave him now, he wondered, and returned to the letter.

> *"Before things start getting difficult for me, I'm going to find a place to live, get a job, and be ready for the baby when it comes. I know it's your baby too, but here's what I feel and what's best for both of us. I don't want you to get involved with the baby at all.*

The way our lives are, that wouldn't be fair to me, you, or our son or daughter. I hope to find another man I can love, one who will be with me all the time. If that happens, and he wants to marry me, you and I will have to get divorced, or we can get divorced sooner if you meet someone yourself. That may be better for both of us. Please, Jimmy, I don't want you to be trying to find me because we couldn't get together again if you did. But I promise that if you let me be and we have a son, I'll send you his picture and let you know if he's growing up to be a baseball player. I won't stop him from doing it if that's where his heart is. But I won't tell him that Jimmy Diamond is his father, and if I marry soon enough he won't have any reason to ask. So I'm saying goodbye to you with a hug and a kiss. Take care of yourself and just try to forget about me. You're a good man, Jimmy, and you'll be a wonderful husband for the right woman."

It was signed, "Love, Heather," and there was a P.S. reminding him to pay the rent to Mr. Dudley within the first three days of the month.

Diamond put off the light in the kitchen and went to lie down on the living room sofa. All sorts of thoughts raced through his mind, most having to do with finding Heather and letting her know that he wanted to be fully involved as the baby's father when it was born. He told himself at first that he didn't want to sleep in their bed that night, not after this. But he soon remembered that Hoby Bailey would be watching his play carefully at infield practice in the morning, and he needed as much rest as he could get.

Years later, if you were fortunate enough to own a Jimmy Diamond baseball card, of which only eight, over thirteen years, were issued by Topps Bubblegum, you could read the following:

James Matthew Diamond, Jr., born September 6, 1964; Height 5'11" Weight 180; Bats Right, Throws Right; Philadelphia Phillies, 1985-1998; Career Stats: Games, 2012; Hits 2483; Runs 1489; Doubles 611; Triples 117; Homers 240; RBI 1005;

*Avg .322; Most Hits Season (NL), 1988-89, 1992-93; Most
Doubles Season (NL), 1987-90, 1993; Gold Glove, 1987-92.*

And if you were able to follow his life during Diamond's baseball
career, you would know that for months after Heather left him, he tried
to locate and contact her, but was unsuccessful. He was told by her parents in Texas that she had not been in touch with them, and they were
not even aware, they said, that she walked out on him.

Through it all, Diamond's play remained at a high level. Whenever
anyone asked about Heather, he said she had returned to Florida to finish
her nursing studies. It startled him that a week after he was called up to
the big leagues that September, he received a note from Heather, written
on her own stationery, and postmarked from the Empire State Building
in New York. She congratulated him on having his dream come true, let
him know she was fine and said the baby was due in about four months.
She didn't say whether she was expecting a girl or a boy. Diamond figured
that someone in the Phillies minor-league family was in touch with
Heather—probably a player's wife or girlfriend with whom she remained
friendly—and he understood that there was no reason to believe she was
living in New York. She may have simply been visiting there, he realized,
or given the letter to a friend to mail from the City.

Shortly after spring training got under way in February of the next
year, a front desk clerk at the Florida hotel where the team was staying
gave Diamond an envelope that was unstamped and had no return
address. In it was a note from Heather, again letting him know she was
well and enclosing a picture of a baby boy. "He looks a lot like you,
Jimmy," she wrote, but did not reveal the baby's name.

Diamond asked the clerk to tell him who left the envelope. The clerk
said it must have been given to someone on the evening shift and that
he found it in the player's mailbox that morning. Diamond's attempt
to get more information from any of the staff that reported for duty at
8:00 p.m. was unsuccessful and met only with frustration.

A registered letter from a law firm in Las Vegas arrived in June. It contained divorce papers and instructions on how Diamond should fill them out. The letter pointed out that Heather was not seeking either alimony or child support. Also enclosed in a separate sealed envelope was a note from Heather in which she said that a divorce was the best thing for both of them, and told him that she was dating "a good man" who wanted to marry her and adopt the baby.

"I'll always love you, Jimmy," she wrote, "and I promise you again that I'll let you know what your son chooses to do when he grows up."

A year later Diamond met Katherine Price, a physical therapist who worked in the office of the team doctor, and they were married a week before Christmas. Katherine had also been through a divorce and brought with her a two-year-old son, Kyle. The marriage was a good one, and Diamond felt totally fulfilled. He was buoyed by the fact that Kyle, showing marvelous athletic ability from the age of four, learned to love baseball and became an outstanding shortstop. In his last year of high school, Kyle batted .477 and led his team into the final game for the State championship. Diamond recognized his stepson's potential and discussed with him the choice between going on to college or playing professional baseball. When Kyle opted for the latter, Diamond, who was then in his fourth year of coaching and managing in the Phillies minor league system, prevailed upon the Club to draft him and assign him to their Single-A team in Bradenton.

Five years later, in September of Diamond's fourth year as the Phillies manager, he and Gary Sherman, the general manager, agreed that Kyle was ready to play major league baseball. He was called up to Philadelphia where he served as a utility infielder for the last few weeks of that season and for the season that followed. It was common knowledge that he was being groomed to take over the shortstop position if Buddy Walters opted for free agency at the end of the year and was signed by another team. The Phillies were picked to finish first in their Division that year by four of the six local writers who followed the team and by several of the more popular national baseball magazines. Instead, due mainly to injuries to the pitching staff, the team finished a distant third and essentially bowed out of the race in mid-September. There was no baseball played in Philadelphia in October, and the media needed someone to blame.

Meanwhile, over the years, Heather periodically wrote to Diamond about their son, never revealing his name, each letter usually arriving from a different part of the country. She informed him that he was pitching in Little League, and later, for his middle school team. Diamond was happy to learn that in high school the coach converted him to shortstop and that he was elected team captain in his senior year.

"He's a strong, handsome boy, Jimmy," she told him in a note written on light pink stationery that had her initials "HN" at the top in a flowery pattern, "and he'll be going on to college next year. I'm not sure what he'll want to major in, but I do know he wants to keep playing baseball." And, when four more years had passed, Heather notified him that their son had signed a contract to play with a minor league team, but she didn't say which one.

Tommy Hanover, owner of the Philadelphia Phillies, waited until the day before Thanksgiving before announcing his manager for the next baseball season. The beat writers for the city's two major newspapers and all the sports talk show hosts had been on his case from mid-September, even before the team was mathematically eliminated from making the playoffs, to let the fans know whether Jimmy Diamond would be brought back to manage the team for another year. Everyone who still bought a ticket to the ballpark or who cursed himself for having laid down top dollar earlier for tickets to games that had no meaning or excitement any more, could see that the players had thrown in the towel and were just waiting for the season to end.

Hanover witnessed the same scene, but he'd been in baseball long enough to know that the team's performance couldn't always be laid at the feet of the manager, whether it failed to live up to expectations or overachieved out of the blue. The Philadelphia media upped the pressure on him during the World Series, mostly asserting that the delay in announcing a new deal for Diamond meant that he was certain to be fired. It was considered almost a sure thing that he would not be wearing a Phillies uniform when spring training rolled around. Names of potential new managers were offered the fans for their consideration and consumption almost every day. Many a sports writer ventured to predict that the delay was a sure sign one or both of the managers whose teams were then fighting for the title of baseball world champion would be interviewed for the job as soon as the Series concluded.

Diamond arrived at the team's stadium on a cold Tuesday morning, two days before Thanksgiving, having flown in from his home in Minneapolis the night before. The phone call summoning him to Philadelphia came from Gary Sherman just several hours before Diamond drove to the airport and hurried onto a flight ready to depart. When he got off the elevator on the floor housing the team's general offices, he was surprised to find all of the desks in the open area deserted, and only Sherman at work in his office.

The GM greeted him without leaving his chair. "Hey there, Jimmy, good to see you. Get here this morning?"

"No, I didn't want to take a chance with U.S. Air. They do better at night than during the day. I got a room at the Holiday Inn when we landed, had seven hours shuteye, and feel great. Where is everybody?"

"The boss told them all to take today and tomorrow off, stay home, and cook. He did the same thing last year, so now it's a tradition. He's waiting for you in his office, but tell me first what you think of Jason Mason."

"I think he must love his parents very much since he kept the name they gave him. He could have changed it legally and stopped people from laughing at him when they heard it. If it was me, I might have beaten up my old man as soon as I was sure I could."

"Never mind that, what do you think of him as a ballplayer?"

The question from Sherman wasn't unusual. Whenever the GM's constant search for players pointed to someone whom he felt might be a good fit for the Phillies on the basis of offensive or defensive statistics, raw talent or leadership qualities, he found his way to the manager's office hours before game time and asked for an opinion. Diamond usually had one to give.

"I'll tell you what, Gary. If you're still here when I come out and I've got a smile on my face, I'll talk to you about Mason. But if the corners of my mouth are pointing at the floor, what I think of Mason will be my secret. So if my opinion is important to you, wish me luck."

Sherman got up and offered his hand to Diamond. "I do wish you luck, Jimmy. The boss hasn't asked me for any input about keeping you to run the team, which in my position doesn't make me feel too good, but I'm sure it's because he knows how much I think of you. He's made up his mind himself on this one."

"Thanks, Gary, I appreciate it. I know that when the manager gets canned, plenty of times the guy who hired him gets pushed out the door too. What the Club has done the last two seasons wouldn't get you voted GM of the year, though I never had any real disagreement with the twenty-five players you put on the field for me. You did the best you could when some of the ones we counted on at the beginning got hurt or didn't produce for one reason or another. So if Tommy lets me go, I hope you stay. Anyway, I'd better get in there and see what he has to say."

Hanover greeted him in a loud, friendly voice. "Come in, Jimmy, sit down. Take the chair on the right side of the desk and I'll hear you better." He waited for Diamond to take a seat before continuing. "Sorry about dragging you here just before the holiday but I wanted to have a talk with you and move on."

"It's okay, Tommy. I've got a flight back at one o'clock. Ellen's got everything under control at home."

"Good. Jimmy, this was my twenty-fourth year as owner of the Phillies, and you know how many times we've been in the World Series?" He didn't wait for an answer. "Twice. Twice is all. And do you know how many we won? Of course you do. None, an easy number to remember. So what are we going to do about that?"

Diamond didn't say anything. He knew Hanover well enough to realize more was coming, that he wasn't asking for an answer.

"I'll tell you what I want to do: I want to use this offseason to put together the best team we can. I'm ready to trade anyone we've got if it will help us win. And I'm willing to go to the vault and pay for a free agent or two if that's what we need. This is my silver anniversary coming up, and the only way I can celebrate is by our getting into the World Series and winning it." Hanover paused several seconds while looking straight at Diamond. "That's what I want from my manager next year, a championship team. Can you give me that, Jimmy?"

"I can bust my ass trying, Tommy, that's all I can say." But then Diamond realized that Hanover was still conducting a one-way conversation.

"You were a great ballplayer for this club, for thirteen years, and I never saw the day you didn't give it all you had. You played hurt when you could've been sitting it out, you taught the young players to respect the game, and you led by example. I never saw the time you didn't hustle down to first on any ball you hit. I always felt you'd be taking over our team some day. But the best we've done in your five years as manager is second place two years ago. We both know everyone expected us to finish on top this year, but you can't lose two of your starting pitchers to elbow trouble and keep winning games, can you Jimmy." He stated it as a fact, not a question. "No way," he continued, "especially when they break down just after the trading deadline. There was no way we could replace them."

Hanover got up from behind his desk, stepped over to his office window and looked out at the empty ballpark. "I know you're a good manager, Jimmy. You won a lot of games for us in the minors and the title with Mobile in the Southern League. We groomed you for this job and I wanted you to stay with the organization as long as you were in baseball if you could handle it."

Diamond was sure he knew what was coming. He was getting the big buildup before the axe came down. Tommy couldn't look him in the eye when he fired him.

"There are a bunch of writers out there who figure they're smarter than me," Hanover continued, turning back toward Diamond. "They're ready to dump you if they could, and they're betting that's what I'll do. But that's not how I feel about it, and since I'm the guy who pays the bills I'm just going to have to disappoint the whole lot of 'em. I'm extending your contract for two years, with fifteen percent more each year. Are you okay with that?"

Diamond gave his employer a big smile. "That's fine, Tommy, as long as I can keep the same coaches, and like I said before, I'll bust my ass to get us a winner."

"I know you will. But Gary and I have been talking about letting Cavalho manage in Single-A. It's about time he got that experience."

"You're right, but let him stay with me one more year. He's a good bench coach and I want him around when we win that championship."

"Alright, Luis stays. So get out of here and go on back to Minneapolis, but call me on Monday. That's when we start building a team."

As soon as Diamond shut the door behind him, Sherman came out of his office and saw the smile on the manager's face. He reached for Diamond's hand. "Congratulations. I'm glad the boss made the right decision."

"Thanks, Gary, I'm happy as a pig in slop. He gave me another two years. And yeah, I think Jason Mason is ready to bust out and show what he can do. He's someone you and me and Tommy should be talking about next week. Right now, though, I've got a plane to catch."

"Happy Thanksgiving, Jimmy."

"You too, Gary. Have a good one."

During the winter months of the "hot stove league," the Phillies were one of the more active teams. Sherman and Diamond had a number of long telephone conversations about the players to let go, others to pick up in trades, if possible, and about the free agents offering their services to the highest bidder. Whenever they agreed on a move they hoped to make, Sherman took their plan to Tommy Hancock for his approval to be certain the owner understood the financial consequences of the deals they had in mind. Hancock proved his willingness to spend money, allowing Sherman to beef up the bullpen with two proven relievers and to sign Jason Mason to a three-year contract as the club's right fielder.

Management felt good about the team it brought to spring training, and the exhibition games in March resulted in even greater confidence going forward as the two starting pitchers, whose elbow troubles the year before had derailed the team, showed they were ready to resume their regular turns on the mound. The Phillies roared through the first half of the season, and by the middle of July they had an eight-game lead over both the Mets and the Braves. They were on a pace to win over a hundred games, a feat they hadn't accomplished in all of Hancock's twenty-four years of ownership. In the clubhouse, some players were already speculating about which team in the National League would be the wild card entry and their first opponent in the playoffs.

As the July 31 trading deadline approached, Diamond, Sherman and Hancock conferred several times about whether they should be considering any other moves that might further strengthen the team. Some minor trades were discussed with other clubs, but management didn't consider it a loss when none of them reached fruition. Then, four days before the deadline, Buddy Walters, the team's All-Star shortstop who turned down more money from Kansas City to stay with Philadelphia on a new one-year contract, cried out in pain after swinging awkwardly at a pitch that fooled him completely. He was attended to by the trainer and Diamond, and was removed from the game, replaced by Kyle. X-rays taken immediately showed he had seriously strained an oblique muscle in his abdomen. The team's experience with this type of injury in the past left no doubt that Walters would be unable to return to the lineup for at least two months. If the Phillies were going to maintain their lead, win the Division, and play their way into the World Series, they would have to do it with a different shortstop.

On the day Kyle took over for Walters, he had a .221 batting average. He had appeared in thirty-six of the team's 101 games as the sole infield utility player, and was having a disappointing season. Sherman and Diamond were concerned not only with his low average but also with his lack of power, evidenced by just two home runs and fifteen runs batted in. Kyle had also made seven errors in the field, just three shy of those charged against Walters in ninety-three games. It was difficult to envision him taking over at shortstop on an every day basis if Walters jumped to another club the next year. In any event, another shortstop, to play regularly or take on the utility role behind Kyle, was needed right away.

Diamond was always aware, after receiving Heather's last letter, that their son had signed with some team to play professional baseball. But there was no way he could follow his progress without knowing his name or the club he was on. Now he realized that circumstances had given him at least a chance to find out where his son was playing and whether he was ready to move up to the big leagues.

"Here's what to do, Gary," he told the GM after the team lost its second consecutive game to the last place Pirates. "Contact every team in both leagues and see who can offer us a shortstop from either their major league roster or their Triple-A farm team. Let that college girl you hired into the marketing and PR department work with you. What's her name?"

"Debbie Newton."

"Okay, if anyone from Triple-A is available, tell Debbie to find out what she can about whoever it is. I mean where he comes from, his birthday, his parents' names if they have it."

"What's all that for?"

"I'm looking for a particular kid I've heard about, but I forgot his name and who he plays for. I think I'll know it if I hear it again but the other stuff may help."

"All right, with any luck we'll know what's out there by tomorrow night."

The Phillies closed out the series with the Pirates with a victory, sparked by Kyle's three hits, including a bases clearing double. Diamond gave him a quick hug in the dugout, and said "That's my boy," but not loud enough for anyone else to hear.

That night, after an early dinner, he joined Sherman and Debbie Newton in Sherman's office. "Here's what we've got," Sherman said, "three choices to consider."

Diamond, impatient, interrupted. "Any in the big leagues now?"

"I was about to tell you that, Jimmy. Sit back and relax. Debbie and I will lay it out for you." He waited a few seconds before continuing. "Seattle will let us have Manny Marosco for a couple of prospects, one from Triple-A, one from Double-A. Marosco has played mostly second base for them this year, but he knows his way around shortstop."

Diamond spoke up again. "Yeah, I know, I've seen him play. Throws funny, but always gets it there on time."

"As I was saying," Sherman went on, "the main problem I see is that he's going on thirty-four and has been on the DL already this year for three weeks with a pulled groin. So how dependable he'd be we don't know."

"Okay, next," Diamond said.

"The Twins have got a kid in Wichita," Sherman said. "Darryl Coburn. It's his second year there. Right now he's hitting .317 and has fifteen home runs. So he's on a pace to hit twenty-five, which is damn good for any shortstop, and the park he plays in is no band box. He's got a healthy arm, but he's thrown a few souvenirs into the stands back of first."

"What else do we know about him?"

Sherman pointed a finger at Newton who looked down at a paper she was holding.

"He's twenty-four years old, Mr. Diamond, and grew up in a town in Oregon, called Milton."

"Do you have his birthday?"

Sherman gave Diamond a quizzical look but didn't say anything.

"Yes, he was born on January 9, 1986."

That could be him, Diamond thought. Heather told him in September that the baby was due in about four months.

"Anything about the parents?"

This time Sherman's patience deserted him. "Come on, Jimmy, what's that got to do with anything?"

Diamond ignored him and nodded at Newton. She understood that he wanted her to continue.

"Very little," she answered. "The Twins said they believe his father's an executive in a farm machinery company. They don't know anything about his mother. Someone was supposed to get back to me with their first names, but I haven't heard anything yet."

"Okay, who's the last one?"

"Another kid in Triple-A," Sherman said, "in the Cubs system at Akron. He's tall and rangy and covers a lot of ground. They compare him to Luis Aparicio, if you remember him, and a little with Cal Ripken too."

"That's pretty good company to be in, but the Cubs are giving you a selling job. Why would they want to move him if he's that good?"

"I asked the same question. They say he's a pure shortstop who doesn't want to play a utility role in the infield. He's afraid moving around will hurt him when he's at short. Since they're counting on Rafy Trinidad being their shortstop for at least the next three years with the new contract he signed, the kid is expendable."

"Sounds a little like a prima donna. What's his name, anyway?"

"Matthew Norris."

Matthew, Diamond's middle name. Heather could have done that for him, he thought, even though she might never want him to know.

"And where's he from?"

"Tell him what you've got, Debbie."

"He grew up in Texas," Newton said. "The name of the town is Hopedale. It's very small, population about three thousand. It was hard to find on a map, but it's about halfway between Houston and Dallas. The family still lives there."

Diamond felt himself getting excited, but without wanting Sherman or Newton to be aware of it. He knew Hopedale. It was about fifty miles from where Heather's parents lived, and about eighty miles from the army base where he was stationed when he met her. He had driven through the town once with Heather while he was courting her. She probably returned to Texas when she left him, he figured, met her husband somewhere around there and settled in Hopedale after they were married.

"How old is he?" he asked.

"He's twenty-four, Jimmy, same as Coburn with the Twins," Sherman said.

Newton filled in the rest. "Actually, he was born just two weeks before Coburn, near the end of December." She looked at her notes again. "On the twenty-seventh."

That still fit, Diamond thought. Heather had said the baby was due "in about four months." That could have put his birthday in December. If either of the two players was his son, the chances were greater that it was Norris.

"What do his parents do? Do we know?"

"No, the Cubs have nothing on that," Newton said.

"The Texas kid sounds more solid," Diamond said. "I think I'd go with him. What are the Cubs asking in return?"

"Wait a second, Jimmy," Sherman said. "Don't you want to know about his hitting?"

Diamond realized he had spoken too soon, that he was almost convinced Norris was his son. "Of course," he answered. "Sorry, Gary, my mind was wandering. I was starting to think about tomorrow's game."

"He's not a long ball hitter like Coburn. He had seven home runs last year and he's on that same pace this year. The good news is that he's a solid contact hitter and is leading the Mountain League in base hits right now with a .322 average. The bonus is that he's got good speed and would probably have at least twenty-two stolen bases this year if he stays where he is."

Diamond thought back to the four years he led the National League in base hits and the eight—or was it nine?—seasons he'd won a gold glove at shortstop. The boy sounded like a chip off the old block.

"So that's the good news. What's the bad news?"

Sherman laughed. "I didn't mean there had to be bad news too. None that I'm aware of."

"Well, then I feel even stronger about him. If the Cubs aren't trying to rob us blind, make the deal and get the kid here right away."

"Who are you going to play when he's here," Sherman asked, "him or Kyle? That's a pretty sensitive situation. Kyle's your stepson and he's been with the club for almost a year. If you sit him down for this kid, it could be a morale problem and you know how those things can spread."

Diamond didn't hesitate before answering. Sherman's question bothered him but he spoke calmly. "You know that's my territory, Gary, not yours. You get us the players, I make out the lineup. But the answer is that Kyle gets the call, and he stays in there as long as he does the job, both ways. Maybe he turned the corner tonight with those three hits. But if his batting average stays where it's been so far this season, we'll have to see what Norris can do."

"Will you get any pressure at home to play Kyle, regardless?"

"A lot of people question some of the moves I make, even Katherine. That goes with the job. But like I just said, I make out the lineup, no one else."

The Phillies had a day off after the Pirates series, but had to use it to fly to the west coast for games against the Dodgers and Giants. Diamond scheduled a practice for four o'clock that afternoon in Dodger Stadium, three hours after the team arrived in California. As the players were putting on their uniforms in the clubhouse, a young man carrying a small Chicago Cubs duffle bag entered the room and was looking around, not sure where to go. Kyle saw him and went over to greet him.

"Hi, I'm Kyle Price, and you must be Matt Norris. Welcome to the Phillies. We're taking the field today in about an hour for practice, so let me introduce you to the guys, and then you'll want to speak to Sergio, the equipment manager, about getting a uniform."

They shook hands and Kyle led Norris around the room to meet his new teammates, all of whom greeted him warmly, most with words of encouragement. At the equipment counter, Sergio had a uniform all ready for him. "I know your size from information they already gave me, so those should fit. And the lowest number we're not using is twenty-nine, so you got it unless you gotta have a different one to feel good."

Norris smiled and waved his hand. "No, that's fine," he said.

"You've met everyone except the manager," Kyle told him. "He's Jimmy Diamond and he's my step-father. You'd probably find that out from the guys at some point, but I want you to know it now because we're the two shortstops on the team and he decides which one of us plays."

"Thanks," Norris said, "I didn't know that."

When they entered the manager's office, Diamond was on the telephone. He held one finger up in the air to show he was about to finish the call, and, as he alternately spoke and listened, looked Norris over carefully. He saw a young ball player about his own height but with larger shoulders and a thicker neck. He had long eyelashes, like Heather's, and lips that reminded Diamond of her also, but he couldn't see anything of himself in Norris's face. He remembered Heather telling him that their baby boy looked a lot like him and he expected to see that for himself when they met. But his disappointment was quickly tempered by his realization that twenty-four years had gone by since her description.

Diamond had already decided that he would not tell Norris he was his father. He had to keep the secret out of respect for Heather's feelings, at least until he had the chance to talk to her about it. And he didn't want the team to get mixed up in it and think he was favoring his son if he had to replace Kyle at shortstop with Norris.

He got off the phone and was careful to speak to Norris as he would to any player called up to the big leagues. He told him it would be a good idea to say little but to observe everything, both on the field and in the clubhouse. "You're part of the team as of right now. That means you don't shy away from celebrating on the field with the guys when we win. I'm not going to play you in our next two games unless I need you in an emergency, so find yourself a seat in the dugout and relax. You're last in line for batting practice, and you get six swings like everyone else."

Diamond reached into a thin leather file on top of the desk and pulled out a sheet of paper. "Here are all the rules," he said. "Do yourself a favor and memorize them all tonight. If you've got no questions, Kyle will show you your locker and you can suit up. We'll give you some infield drill and then let you get those six swings in the cage. Glad to have you with us."

Kyle stayed hot. Over the next three weeks he batted .321 and had several timely hits, including a walk-off home run against the Cardinals in the twelfth inning. That hit capped the team's comeback from a six-run deficit and gave it the momentum to keep its five-game winning streak alive and extend it to eight. Several games in the streak were "laughers" for the Phillies, and Diamond took advantage of the opportunity to insert Norris into the game in the late innings. There were small celebrations in the dugout after his first major league hit (a two-hop grounder up the middle), his first extra-base hit (a double, which also gave him his first two runs batted in) and, to his embarrassment, his first error on a no excuse drop of an infield popup.

It was clear, however, that Norris knew how to play shortstop. He covered the same ground as Kyle but his strong arm gave him a better chance to throw out a hitter from deep in the hole. Although his defensive skills impressed Diamond, as did his speed on the base paths, he realized that Norris was not as advertised by the Cubs but rather a work in progress

In the last week of August Kyle cooled off quickly and had just three hits in his next twenty-three trips to the plate. Diamond gave him a two-day break, but Kyle's sudden ineffectiveness continued when he returned to the lineup, and he batted just under .200 in the team's games that week. It was time, the manager decided, to find out what Norris could do over an extended period, and he notified Norris in the clubhouse that he'd be in the starting lineup the next day for the opening of a series in Florida. Diamond knew there would be less pressure on the rookie getting this chance away from the Phillies' rabid hometown fans. He also spoke to Kyle, reminding him that baseball was a streaky game within a long season and encouraging him to keep doing his work every day.

As he left the ballpark that night and walked toward the bus waiting to take the team to the airport, Diamond noticed Kyle and Debbie Newton in the front seat of her car in the parking lot. Minutes later, the bus driver blew the horn several times, signaling that it was about to leave, and the manager's stepson was the last to board. Thinking about it, Diamond recalled that he had seen the two of them together on several other occasions.

Norris's play in the three games at Miami was impressive, but not outstanding. Although he had just three hits in eleven at-bats, he hit the ball hard most of the time and struck out only once. On the defensive side, he played errorless ball and covered his position smoothly. He twice started exceptional double plays with hard, accurate throws to second that gave Gerry Small, his infield partner, plenty of time to avoid the sliding base runner and make the relay throw to first.

In the next series, at Pittsburgh, Norris had a surprise bunt single to start the winning rally in the first game. Two days later he stroked a ninth inning double in the rubber game that put runners on second and third from where they scored on a two-out hit that put the Phillies ahead by one run. The team's closer was perfect in the last half of the ninth, and everyone was feeling good on the flight to Milwaukee, the last stop on the road trip.

It all came to a grinding halt for Norris in the four contests with the Brewers. His offensive statistics took a sharp drop as he was hitless in two of the games, struck out six times in the series (four of them coming with at least one runner in scoring position) and was picked off first on one of the few times he managed to reach base. It was clear that the rookie's performance at the plate affected his play in the field as he was charged with two errors and looked shaky on several throws that were dug out of the dirt by his first baseman.

It hurt Diamond to watch Norris's play, like the helpless feeling a father would have witnessing the ineptness of his awkward son in a Little League game. In his heart, Diamond knew that he wanted Norris to have a good game every day, to play better than Kyle, to be accepted by his teammates as the Phillies' regular shortstop and to be in the lineup when the post season began. He even found himself recalling the thoughts he had years earlier, imagining the team in the World Series and his son either delivering the winning hit or making the spectacular play that would bring them the world championship. But he knew that at this point in time, with just fourteen games remaining to be played, he owed it to Kyle to write him into the starting lineup. Sherman had been told by the medical staff that Buddy Walters' injury was not healing as quickly as anticipated and that his recovery would not be complete until after the World Series.

The time Kyle spent on the bench did him a world of good. He was eager to try and regain his role as the team's shortstop, and the energy he brought to his play was evident to his teammates, to Diamond, and the Phillies coaching staff. Although Diamond wanted to give Norris another chance to compete for the position before the start of the play-offs, Kyle's performance put such a move out of the question. It was clear from both their conduct and conversation that the players and coaches believed Kyle had won the competition over Norris to start at shortstop. Diamond realized that substituting Norris for Kyle again could be totally disruptive as the team finished the regular season and got ready to meet its first playoff opponent.

With the best record in the National League, the Phillies were at home to play the Colorado Rockies in a best of five series. In storybook fashion, the Rockies had won their last ten games to overtake two teams and capture the wild card on the last day of the season. But their heroic struggle disrupted their normal pitching rotation, leaving their best starter unavailable for the first two games, and the Phillies eliminated them quickly with three victories in four games. Kyle's contribution to the offense was minimal without being disruptive, and his defense, although effective, didn't include any highlight plays that gained a spot on Sports Center later at night.

The National League Championship Series, pitting the Phillies against the Houston Astros, opened in Philadelphia also. The two games played there were both pitching duels, the Astros winning the second game 2-1 after losing the first by the same score. Kyle had no hits in either game and, with the tying run on third, made the final out in the Phillies defeat.

When the series resumed in Houston two days later, Diamond put the same lineup on the field in each of the three games played. His team claimed only one victory and found itself just a game away from elimination. Although Kyle had three hits and a respectable batting average for the three games in the Astrodome, his failures at the plate came, for the most part, with runners in scoring position. On two occasions the hitter ahead of Kyle was walked intentionally, loading the bases. Unfortunately, Kyle validated the Astros' strategy each time by striking out and ending the scoring threat. The Phillies lost each of those games.

On the return flight to Philadelphia, Diamond changed his mind several times while trying to decide whom he would play at shortstop when the series continued. On the one hand, he didn't think it would be fair to pull Kyle out of the lineup and seemingly blame him for the predicament the team was in. The local media might question the move and would be in a position to rake him over the coals if Norris turned out to be the catalyst for the defeat that ended the Phillies season the wrong way. On the other hand, he knew he was looking for an excuse to have Norris at shortstop in the World Series, putting him in a position to bring Diamond's fantasy to fruition. Diamond felt that the announced pitching matchups for the next two games were both in his team's favor, and he was confident that his players, strongly supported by the sixty thousand fans shouting and waving their white towels, would respond with winning performances. If he was right, Kyle's presence in the lineup for the two games could settle the matter and require him to be back at his infield position when the Phillies met their American League opponents in the World Series. But if Diamond switched to Norris "because I think we need more offense out there," and his team sent the Astros packing, he'd be able to keep his son in the lineup when the championship series began.

Five hours before the scheduled start of Game Six, Diamond met in his office at the ballpark with Luis Cavalho, his bench coach and closest friend in baseball. He took pride in the fact that he was responsible for getting Cavalho, his former minor league teammate, to recognize the doors that might open for him if he chose to explore a career in baseball and remain in the United States instead of returning to Puerto Rico and an uncertain future there.

In the same month that Diamond was called up to the big leagues to play in Philadelphia, Cavalho was summoned to the manager's office in Scranton and told that the club would not be offering him a contract to return to the team for the next season. As Cavalho was aware, the Phillies had a power hitting center fielder on their Double-A roster in Reading and he was being promoted to Scranton the following spring. When he learned of Cavalho's situation, Diamond spoke to the coach in the Phillies system who played with his father and who was still employed on the club's entry in the rookie league. He urged him to use whatever connections he had to obtain a minor league position for Luis, and the coach was able to come through. Starting as both an outfield and base running instructor for the Phillies Single-A team in Tallahassee, Cavalho worked his way up to being a third base coach, returning to Scranton in his final minor league assignment. Two years later, Diamond persuaded Gary Sherman to bring Cavalho to Philadelphia as his bench coach.

"Luis," Diamond said when Cavalho had settled into his chair, "I've decided to put Norris at shortstop and bat him seventh. We need his bat in the lineup."

Cavalho was stunned. His anger came immediately, confirmed by the tone of his voice. "You're kidding, Jimmy. You can't do that to Kyle. It'll look like you're blaming him for the fact that we stunk out the joint those last two games in Houston. We left ten runners in scoring position in the fourth game and twelve in the fifth. It wasn't just Kyle. No one was getting a hit when we needed it." Cavalho paused for a few seconds, raising his voice even louder when he continued. "Jimmy, you'll kill the kid if you make it look like it was all his fault. He'll feel he let the whole ballclub down. And he's your stepson, for Christ sakes. Don't do this to him. Your wife will hate you for it and the whole team will be wondering what the hell is going on. If you make that move, I think a lot of the guys will lose their focus on what we've got to do today and tomorrow. That could hurt us the most."

Diamond was unprepared for Cavalho's outrage and passion. He knew his bench coach was right, but while raising the fact that he shouldn't hurt his stepson, Cavalho was unaware that Diamond was trying to help his own son.

"I thought we should get Norris into a game now and see what he does at the plate under pressure. If he looks good, I wouldn't be afraid to use him in the Series."

Cavalho stared at Diamond, shaking his head from side to side before answering. "Jimmy, do I have to tell you it's a little early to be worrying about the goddam World Series? If we lose today or tomorrow, we'll be sitting at home in front of the TV when the Astros start playing next week. All the pressure is on *us* today and you're talking about sticking Norris out there. He's been up here for how long—just a month—he's still raw. He doesn't know this kind of pressure. He could piss his pants out at shortstop, afraid he'll screw up on a ball hit to him and cost us the game. And if that ever happened, it could ruin the kid, set him back for a long time. We lose the game because you play a Triple-A ballplayer at short, you'll never hear the end of it. It makes no sense to take Kyle out of there."

Cavalho got up and walked toward the door. Before opening it, he turned around to face Diamond. "You're the manager, Jimmy, and it's your call. I just had to be honest with you about it."

Any suspense for Phillies fans about the outcome of Game Six ended early. The team scored five runs in the first inning, four more in the second, and had an 11–1 lead with the game just three innings old. Diamond thought over what Cavalho had said and winked at him in the dugout as he went to post the lineup card on the wall next to the bat rack. Kyle started at shortstop, walked both his first and second time up and then went hitless in two official at bats. He was replaced by Norris in the eighth inning when Diamond, sitting on a 15–2 lead, pulled four of his starters from the game. In his one at bat, Norris lined a double down the left field line. In the field, his only chance came when he leaped high in the air to snag a line drive and rob the batter of a hit.

The Astros looked like they knew what fate awaited them as they got ready for the deciding game of the series. They realized that the Phillies pitcher who had given them just four hits in Game Three, and had beaten them twice during the regular season, was matched against their own pitcher who was knocked out of that same game in the fourth inning. The momentum they tried to establish by scoring two runs in their first at-bats went up in smoke when the Phillies scored three runs of their own in the last half of the inning, all driven in by a Jason Mason home run with two outs. Philadelphia scored single runs in the third, fourth and sixth innings while the Houston hitters encountered only futility in their attempt to put more runs on the board. The 6–2 score in favor of the home team after seven full innings was the final score of the game as two Phillies relievers each pitched an inning without allowing an Astros hitter to reach base. Kyle played the entire game, getting a single in four trips to the plate and fielding his position cleanly. When the final out was recorded on a fly ball to center field, Diamond and Cavalho hugged each other for several seconds before joining the rest of the team on the field to celebrate their winning the National League pennant.

For the third consecutive series, the World Series of baseball, Philadelphia opened at home, hosting the American League champion Texas Rangers. Tommy Hancock went all out for the occasion, providing red, white, and blue bunting that was draped not only in front of the box seats located along the first and third base lines, but which also hung directly below the entire area set aside for the media in the second deck. Hancock arranged for the installation of a giant American flag that covered a large portion of the center field wall until it was rolled up and removed just before the start of the game. Military units from the Army, Navy, Marines, and Air Force, accompanied by a marching band from the nearby Fort Dix, New Jersey Army base, assembled in the outfield. At the appointed time they marched in step toward home plate as the band played the popular fight songs of each of the armed forces. The singing of the National Anthem by Mariah Carey followed immediately. With incredible timing, three Air Force jets roared over the stadium just as she reached the last note.

When the cheering died down and the crowd took their seats, the managers of the two teams were introduced. Diamond and Terry Granger, skipper of the Rangers, met at home plate, shook hands, and greeted each of their respective players who were not in the starting lineups as they were introduced to the fans and came jogging out of their dugouts. The starters were called out next to the applause of the crowd, with Jason Mason receiving the loudest ovation and waving his cap in appreciation in all four directions. Joey Townsend, the Phillies eighty-three-year-old Hall of Fame first baseman, then walked slowly onto the field to throw out the first pitch. Stopping halfway between the mound and home plate, and smiling broadly as he rotated his arm several times, he threw the baseball into the glove of the team's catcher. The fans cheered him loudly, many of the older ones with tears in their eyes, as he retreated toward the first base dugout. Finally, a nine-year-old boy in a wheelchair, introduced as the baseball whiz in his hospital's cancer ward, was brought to the plate and given the microphone. "Play ball," he hollered, and the World Series had begun.

The two clubs had their best pitchers on the mound for the first game. Although a tight pitchers' duel was expected, and neither team scored a run through seven innings, each had collected nine hits to that point. It was only the inability of both to produce a timely hit with men on base that resulted in the presence of fourteen goose eggs on the scoreboard.

In the top half of the eighth, Texas put a man on third with two out. The next batter hit a bouncing ball headed for the shortstop hole. The Phillies third baseman reached it but had it bounce off the fingers of his outstretched glove. Kyle, who was running to his right, stopped in his tracks, turned back toward second and grabbed the ball out of the air with his bare hand. Coming down on his left foot, he fired it to first in time to beat the runner by half a step on a bang-bang play. The crowd roared as the umpire pumped his fist once to signal the out, and it gave Kyle a standing ovation as he crossed the infield to the Philadelphia dugout.

The Phillies' leadoff hitter in their half of the same inning blooped a ball down the right field line which fell just out of the reach of the three Rangers, allowing him to reach second base with a double. Diamond called for a sacrifice which was executed successfully, moving the runner to third. He considered pinch hitting for Kyle, who was hitless to that point, but decided that his stepson deserved the opportunity to drive in the go ahead run on the basis of his sensational defensive play earlier in the inning.

The Texas manager pulled the starting pitcher and brought in his fireballing closer, hoping to induce two strikeouts and get out of the jam without allowing the Phillies to score. The move didn't persuade Diamond to change his mind about using a pinch hitter, and when the closer started out a little wild, missing the strike zone with his first three pitches, Diamond was certain the next pitch would be a fastball over the heart of the plate. He signaled that Kyle had the green light to swing at it if it looked good. Kyle did just that, but got slightly under the ball and hit what the game announcers called a "major league popup" in the infield. His confidence bolstered by the comeback, the Texas pitcher struck out the next Phillies hitter on four pitches, deflating the crowd's enthusiasm. The game entered the ninth inning still tied at zero.

It took Texas just two batters to score a run. An infield single was followed by a drive to right center field that split the two outfielders and gave the speedy runner enough time to race around the bases and beat the relay throw home. No further damage ensued, and the home team's fans were up on their feet immediately, shouting support, clapping their hands and waving their towels in the air, virtually demanding a come-from-behind rally. The noise must have awakened the gods who looked after the Phillies all season because Jason Mason followed a one out single with a first-pitch drive into the third row of the centerfield bleachers for a Philadelphia victory. He was met at home plate by the entire team with each player anxious to make physical contact with some part of his body. Many of the fans were reluctant to leave the park, staying to watch the home run and the celebration replayed several times on the giant scoreboard.

The fans who attended Game Two of the Series were not treated to the same reward that was bestowed on those at the ballpark a day earlier. The Texas heavy hitters were in good form from the start and their team led 11–3 after five innings. Philadelphia tried to make a game of it by scoring four more runs in the sixth, but the Rangers answered with three runs of their own in the seventh inning. Empty seats were soon visible all around the stadium as droves of fans gave up on the team and left early to beat the traffic.

Diamond rested several of his starters for the final two innings. Norris, inserted at shortstop, hit a drive to right field that had home run distance but sliced foul and into the seats as it neared the fence. On the next pitch, he stepped into a slider as it hugged the outside edge of the plate and singled to left field. The at bat impressed Diamond who turned and gave a thumbs-up to Cavalho as Norris ran to first. Diamond was also aware at that moment that Kyle had one hit to show for the two games.

The festivities in the Rangers ballpark in Arlington that preceded Game Three were on a par with those that took place earlier in Philadelphia.

Borrowing from the State's rich football tradition, Grantland Hoban, the team's owner, arranged for a dozen beautiful cheer leaders on each side of the field to entertain the fans whenever there was a lull in the scheduled activities. The National Anthem, sung by Tony Bennett, followed a recording of "God Bless America," with the voice of Kate Smith still sounding marvelous over the stadium's speaker system.

Diamond felt confident about regaining the lead in the Series. His starter had already beaten the Astros twice in the earlier playoff round, allowing them a total of just ten hits in fourteen innings pitched. The Texas starter had won two games and lost one in the post season to that point, but had an unimpressive earned run average just below 4.00. However, as so often happens, the statistics shown on paper were completely reversed in the playing of the game, and the pitcher with the outstanding record suddenly reverted to what seemed an imitation of his less accomplished opponent. Diamond watched with increasing alarm as the Phillies hurler was touched for six runs in just five innings before handing the baseball over to his troubled manager after walking the first batter he faced in the Texas sixth. The Phillies relievers allowed no runs the rest of the way, but the team was held to a total of three runs and never threatened to overtake the early Texas lead. Kyle went hitless again, his batting average falling to .091.

In the manager's office after the game, Cavalho agreed with Diamond's assessment that the team looked flat on the field. "In the dugout too, Jimmy, there wasn't a whole lot of chatter," he added.

"I think I'll make a couple of changes tomorrow, and I may shake up the batting order too. Something's missing there. I don't know, I'll sleep on it if I can get any sleep."

Diamond posted the lineup for Game Four shortly after arriving at the ballpark in the middle of the afternoon. He wanted to give his players plenty of time to digest the changes he made, both in the insertion of a different catcher and left fielder, and switching the order in which several of the players would bat. He intended to start Norris at shortstop also, but changed his mind at the last minute when he decided, based on that day's pitching matchups, that a stronger defense was going to be more important than additional offense. He still felt Kyle was a better fielder, overall, than Norris, but his patience was wearing thin on Kyle's continued ineffectiveness at the plate.

Diamond was half right about the Phillies offense. The team had eight hits to go along with five bases on balls, but continued its frustrating habit of not getting the big hit when needed, and leaving men on base. After scoring two runs in the first inning, the team led the Rangers until there were two outs in the last half of the ninth with the score 5–3 in its favor. Then, with a suddenness that energized both the players and their fans, the home team put together a double, a single, a stolen base, and another single to score two runs and tie the game. Every hit came with two strikes on the batter, putting Philadelphia just one strike away from victory each time. The roar of the crowd, which was finally given a chance to vent its emotions, was sustained through the Phillies scoreless tenth inning and seemed to foretell the inevitability of what was to follow. The Texas cleanup hitter, batting first, looked at one pitch from the new reliever and deposited the next one into the mitt of a fan in the left field bleachers who wore the same number "22" on his newly purchased Rangers jersey as the ballpark's hero of the moment.

Shortly after the game ended, the Texas manager announced to the media representatives crowded into the clubhouse that he would not be giving his Game One pitcher a second start the next day in Game Five. Instead, he would save him in the event a sixth game was necessary, allowing him two additional days of rest. When Diamond learned who would be on the mound for Texas, he made up his mind to have Norris at shortstop. In four games, Kyle had two hits and a .143 batting average.

Before his team took the field for Game Five, Diamond gathered the players in a close circle in the clubhouse and gave a short speech:

"We have to win three games in a row to be world champions," he began, "and everyone in this room knows we can do it. If Texas could do it, we certainly can because we've got a better team. But we can't win three games in one day. So I don't want any of you out there trying to win this game by yourself. Just do your own job, the one you've been doing all year, and don't put any extra pressure on yourself. A few hits at the right time and we'd probably be up three games to one ourselves. We've got the better pitching going for us today, so let's give Rudy some support." Several players started moving away before realizing that Diamond hadn't finished. He paused several seconds before banging his fist into an open palm and saying, "Then we can go play some more baseball back in Philadelphia." There was a loud cheer, and the players got ready to go about their business.

When the World Series was over, and both the media and the fans had time to digest everything that had taken place in the two ballparks over the course of nine days, most of the written and spoken words seemed to focus repeatedly on the ninth inning of Game Four and the ninth inning of Game Seven.

The Phillies took Diamond's pregame pep talk to heart and beat the Rangers easily in Game Five, scoring three runs in the first inning and shutting them out 7–0. Texas managed only three hits in the game, had a total of ten strikeouts, and gave their fans nothing to cheer about. Its dream of winning the World Series in front of the home crowd wasn't realized. Diamond started Norris at shortstop and was pleased to see him single twice and handle six chances in the field effortlessly.

Back in the "city of brotherly love," the team showed no mercy for their Texas brothers in Game Six. Cheered on by their fans, many thousands of whom came dressed in the red and white Phillies colors, they crushed the Rangers 16–3. This time, Diamond pulled Norris out of the game after six innings and let Kyle finish up. The final statistics showed that Norris singled twice in four trips to the plate but left two runners in scoring position by making the final out of the inning each time. He also committed an error on a ground ball hit directly at him. Kyle had two at bats, leading off the seventh inning with a double to center field, and driving in the last Phillies run with a two out single in the eighth inning. He made a sensational play at short on which he dived to catch an errant throw from his second baseman on a potential double play ball and rolled his body over in time to kick the base with his heel for the out.

After the game, the Texas "ace" told the writers gathered around his locker that six days' rest after pitching the opening game of the Series was too much and was obviously a mistake. Egged on by some of the questions, he threw his manager under the bus by saying that he wanted to pitch Game Five and had said so back in Texas, but was overruled.

Diamond didn't expect to get much sleep that night, and he was right. He was facing the biggest game of his life as a manager, and he couldn't decide who he should send out to play shortstop. In his heart he wanted it to be Norris because he felt certain the Phillies would win and Norris's presence in the lineup would give him the chance to fulfill Diamond's fantasy that his own son was instrumental—was the hero—in winning the World Series. But Diamond knew that having the team beat Texas, that getting Tommy Hancock the championship he coveted was the all important thing, and he realized that his emotions were distracting him from the decision that had to be made on the basis of which player, Norris or Kyle, would best help the team win.

The players had been told to be at the ballpark at three thirty that afternoon. After finishing breakfast shortly after eleven o'clock, Diamond made up several excuses for getting to the ballpark early, kissed his wife, and reminded her to leave for the game before the traffic got heavy.

"Good luck, honey," she said, "and tell Kyle I'll be rooting as hard as I can for him."

"Yeah, okay," he answered, and left.

When he entered the clubhouse just after noon, Diamond was surprised to see Luis Cavalho, in uniform, in the room shared by all six of the coaches. "What are you doing here so early?" he asked.

"I've been here since ten o'clock, Jimmy. Kyle was here and I was throwing him some batting practice. Those two hits he had last night were no fluke. I've been working with him, and I'm pretty sure we finally figured out his problem. He asked me to come in this morning and let him hit so he could feel more confident about how we fixed his stance. He ripped the ball all over the park, and into the seats too. Feels real good about himself now. I sent him home to get some more rest."

"I haven't decided who starts at short, Luis."

Cavalho had been taking some personal items out of his locker and stuffing them into a duffel bag while he spoke to Diamond. He stopped, and looked at his manager.

"Jimmy, sit down a minute, will ya?"

Diamond took a deep breath and walked over to the white plastic chair in the corner of the room. He anticipated what Cavalho would tell him and wasn't sure he wanted to hear it. "Okay, I'm sitting," he said.

"Jimmy, anything I say to you is said totally with respect. You and I both know I wouldn't be here today if it wasn't for you. Maybe I'd be sweating in the sun back in Puerto Rico shoveling some cement into place or carrying lumber up a flight of stairs to my brother-in-law. I've had a good life here in the States on account of you and I'll never forget that." Cavalho stopped long enough to pick up another chair and bring it closer to where Diamond was sitting. "But if you're trying to decide who to play at short today, I can give you my two cents worth one of two ways. I can lay out the reasons I think Kyle should be out there or I can just say I think you'd be crazy to give Norris the nod over him. Which'll it be?"

"I'll go with being crazy, Luis. I know every statistic you can throw at me. I've gone over all of them in my head a hundred times and was awake most of last night thinking about it. But sometimes every number you can come up with on paper doesn't add up to the answer. In the end I've got to go with what my gut tells me." He got up and walked to the door. "I'm going into my office to ride the bike a while."

"And make sure your gut remembers that Kyle's your family and he's got more experience than Norris."

Diamond didn't answer.

An hour later Diamond came out of his office wearing his uniform and found Cavalho talking to the clubhouse attendant. "Luis, I feel tight as a drum. Get a bag of balls and let's go outside. I want you to hit me some grounders at short."

"We haven't done that for a while. You sure you're up to it?"

"Yeah, I'm sure. Just hit them all where I can reach them. It's not a good day for a heart attack."

The workout loosened him up. When it was over, Diamond took a shower and got himself a fresh uniform. Sitting in his office, he made out the lineup card, leaving only the eighth spot in the batting order blank. It would be filled by either Kyle or Norris when he made up his mind.

At four o'clock, as the players were dressing and relaxing in the clubhouse, Diamond went back out on the field. He liked to watch the empty stadium begin to come alive as the ushers dusted off the seats in anticipation of the fans who would be allowed to come through the gates in an hour, and the grounds crew removed the tarpaulin covering the infield. While he watched, the batting cage was wheeled into place and the Rangers came onto the field at four thirty to take batting practice for the next forty-five minutes. Diamond observed them from the dugout for a while and then returned to the clubhouse to make sure all his players, especially those being cared for by the trainers, were ready to go. At the appropriate time he sent them onto the field for their own batting practice session. He took his place behind the cage to observe their swings and make any comments he thought were helpful. Cavalho stood there also, neither saying a word to the other. Kyle and Norris were the last to take their cuts, both hitting a series of sharp drives to the outfield.

As Diamond headed back to the dugout, Hancock and Sherman came onto the field through a door along the first base line.

"Well, Jimmy, here we are," Hancock said. "This is everything we worked for, starting last Thanksgiving. I know you and the players are going to bring us the championship. But good luck, and have a great ballgame."

"That goes for me too," Sherman said.

"Thanks, Tommy. Thanks, Gary. We'll bust our butts to win."

The stadium was already mostly full. Several members of the grounds crew were busy laying down the foul lines and batter's box with white chalk while two others were raking the dirt around the mound. Diamond looked over to the section of the grandstand where the players' wives sat and saw Katherine studying her program. In the hour that had just passed, he found himself leaning toward starting Kyle at shortstop just for the experience factor and hoping Norris would be able to enter the game at some point and do something to win it. As he was about to step down into the dugout, Diamond heard his name called and saw a stadium usher coming toward him.

"Mr. Diamond," he said, "I was asked to give you this envelope by a woman on the third base side. She said it was important, and the woman with her showed me a Phillies ID."

Diamond took the envelope and thanked the usher. He went into the dugout, sat down and opened it. Inside was a note on personal stationary he immediately recognized as Heather's from the initials "HN" at the top. It read:

"Dear Jimmy,

I'll be watching the game tonight and I wish you good luck. I know how much it means to you. We have a flight home early tomorrow morning, but I want to see you before I go. I'll wait for you in the lounge at the players' entrance after the game.

Love, Heather"

She's here to see our son, Diamond thought immediately. Then it occurred to him that he had never even considered the idea that Heather might be at the ballpark for any of the previous six games. And especially those played in Texas if, as he had assumed, there was a good chance she was living there. But maybe, if she attended, she was afraid of upsetting him with any talk about their Matthew while the Series was still ongoing. Tonight it would all be over, and she had come from wherever she lived to see the game. In that case, how could he not start Norris? It was true that Kyle was steadier in the field than Norris, and maybe the Phillies pitchers felt more comfortable with him out there, but the ability to score runs counted also, and Norris was hitting .375 to Kyle's .250. When you came right down to it, the two shortstops were pretty much equal in talent and Kyle's experience was not that much greater than Norris's. Neither had seemed phased by playing in the post season, including the World Series with all the pressure that mounted game by game. And Cavalho had pointed out to him—twice he recalled—that Kyle was family. Well, his own son was closer family than his stepson, even though he had known him for only three months. When Diamond brought the lineup card out to the umpires at home plate, Norris was listed at shortstop, batting eighth.

Game Seven pitted the Phillies' losing pitcher from Game Three, who had given Texas six runs in five innings, against the Rangers' hurler from Game Two who was battered around through five plus innings in his team's 14–7 win. The game was scoreless for the first five innings, and it was clear that this time both pitchers had brought their best stuff to the mound.

In the sixth inning, Norris failed to get the ball thrown to him by his second baseman out of his glove quickly enough to complete a double play at first. The misplay extended the inning, and apparently upset Philadelphia's pitcher who gave up four consecutive hits before getting the third out. His lapse resulted in Texas putting three runs on the score-board before it was over. The Phillies fought back, scoring single runs in the sixth, seventh and eighth innings to tie the score, the last one driven in by Norris's clutch double off the right field fence. The stadium crowd was back in the game, standing and cheering for their heroes.

Diamond brought his closer in to pitch the ninth, gambling on getting a scoreless half inning out of him and counting on the team's momentum to find a way to win the game in their own at bats. With two outs, the closer walked the next Ranger on a very close 3–2 pitch. When the umpire's right hand didn't go up, the pitcher kicked at the dirt on the mound to show his disagreement. That prompted the umpire to remove his mask, step in front of the plate and holler something out to the mound. Diamond ran onto the field, made sure his player didn't say another word and told him the team couldn't afford to lose him to an argument. On the first pitch to the next Texas hitter, the runner on first stole second on what looked like a bad call to the entire Philadelphia bench. Diamond ran out again and disputed the call until he himself was warned that he'd be thrown out of the game if he persisted in arguing.

On the steal, the Texas cleanup hitter, whose home run had defeated the Phillies in Game Four, took a called strike at the plate. Cavalho suggested to Diamond that he be given an intentional walk to set up a force play at any base. But Diamond was aware that the player had gone hitless in his last seven at-bats, and preferred pitching to him rather than to the on-deck hitter who already had singled twice in the game. He called for time and made a slow trip out to the mound where he reminded his closer that the batter was a notorious low ball hitter. He also passed the word to his second base combination to keep the base runner from getting a good lead.

As Diamond watched, taking a deep breath before every pitch, the hitter fouled off several balls while also looking at three others outside the strike zone and working the count full. On the next pitch, the ball was hit sharply up the middle, past the pitcher's late attempt to stop it, headed into center field. Norris raced to his left, dived for the ball and got it in the webbing of his glove. He got to his feet as quick as he could, and without setting himself, cocked his arm for the throw to first. Diamond and Cavalho, seeing that the throw would not beat the runner, were shouting at him to hold the ball. But Norris couldn't hear them over the noise of the crowd and fired it as hard as he could. The ball was too far away for the first baseman to reach, and bounced into the Phillies dugout, allowing the runner on second to score.

The ballpark was suddenly quiet, as if all the air had been let out of the bag. Everyone realized, even as the third out of the inning was made, that the Phillies had only one chance to score at least one run or their quest for the championship was over.

Texas brought its closer into the game to nail down the victory. The program listed him at six feet, four inches tall and weighing 247 pounds, but on the mound he looked even bigger. As he began taking his warm-up pitches, the fans started coming to life again, and their cheering and hand-clapping was at full throttle by the time the umpire told the first scheduled hitter to step into the batter's box. The closer's task appeared to be significantly enhanced by the fact that the Phillies bottom third of the batting order was due up to the plate.

There was a loud shout from the crowd as the ball hit by the team's third baseman rose in the air toward left field, but the announcers in the booth could tell immediately that it wasn't hit hard enough to leave the ballpark. The left fielder moved back to the warning track and casually gloved the drive with one hand.

Norris was next. He tried to disrupt the pitcher's rhythm by stepping out of the batter's box twice, feigning an eye problem, just as the closer was ready to start his windup. Although he incurred the wrath of the Texas battery, both pitcher and catcher telling him to "get your damn ass in the box," he succeeded in inducing a walk and a free trip to first base.

Diamond sent Kyle up as a pinch hitter for the pitcher. Norris sensed that he had unnerved the closer and began dancing off first base, moving his body back and forth as he took his lead. The crowd on that side of the stadium saw what he was doing and tried to further upset the pitcher by shouting some choice epithets at him. When the first two pitches to

Kyle were off the plate, giving him the advantage in the count, Norris was certain that his bouncing around affected the pitcher's concentration and his ability to throw strikes. He also felt that the crowd noise, now more deafening than ever, was helping to rattle the Texas closer. On the next pitch, Norris faked a steal of second base with several steps in that direction, but then had to turn and dive back into first when he heard the word "Back" shouted by the first base coach and saw an attempted pickoff throw coming from the strong-armed catcher. The umpire moved quickly toward the base and was in a good position to see Norris's out-stretched hand inches away from the bag as the fielder brought his glove down on it. After the "Out" call was given, followed immediately by boos and catcalls from all over the park, there was nothing Norris could do but jog off the field with his head down.

Kyle now stood as the last barrier to a Texas celebration, and the fans, by their near silence, signaled the absence of any hope in a miracle. But on the next pitch, the enormity of Norris's gaffe was reintroduced to Phillies Nation when Kyle drove the ball on one bounce off the wall in right center field and raced around the bases for a triple. Everyone realized that the hit would have tied the game and put the tying run on third with only one out. The radio and TV broadcasters in the booth tried to stay positive, reminding their listeners that the potential tying run was "only ninety feet away," and that the team had led the league in comebacks when behind after eight innings. But whatever hopes still survived at that point were crushed for good when the second pinch hitter of the inning dribbled a ball back to the mound and slammed his bat into the ground as the pitcher underhanded a throw to first for the final out.

Jimmy Diamond knew the agony of defeat from earlier managerial assignments and pennant races. He gathered his players together in the clubhouse and told them to take pride in the year they'd had and to look forward to playing their way into another World Series the next season.

Then he walked around the room and had short conversations with each of the players in which he thanked them for their individual contributions to the team's success. He put his arm around Norris's shoulder and told him he knew how hard he tried to win the game. "That stop you made out there was one of the best I've seen. I know how hard it is not to try and finish off a play like that by getting the out. It just takes a little more experience. You'll get there."

Before going into his office to dress, Diamond took Cavalho aside to speak to him.

"When we're both older, Luis, with gray hair, we'll talk about this game and I'll tell you something you don't know today. I know how you feel about my decision, and I'm sorry how it worked out, but I think you'll understand later on."

"It's okay, Jimmy, we'll do it next year."

He wanted to tell Cavalho he'd be managing his own team in the minors next year, but decided to leave word of the promotion to Hancock or Sherman.

"Yeah, Luis, you're right. Listen, I'll see you at the breakup dinner tomorrow night."

Diamond could feel the tension building as he walked the long passage from the clubhouse to the lounge at the players' entrance. It was a large room with a number of plush-looking chairs, two sofas, and a coffee machine, always stocked, that dispensed individual servings in several varieties. It was where wives and girlfriends could wait for players after the game while they showered and dressed. He couldn't help wondering if Heather had changed so much in twenty-five years that he might not recognize her. And he hoped he wouldn't see a sign of disappointment or surprise on her face when she first looked at him.

There were several women in the lounge when Diamond entered, but the one furthest from the door rose immediately from her chair and approached him. He knew it was Heather.

"Hi, Jimmy," she said, and opened her arms to hug him.

"Hi, Heather," he answered, and they embraced warmly for several seconds.

When they moved apart, he smiled at her and told her she looked marvelous. She returned the compliment and suggested they sit down. Neither sofa was occupied, and Heather led him to the closer one.

"I'm sorry about the game," she said. "I know how much winning it would have meant to you."

He wasn't ready to talk about that yet, to spoil their reunion recounting Norris's mistakes. "Where are you living?" he asked. "Still in Texas?"

"Oh, no, we moved out of Texas the same year we got married. It's been over twenty years in New Mexico."

"Well, I was in Albuquerque once . . . for two days." He smiled again.

"We lived in Gila for the peace and quiet while my husband wrote his doctorate thesis. Now we're farther north, outside of Santa Fe. He's a scientist and works at Los Alamos. That's where they did all that atom bomb stuff in World War Two."

"Yeah, I remember reading about that. What about you, do you work? Did you ever finish up nursing school?"

"I did finish, and I worked at it for four years, mostly part time, but then the kids began to need me more and I stopped."

"You said 'kids.' How many?"

"Three. Two boys and a girl."

"Is your other boy a ballplayer too?"

"No, he's into soccer and tennis, but he's pretty good at both of them." They looked away from each other for several seconds, saying nothing.

"So you're going back tomorrow morning, you said."

"Yes."

Diamond nodded his head up and down in response. Heather spoke again. "Well, I know you have a wonderful stepson, and I've been told he's an excellent shortstop."

They were back to baseball. He figured it was time to try and make her feel better about Norris's performance before she left. "He is a good shortstop, just like our son, but my gut and your being here told me to play Matt tonight."

Heather looked slightly confused. "I don't understand," she said.

"I had to make a decision between Kyle and Matt, and I was sure you'd come all the way to see our son play."

"Jimmy, I came here to see my daughter. Our son is at home in New Mexico. In fact, he's been home since the middle of July when he tore his Achilles heel."

"But Matt . . . I thought he . . ."He stopped speaking and stared at Heather.

"I can't imagine where you got that idea," she said.

Just then the lounge door opened and Debbie Newton came over to the sofa. "Hello, Mr. Diamond, I see you've met my mother."

It was like the aftershock following the earthquake.

Heather looked at him and spoke before he could answer. "I came here to see Debbie," she said, "and to meet her boyfriend. They seem to be very serious about each other."

"We are, Mr. Diamond. And Mom thinks Kyle is just terrific. She invited him out to New Mexico this winter. We were both glad he was able to get into the game tonight, but it's so sad that we lost."

HOT CORNER BLUES

*"I've had a pretty good success facing Stan (Musial) by throwing
him my best pitch and backing up third base."*

—Carl Erskine

SEVENTH INNING STRETCH. Damn. Better get something going now or
we'll be looking at Rosado and Gilman on the mound in the eighth
and ninth. If we can tie it with two runs here, Connelly will throw someone else out there if they don't get the lead back in the eighth. Who the
hell expected a 3–1 squeaker with us starting Manley and them pitching
Perez? Shit, they both have ERAs in the low sixes.

"Come on, Andy, give us a hit. This guy's running out of gas. Get
on, baby."

I don't think Red's gonna want him to lay one down. Third baseman's watching for it. Let's have it, Red, scratch your nose or your ear
over there. Nope, no bunt on this pitch anyway. Okay, Andy, watch my
hands. No bunt, but lay off until the ump calls a strike.

"Goddammit, give us a break, ump. That was below his knees. Bend
down and watch the damn pitch. Okay, Andy, shrug it off, the next one's
yours."

Lazy bastard. Get your fat ass down and look at the ball. The League would dump this clown in a minute if it could. The strike zone don't mean shit to him. You're on your own, Andy. Throw him a curve, Perez, throw him a curve. Hey, thanks baby, just what we wanted. Attaboy, Andy, good hit. Kid can put the outside curve into right like he was tossing it there himself. No one up loosening yet but that'll change if Starr gets on. He's watching me to see if there's a bunt on. We're two runs down, Kevin, not one. You know Red never bunts two runs down. Hit away.

"What's the matter, Perez? Arm getting heavy? You'll be resting it in a couple of minutes, man, soon as Kevin boy racks you up. Put it in gear, Kevin, drive this wreck off the lot."

I'd have bet against Kevin getting rung up twice by Perez today. He's only got three K's for the game. Don't know if he really painted the black on those called third strikes to Kevin or the dumb ump painted it for him.

"Come on, Kevin, Andy's got a message for me. Send him over here."

Hey, that was a pitch he should've turned on. What's he waiting for? Maybe he didn't get his sleep last night. Check the signs again, Kev. Nothing on. Just pick your pitch and hit it. If it's hard into left or center, Andy holds at second. Good arms out there. But the guy in right's probably thinking about his next at-bat. Needs a hit to keep his streak going. I'll take my chances if it goes that way.

"Good eye, Kevin, good eye. Drop it down this way, baby."

Ha! That brought Perini in a couple of steps. Slap it past him, Kevin. Andy ought to be taking a bigger lead. Perez has no move to first. Wake up, Red, tell Dutch to talk to him. Get him off that base for Chrissake! Another fastball, one and one. Thought he was going after it.

"Stay loose, Kevin, he's throwing prayers up there. Take him deep on the next one, baby. Come on, Perez, show the fans your gopher ball. That's what they came for."

Wow, terrific stop back there. That rookie Domozych's got all the tools. Reminded me of Pudge Fisk on that one. Real quick! Two and one now. This ought to be your pitch, Kevin. Give it a ride if it's in there. Look at Connelly. He's parked right next to the dugout phone. He'll be on it if Kev reaches. Goddammit, Andy, get off the base, stretch that lead. Bingo! Into right, and it's gonna fall! Come to Poppa, Andy. Watch me, watch me!

"Come on, Andy, move it! Come on!"

What the hell did he slow down for at second? Now McFee's got a chance to make a play. Oh shit, this is a bullet coming in and right on line. Watch me, Andy. Go for the outfield side of the bag.

"Leg it, leg it! Hit the dirt! Safe, he's in there. Oh bullshit, ump, he had the base before the tag. His left hand was on the corner before Perini put a glove on him. Oh bullshit, you just blew the goddam call. Get in the ballgame, for Chrissakes!"

Red could've come out here and made some noise. Would've taken some of the heat off me. Probably pissed that I waved Andy over on a hard hit single. But he'd have made it easy if he took a bigger lead and didn't hesitate halfway. I'll catch hell in the papers if that kills the inning and we lose it by a run. But the goddam writers never saw what really hurt the play. All they know is I waved him over and he didn't make it so it's my fault. Looks like Connelly's gonna stick with Perez as long as he got the out. Someone's up warming, now two of them. Maybe Trinidad will come through and get me off the hook. Rafey could lay one down and beat it out where Perini's playing him. Red can see the same thing but he's not calling for it.

"Come on Raphael baby, it's garbage time. You can hit this guy. Unload, kid."

Good lead, Kevin, but don't go too far. Looks like Red woke up and knows why Andy got thrown out. Rafey's due for a big hit. He'll sit on a fastball here. And there it is! Up the alley in left. This'll score Kevin.

"Keep coming, Kev. All the way, all the way."

Oh, shit! How'd Spencer cut that ball off so fast? It would've rolled to the wall. He's throwing it in and Russo's right there for the relay. Kevin's too slow to make it home. One out, I've got to hold him at third or he's in trouble.

"Hold it, Kev! Stay up, stay up. Hold it right here . . . Oh shit!"

Ball ticked off Russo's glove. Goddammit, if I'd sent him, he'd have made it. Russo had to go fifteen feet to pick it up again. Great! Now the shortstop makes me look like an idiot. Half the park figures he'd have scored even if Russo handled it cleanly and made the throw. And 20/20, the rest of them wish I'd taken the chance and waved him in. I'll be meat for the goddam writers, a two-time loser. "When's the team gonna get a third base coach who knows what the hell he's doing?" That's what I'll be reading tomorrow. Bastards, all of them.

"You'd've been a dead duck, Kevin, if I'd sent you and they handled it cleanly."

Connelly's seen enough of Perez. Who's he bringing in? Son of a bitch, he's calling Rosado. He wants this game bad if he's asking the lefty to get him five outs. That means Red'll probably pinch hit Montanez. Yup, here he comes. Kid's been great off the bench this year. Hitting up around .350 off southpaws. Second and third. A base hit to the outfield and this game's even. Connelly's got the balls to put Montanez on and go for two, but I don't think he will. A free pass could haunt him if that wins it for us. He'll go for an out even if the run scores from third. What about a runner for Kevin, Red? He's done a helluva job catching Manley, but right now we need some speed. Send Goodwin or Klinko out here. Hey, it's his call. Play it the way you want, Red. Rosado looks shaky on those warm-ups. Fastballs low and curves not breaking a hell of a lot. Probably not enough tosses in the pen. Red wants me to talk to Montanez. Whisper in his ear for him to take a strike before he swings at anything. Okay, Red, will do. Monty wasn't too happy about it. Said Red knows he likes that first pitch. Better make sure Kevin knows what's up.

"One away, Kevin. Infield's not playing in. If it's anywhere on the ground, take off. On a fly ball, tag up right away and listen to me. 'Go' means go like hell and be ready to slide. 'Now' means take a few steps down the line like you're going, enough to draw a throw. But heads up. If the ball gets away and you can score, take off. You got it? Keep your eye on Rosado. He'll pitch from a stretch. He may fake a throw to second and try to catch you leaning, so stay close to the bag. When he delivers, move off but don't wander down the line. Domozych would love to pick you off. He'll have you diving back into third for your life."

I've got a good feeling here. It's about time we broke through on Rosado. He's been handling us lately like we're Little Leaguers. Rollins is on deck. Not much in the clutch, but Red won't hit for him and move someone else into center, not yet. If Kevin's got a chance on a fly ball, I'm sending him. I still wish Red had put in a runner. Dammit, that strike to Monty was a straight fastball down the pike. I'll bet Red's sorry he gave him the take. May be the best pitch he'll see. Here comes slider time. Rosado won't show him another heater unless he gets behind on the count. Shit, now Monty's in the hole. Missed that slider by a foot.

"Cheat a little down the line, Kevin. Remember, anything on the ground, you go. Come on Monty, just takes one, meet it, baby."

Good, he shortened up on the handle the way Red's been telling him with two strikes. Kid learns fast and the pressure don't bother him. Good eye, Monty. Look for the same pitch. He'll keep it inside on you. There we go, two and two. What's bothering Rosado? That's three times he shook off the sign. Probably wants to throw a change. Now Domozych's out for a conference. May be doing it just to try and spook Monty, get him anxious. Break it up, ump, let's get going here. I'm still guessing changeup. Hit one, Monty. Fly ball. Shit, is it deep enough to left for Kevin?

"Tag up, Kevin, I'm sending you. Cream him if he blocks the plate. Make him pay. Get set . . . go!"

Move it! Dig! Dig! It's close. Drop it, you bastard! Shit! Double shit! Should've had two runs in and going for more. Worse goddam inning I've ever had and none of it was my fault. Oh boy, here it comes. Go ahead, you freaking boobirds, let me have it. As if any of you knew what the hell really went on out there. Just blame the coach, you assholes. I ought to tip my cap and give them something to really holler about. Screw it, let me just get in the friggin dugout.

TRADE-OFF

"When they start the game, they don't yell, 'Work ball.' They say, 'Play ball.'"

—Willie Stargell

HELL, MURPH, NO one's asked me about that for ages. Most of the characters who were involved aren't even around anymore. But you've always been straight writing about the ball club, and as long as we're stuck here until another crew shows up to put this damn plane in the sky, I'll tell you what I know about it. This comes from what I heard back then and from people I've spoken to who picked up pieces here and there and passed them on to me. But if you do a story on this, you've got to agree not to mention my name.

You know the year we're talking about, right? Okay, well the Sox and Yankees were playing three games over the weekend at Fenway in July when it happened. The Yankees took the Friday night game 6–2, with DiMaggio getting the big hit, a three-run homer that put them ahead for good. Williams had two doubles, the second one just about a foot short of clearing the fence and landing in the Sox bullpen. But things turned around on Saturday afternoon. We won that one 9–3, and it was the

Kid's two homers, mainly the grand slam, that led the way. Joe D. was pretty much the whole Yankee offense, hitting two balls off the Green Monster in left for doubles and a mammoth shot half way up the light tower. He drove in all of their runs.

Tom Yawkey and Dan Topping watched both games from separate owners' boxes upstairs on the third base side of the field. When the Sox got the final out on Saturday, Yawkey went over and invited Dan to have dinner with him that night. Topping agreed, and Tom told him they'd meet at the Garden Café, a small bar and dining room in the Kenmore Hotel. That's where the Yanks stayed when they were in town, and both Yawkey and Williams kept a room there for the whole baseball season.

Most of what they talked about over dinner was that year's pennant race. Each of them kind of boasted about his own team and predicted it would finish first, but they could both see that with a little bad luck or a slump or two at the wrong time, they could be lucky to finish in the top half of the division. Anyway, at some point Topping said that if Williams was playing in Yankee Stadium, he'd have hit three home runs that afternoon instead of two, and another one on Friday night, referring to the ball Ted hit off the bullpen fence. Yawkey chuckled at that, and after thinking about it for a few seconds said he didn't want to take anything away from DiMaggio, but that the fly ball homer Joe hit the night before would have been caught by the left fielder if it was hit in the Bronx.

Topping picked right up on that. "You know, these two guys were really meant to play their careers in each other's ballpark," he said. "If Ted played his home games in the Stadium, and Joe played his here at Fenway, they'd both have a chance to break the Babe's record."

Well, what Topping said lit a fire under Yawkey real fast. "You're right, Dan," he told him, and leaned forward to look the Yankee owner straight in the eye while he spoke. "And what a thing it could be for baseball if those two were battling each other every year to see who could hit sixty-one out of the park. Attendance would be up all over the league, especially at your ballpark and right here. I'd have to hire an architect to see if there was a way to add at least ten thousand seats to Fenway. Ticket sales would go through the roof."

I've no idea, Murph, whether those two guys were having drinks during the course of their dinner, but they were there for over three hours so I suspect they did. I can only guess that Yawkey, a southerner, would have gone for bourbon and Topping would have asked for Scotch. What I do know is that it was after they'd sat in the restaurant all that time that Topping proposed trading DiMaggio for Williams, straight up. "I'll give you the greatest player in the major leagues today," he told Yawkey, "and you give me maybe the greatest hitter of all time."

"There's no maybe about it," Yawkey shot back. "There's no one around who can hit like Ted, and never was. But we're talking just those two, right?"

"That's what I said, just Joe D. and the Kid."

"Don't you have to check with Del Webb?" Tom wanted to know. "I thought he owns fifty percent of the team."

"Don't you worry about him," Topping told him. "Leave that to me."

Yawkey took his time before answering, bobbing his head this way and that like he was lining up all the pros and cons of the deal in his mind's eye. "Okay then, I'll do it," he said finally, "but on condition that no one finds out about it until after tomorrow's game."

"Agreed," Topping answered. "We can announce it after the Yankees leave town."

"Well, then I'd say we're all done here and it's time to go to bed." Yawkey caught the waiter's attention and signaled for the check.

"I'll drink to that," Dan said, reaching for his glass on the table and gulping down whatever was left.

The fact that it was almost midnight didn't stop Topping from phoning DiMaggio as soon as he got back to his room and telling him about the trade. "You'll play for us tomorrow, Joe, because we don't want word of this to get out until the team has left Boston, and we don't have a good reason to keep you out of the game. But I wanted you to know I did it to help your career. You deserve to have a place like Fenway to hit in, to go for Ruth's record and have a chance of being MVP every year. McCarthy will love it when he finds out he's got you playing on his team again."

DiMaggio reacted just as you'd expect, in that low key way of his, not getting excited at all. "Thanks, Dan. It's been great being a Yankee since I came up. I'll miss the guys and the city, but everything will work itself out. I'm going back to sleep. Good night." That was it and he hung up the phone.

At about ten o'clock the next morning, Yawkey finished the cheese omelette he made for himself and washed it down with his third cup of black coffee. He had a slight recollection of his dream the night before in which DiMaggio led the Red Sox to a pennant, and then to victory in the World Series. Still, knowing how much his wife, Jean, liked Williams personally, he was nervous about informing her of the trade. When he did, he was unprepared for what followed.

"Are you crazy?" she hollered. "You're trading the greatest hitter in all of baseball to the Yankees? I hope you're not serious, Tom. Because if you are, what they've said about Harry Frazee over the last thirty years since he sold the Babe to New York will be a drop in the bucket compared to what our fans say about you. And that will continue for generations to come! Every time the fans hear your name, they'll start booing. How could you be so stupid? Were you drunk? It was Topping's idea, wasn't it? He's probably been waiting to catch you at a time when he figured you couldn't think straight, and last night was his chance. He didn't drink as much as you, did he? Did you two shake hands on the deal? Because if you didn't, then there was no deal. I can't believe you'd have even considered making a trade like that. What do we do with Dom? Take the second best center fielder in baseball and stick him in left? Make him play next to his brother and feel inferior all the time because Joe's the one in center? Couldn't you see that yourself? Any Red Sox fan could tell you that. Well, you listen to me, Tom, you just get on the phone to Dan Topping and tell him the trade is off. Tell him you weren't thinking straight last night when the two of you agreed to it. Tell him you didn't have the authority to make it without the unanimous approval of the club's trustees and that I won't go along with it. Tell him I'm ready to divorce you over this. Tell him anything you want, but make damn sure he understands that Ted Williams isn't leaving this team and going anywhere else."

Mrs. Yawkey didn't wait for an answer. She stormed out of the kitchen, went to the office she had in their apartment and slammed the door behind her.

Dan Topping didn't fare much better that morning. Although Del Webb was furious when he heard about the trade, he managed to control his temper while talking to his partner. "Dan, I think you're forgetting that you only own fifty percent of the ball club, not fifty-one. Any major decision like this is something we both have to agree on. You may know a lot more about baseball than I do, but I know enough not to let Joe DiMaggio out of New York. We're talking about the 'Yankee Clipper' here. What the hell would we tell the Italian population of this city? Hell, it wouldn't matter what we told them, they'd stop coming to the Stadium altogether. And who's going to play center field? Our pitching staff will go nuts if DiMaggio's not out there to save games for them. I don't know how you're going to do it, Dan, and I really don't care, but you'd better find a way to kill that deal before anyone in New York gets wind of it."

At about the same time those conversations were taking place, DiMaggio was walking through the children's area of the cancer center at Beth Israel Hospital, not far from Fenway Park. He'd been asked a month earlier to visit with some of the patients when the Yankees were in Boston and agreed to do it. The doctor taking him around told him about a boy named Dickie Collins, a twelve-year-old who was the biggest Red Sox fan in the ward, and brought Joe over to the boy's bedside. Collins recognized DiMaggio as soon as he saw him, and said the Yankees would be his favorite team if the Red Sox weren't. Joe laughed and said that

Ted Williams was probably Dickie's favorite player. Collins said he was because he was the best player on the team, but that DiMaggio was his second favorite player.

"So what if I was playing for Boston and Ted was a Yankee?" DiMaggio asked.

"Then you'd be my favorite player and I'd be rooting for you to hit a home run every time up," the boy said.

"Well, Dickie," DiMaggio said, giving him a wink he couldn't miss, "you never know, maybe that will happen one of these days and then you and I can be real close friends. Is there anything I can do for you today?"

"Yes, Mr. DiMaggio, I'd like you to hit a home run for me this afternoon, but don't let it beat the Red Sox."

"That's a big order, young man, but I'll see what I can do. Meanwhile, I've got a baseball here I'm going to autograph and leave for you." DiMag signed the ball "To Dickie Collins from Joe DiMaggio" and handed it to him. "And what you can do for me," he told the boy, "is try and get better every day. If that's a deal, let's shake on it." Collins stuck out his hand, DiMaggio shook it and then patted the boy's head where his hair had been shaved.

A half hour later, Williams was walking through the same area of the hospital, as he did on so many Sunday mornings when the team was playing at home. It was something he never wanted the fans to know about. He and Collins were old friends by this time since the boy was in his second year in the ward, and Ted stopped in to say "Hello." Before he left, he promised to try and hit a home run for Collins that afternoon, and found out that DiMaggio had said something about playing for the Red Sox and Williams becoming a Yankee. Ted couldn't wait to get to Fenway Park and find out if there was a rumor of that sort going around. He knew that where there was smoke in the clubhouse, there usually was fire.

Late in the morning Tom Yawkey and Dan Topping agreed to call off the trade they both liked so much the night before. Topping was willing—"reluctantly," he said—to accept Yawkey's explanation that the two of them hadn't finalized the deal with a handshake, and that in any event his wife had the right to veto the trade in her position as a trustee. Of course he was damn happy about not having to tell Yawkey how furious Del Webb was over the trade and that he'd been told to find some way to wiggle out of it. Topping's luck was that Yawkey called him first. And being the fast-thinking executive he was, he kept the pressure on until Tom agreed to send the Yankees one of the Red Sox relief pitchers (who would become a star) in return for a New York utility infielder (who would always underperform).

Topping grabbed hold of DiMaggio as soon as the Yankee slugger arrived at Fenway Park. He told him he had been under the weather the night before and that some crazy impulse he couldn't explain had pushed him into wondering how Dimaggio would react to being traded to Boston. He assured him that no such trade was in the offing or even in the team's consideration. Joe D. accepted the explanation at face value and didn't say a word to any of his teammates about the conversation with Topping the night before.

When Williams asked around the Red Sox clubhouse whether anyone had heard anything about a trade involving him and DiMaggio, the answers he got from the players dressing for the Sunday game were "Not me," "You've got to be kidding," and "That'll be the day." He went to his locker and began putting on his uniform, not certain whether he was happy about the response or not.

The rubber game of the series was tied through seven innings. In the Yankees' eighth, DiMaggio batted with two outs and the bases empty. The Sox pitcher tried to throw a full count fastball over the inside corner of the plate, but missed. The ball was still rising when it went over the Green Monster and past the light tower in the direction of Kenmore Square. In the last half of the ninth, with two out and nobody on base, Johnny Pesky grounded a single to center field, keeping the Red Sox chances alive. Within seconds, fans all around the ballpark were on their feet, clapping their hands and shouting for their hero as Williams stepped into the batter's box. The Yankee reliever tried to fool Ted into swinging at some bad balls but couldn't do it. When the count went to three balls and a strike, the crowd noise was almost deafening. Sox fans were waiting for number nine to win the game with one swing of his bat. But it didn't happen. Ted hit the next pitch on two easy bounces to the second baseman and was thrown out to end the game.

Up in the owner's box Yawkey watched Williams jog back to the Red Sox dugout and then turned to his wife. "I don't know, Jean," he said, shaking his head back and forth, "I don't know about calling off that deal." She gave him one hard look that left no doubt about its message, made a last notation on her scorecard and walked away.

That's it, Murph, the whole story of the greatest trade that never took place. Personally, I think that if it had, one of those guys would have broken the Babe's record before Roger Maris had the chance. Or maybe both of them. Meanwhile, when the hell is that new flight crew going to show up?

HER BEAUTY WAS JUST SKIN DEEP

"I'm getting smarter. I finally punched something that couldn't sue me."

—Billy Martin

YEAH, IT'S REALLY something. I chuckle every time I think how long it's been since the seed leading to this got planted. Fifty years, Emo. Fifty years, and I suddenly hear from this crazy man and he's sending me a present. Without Google—and he must have looked me up there—it probably wouldn't have happened. But the fact he remembered that day at the ballpark fifty years later, the golden anniversary for chrissakes, I mean it shakes me up.

And you know what? When I sit down here in the recliner, rest my head on the pillow and close my eyes, I can remember almost every detail of the trip when I met him.

It goes back to May of 1959. Man, was I ever that young? I was coaching baseball at Holy Cross and we had just a couple of games left on the spring schedule. It was a talented bunch of guys that year, for a change. We'd beaten several of the Ivy League teams, including Yale, which lost only three times all season, and Penn, which averaged over eight runs a game against everyone. They were a powerhouse, but we came out hitting everything, scored ten runs ourselves and almost shut them out. Anyway, out of the blue I got a call from the State Department in Washington, and they want to know if I can come down there because they want to talk to me about a ballgame. It was something they couldn't get into on the phone, the guy said. I'd get plane tickets delivered overnight, and any expenses I had they'd take care of. So we agreed on a day later in the week, and I had no clue what it was all about.

Well, you're my age, Emo, give or take a year, so think back to '59. That's when our friend in Cuba, Mr. Castro, pulled off his revolution against the guy—I forget his name—who'd been the dictator down there. Castro appointed himself the Prime Minister, and in April he came to the States. The biggest news story about him had to do with the pile of chicken bones they found in his New York hotel room after he checked out. Of course you remember that. Everyone does. All the papers had it on the front page. It looked like him and his bodyguards were eating chicken three meals a day. So tell me, who was President then? You got it, Eisenhower. Ike didn't like Castro, or trust him, so he wouldn't even meet with him while he was here. I'm no politician, but afterwards I figured it was a big mistake.

Anyhow, I got to see these three guys at the State Department, one of which was the Secretary for Latin American Affairs. He was a weird sort of guy who never took off his sunglasses the whole time. And he smelled funny, like he'd taken a bath in sour milk. It didn't surprise me when he showed up ten years later in Nixon's cabinet. He was a Nixon type, if you know what I mean. The thing was they couldn't tell whether Castro was going to be friendly with us, like the dictator was, or thought he had a better deal with the Russians. So their idea was to get him to try things our way and let Cuba be democratic. I was going to ask how they thought Ike giving him the cold shoulder helped out the situation, but I kept my mouth shut.

So anyway, one thing they'd found out was Castro was a big baseball fan and had been a pretty good pitcher when he was younger. At that time, though, he was going on thirty-three, and they figured with the revolution and all he probably hadn't played in years. But to make a long story short, they wanted me to put together a team of college guys—no more than twenty-two of them—find myself an assistant coach, and go play a five-game series in Cuba the first week of July. I guess that was supposed to get Castro to like us somehow, maybe remind him the Russians didn't play baseball. They knew it would be hot and humid down there, but still wanted to get the games played as soon as possible. They kept telling me not to worry about being safe, it wasn't a problem. So, naturally I agreed to start putting a team together right away.

That part was easy. First, I got my buddy, Pete Donnelly, from Boston College to coach with me—we Jesuits had to stick together, you know, especially when you're talking a free trip to Havana. Then we made a list of the twenty-five best players each of us could think of from the games that year, and ranked them one to twenty-five. We both took two players from our own teams—you know, a little bonus we gave ourselves—and then worked our way down the list for the rest. We knew we needed at least nine pitchers because all five games were going to be played in a week. So some of the names higher up the list didn't make it if they weren't pitchers. I made up a schedule of practices and intra-squad games we'd play in June, when they were all out of school, and we stayed in an empty dorm at Yale. The government said it was the best housing they could get us.

In the meantime, the weird guy at State, the Secretary, told me the date we'd be flying out of New York, and said we'd spend four days on an island in the Caribbean to practice and get used to the weather. We weren't going to find out where that was until after the plane took off, and we were supposed to never tell anyone which island. He made it sound like the whole trip was hush-hush, keep it to yourself. That was fifty years ago, but no one from the State Department ever got hold of me in the meantime and said it was okay to spill the beans on that, so I never did. I don't want no FBI agent showing up at my eightieth birthday party and telling me I'm arrested for talking about it. Besides, it's nothing important for you to know.

Okay, enough about that. I know you want to hear how we ended up with this thing. We trained on the island for four days, like he said, then had to be at the airport at five o'clock in the morning for the flight over to Cuba. We'd been staying in a big house, all to ourselves, and we were the only ones on the plane, including an old guy from the State Department who was in charge of everything. The only conversation with him usually was when he said "Do this," or "Do that." He sure as hell was no baseball fan.

Of course we'd all been excited about seeing the sights of Havana right away, but it didn't work like that. We sat in the airport for about two hours, with no idea what was holding us up, and then Mr. State Department told us to follow him. We went through a private gate and then we were outside the terminal again and walking over to another plane sitting there. We boarded that one, thinking maybe the whole deal was off and we were going back to the island we'd come from. But it turned out they were flying us from Havana down to Santiago at the other end of the island. That was a five hundred mile flight, I found out later, and that's where we were going to play the first two games.

I remember it was a Friday we got there and the games were scheduled for Saturday and Sunday. In the middle of the afternoon some Cuban guy who spoke real good English showed up in an old beat-up school bus, colored dark red—I never seen a yellow school bus there—and took us on a tour. Santiago's the second largest city there, he told us, and an important seaport. The most time we spent in one place was parked in front of the City Hall because he wanted us to see where Castro gave his speech six months earlier when he said they'd won the revolution. He talked about the building like it was some sort of a shrine, and read from notes that had parts of the speech Castro made there. On the way back to the hotel we drove by the stadium where we'd be playing, and I thought it looked pretty small from the outside.

When we got there on Saturday for the first game, I saw I was right. The place was called Estadio Guillermon Moncada. The reason I remember is because I wrote down the names of the stadiums in this little diary I was keeping, and I asked for some old programs they had from some earlier games. Anyhow, they squeezed twelve thousand people into the place for both games, and that's with a whole lot of standing room. There were no lights for playing at night, and the games started at four o'clock. By then it had cooled off enough so you weren't sweating the minute you stepped onto the field. We did everything right that day, both hitting and pitching, and beat the Cubans 10–3. The players on the other team were all older than our kids, but they were family guys who practiced when they could and played whenever someone arranged a game.

Afterwards they took us to this restaurant with long tables running along two walls. All the Cuban guys sat on one side, and we were on the other side, opposite them. Some of the waiters served just the Cuban players, and other waiters brought us our dinners. We could see our food wasn't the same as theirs, but Mr. State Department said it was because we couldn't handle the spicy stuff they ate. Meanwhile, he sat alone at a small table with the guy who took us on the tour the day before.

Well, about three o'clock in the morning everyone on the American team was wide awake and sick to our stomachs. I knew what me and Donnelly were going through, retching, throwing up, and running back and forth to the toilet. But it wasn't until the morning, when half the team didn't come down to breakfast, and the other half just wanted to drink some coffee, I found out how sick everyone had been during the night. I figured something had been put in our food to cause what it did, and that's why we didn't get the same things to eat as the Cubans. When Mr. State Department said he'd had a great night's sleep, it pretty much convinced me someone wasn't happy about our winning the ballgame.

Anyway, we all stayed around the hotel that day and tried to recover from the night before. Some of our players did better than others, but when it was time to leave for the stadium I could see we were in no condition to play our best. The guys went out there and tried hard, but everything we did looked like it was happening in slow motion. The worst was trying to run after hitting the ball, and our outfielders trying to catch up with fly balls hit in the gaps. The crowd in the stadium had a great time cheering for their team the way they beat up on us. The score was 19–5, and it could have been worse except some of the Cuban guys were moving up a base at a time when they could have had two, or in at least a couple of cases even three. They were too tired to keep pouring it on. So everyone on both sides shook hands when it was over, and they left, probably went home to their families. We went back to the hotel, ordered off the menu whatever we thought we could handle, and flopped back down into bed.

Monday was a travel day, and we had a bus leaving at 10:00 a.m. Our next two games were going to be played in a place called Cienfuegos, about 250 miles away, along the southwest coast of the island. We left on time, right after most of the team finished breakfast, stopped for lunch at a fish shack along the way the driver recommended, and got there just before six o'clock. Some of the guys asked why we didn't fly instead of spending the whole day on the road, and Mr. State Department said the Cuban government was in charge of all our transportation on the island. "How we get there or anyplace else is up to them, not me," he said. "If you've got a complaint, talk to Castro. I'm sure he'll do whatever you say." That was about the funniest thing he said the whole trip.

Anyhow, there wasn't much to see on the ride, but what caught my eye were the American cars that passed us going in the other direction. Most of them were old, some even from before the war, but then every so often there'd be one from the fifties go by. I loved those cars they made in the mid-fifties, and I could tell one from the other pretty easy. Just had to see their grills and tail fins, or the tire guards some wore, or whether they had twin exhausts or what their hood ornaments looked like. It wasn't just the Fords and Chevys. You had DeSotos, Hudsons, Chryslers, Studebakers, Packards, some of the most beautiful cars in the world. You know what I'm talking about, Emo. So I had fun pointing them out for the guys.

The name of the stadium in Cienfuegos was the easiest one for me to remember. It was Estadio 5 de Septiembre, and September 5th is my boy's birthday. It was a lot bigger than the one in Santiago, and you could see they took good care of it. Thirty thousand could watch a game there, and everyone had a good seat. I was impressed when we took the field and saw they had three cameras set up for shooting videotape of the game. One was in the center field bleachers, right on a line with home plate, and the other two were behind first and third.

Our guys did some good hitting in that first game, but so did they. The lead went back and forth almost every inning, and we were down a run going into the ninth. After a beautiful bunt single put a runner on first, our catcher caught hold of a slow curve he'd been looking for and we jumped ahead again 12–11. The Cubans put men on second and third with one out in their ninth, and the next guy hit a bullet I was sure was the game winner for them. But our second baseman—one of the two Holy Cross players I'd put on the team—gloved it with a dive to his right and then touched second before the runner got back. It was a sensational backhand stab and double play. We ran on the field to lift him up and carry him back to the dugout, and I remember seeing the fans behind third standing and clapping for us. It felt good to know they appreciated a great play, and it felt terrific that we'd beaten a team of what I could tell were semi-pros.

The Wednesday game was a whole different story. I'd given our players a pep talk in the locker room about winning that afternoon and wrapping up the series in our favor. We were starting the kid who pitched seven terrific innings in the first game in Santiago, and I knew from watching him in our league at home he was used to going on three days rest. He got through the first couple of innings okay, but then the roof fell in and they began pounding him. I left him in there until the Cubans had six runs on the board in the next two innings, and our three relievers gave up ten more in the four innings they threw between them. All of them got scorched. We had a meaningless rally in the ninth getting a bunch of runs, but the final score was still an embarrassment.

Mr. State Department came into the locker room to let us know the travel plans for the next day, and I told him to get me copies of the video the Cubans took of our two games there. Donnelly couldn't believe all four of our kids could get hit that hard in one game. I agreed with him, and wanted to see if they were somehow telegraphing their pitches. State Department said he'd ask about it, and then told me at dinner there was no video. The stadium manager said those guys were just practicing camera shots. What they were really doing woke me up in the middle of the night. That's when it hit me the guy in center field must have been sending signals to their hitters at the plate, probably holding up one or more fingers when he saw what pitch our catcher was signaling for. The other two guys were just part of the show. So now we'd lost one game on account of food poisoning, and another on them stealing our signs, with the final game coming up on Friday night in Havana.

We were back on the same bus again in the morning, but we knew the ride would be much shorter than the last one, so there was almost no griping about it. For a while we stayed close to a bay on our left side and we could see a long sandy beach there. The driver pointed to it and called it the Bay of Pigs, but it didn't mean anything to me until the Cuban invasion a couple of years later when Kennedy was president. The pitchers who were in the game the day before all felt better about themselves when I explained how our signs were being stolen, and everything was upbeat until we were almost at the hotel. That's when Mr. State Department told us our game on Friday night wasn't going to be played at the main stadium, called Estadio Latinoamericano, which I had been telling everyone about, but at a smaller one in another part of the city. Its name, we found out later, was Estadio Pedro Marrero, and with twenty-eight thousand seats was just half the size of where we expected to play. That was a downer for everyone.

On Friday, our English-speaking tour guide from Santiago showed up and we got driven on the same bus all around Havana to see the sights. We stopped for lunch after a couple of hours, and then spent another hour on the bus listening to him mostly point out more of the memorial statues and buildings around the city. I remember him telling us the population was getting close to two and a half million people, and there were plenty of places where you could see the living wasn't very comfortable.

Again, the biggest attraction for me was the American cars on the streets, and there were a lot more of them here. The tour guide said Cuba used to get most of its cars from Mexico every year, but that while the dictator was there—now I remember his name, Batista—while he was there, they imported cars from the US for the Cubans who had money and could afford them. When the bus stopped across the street from the Presidential Palace, there was a 1954 Buick Roadmaster Convertible, green and white, four portholes on the side, parked right in front. It looked like it just came out of the showroom. If I had the money and could have chosen one car for myself in the fifties, it would have been that one. Instead, I was driving an eight-year-old Chevy my uncle sold me for a hundred forty bucks. The Roadmaster belonged to Castro, our guide said. I asked him if I could walk over and sit in it. He said sure, it was okay if I didn't mind getting shot by one of the three soldiers who were standing there with their rifles at parade rest. That got a laugh from the kids, so I kept the joke going by telling him I'd ask Mr. State Department to arrange for me to get a ride in the car out to the stadium.

"Not in that car," he said. "That car never goes anywhere."

So that was the end of that, and when we pulled away I saw the license plate read "CUBA 1."

The game that night moved along quickly, and we led 8–1 after seven innings. I felt good about the fact we were going to win the series, and I could already imagine the nice write-up I'd get in the Worcester papers—and probably the Boston papers too on account of Donnelly being from B.C.—for coaching the team. I was thinking maybe some college that pays better than Holy Cross might see it and be interested in talking to me about a job.

Before the eighth inning started, some guy in civilian clothes came out on the field and walked over to speak to the home plate umpire. I figured the police on duty near the two dugouts knew who he was because no one tried to stop him. Anyway, after a couple of minutes the umpire waved for me and the Cuban team manager to join them. When we did, the civilian guy first spoke in Spanish to the Cuban manager who kept nodding his head up and down as he listened. Then he told me in English that Fidel Castro had intended to be at the stadium that night but was detained by some important business. He definitely wanted to see the game deciding the winner of the series, so it couldn't be the one we were already playing. Castro said this game and the one scheduled for Saturday night would both be considered practices, or warm-ups, and the deciding one would be played on Sunday afternoon when he could be there. I didn't like what I was hearing, but there was nothing I could do about it. We were two innings away from winning the series, and now it was being taken away from us. I figured the silver lining in it was the guys who hadn't played much so far would be able to get a whole game under their belts without worrying about whether they won or lost. The good news he gave us was the game would be played in the main stadium, which he called the Grand Stadium of Havana. I guess I looked confused because then he said it's what Estadio Latinoamericano was called when it was built about thirteen years earlier, and many Cubans still use that name. Anyhow, since I figured this guy must be close to Castro, I asked him if there was any chance of someone giving me a ride in that Buick convertible in front of the Presidential Palace.

"I will mention it to the Prime Minister," he said, "but as far as I know that car always stays right where it is."

So at least I felt good that Castro knew what I wanted if he was going to send us home with a smile on our faces.

We finished the game, holding on at the end for an 8–6 win after they rallied in their last at bats. The next night we lost by the same score, but our subs got the chance to have some fun for nine innings, and we let four of our pitchers go two innings each. The Cubans used all their regulars, so that gave our players even more confidence. Also, the tour guide told us some of the guys on their club had been good enough to play for Cuba's national team when they were younger. I remembered back in Santiago he said the Cubans expected to beat us in all five games. Anyhow, the fans knew the second game was an exhibition and didn't count for anything, but they filled the ballpark anyway and let us hear it with some cheering whenever one of our guys made a terrific play. I came away feeling they loved baseball for the game itself, and would show up to watch it no matter who was playing.

I'm almost through with this story, Emo. Believe me, I haven't been trying to drag it out, and I'm not going to give you a blow-by-blow description of every inning from the Sunday game. It wasn't one of those games with a lot of action where the crowd is really into it, making a lot of noise and up on its feet half the time. In fact, it was just the opposite. Maybe it's because there were fifty-five thousand people watching us, and the players on both sides had trouble getting rid of their butterflies. It was like we were waiting all game for them to make a mistake and vice versa. Today, the kind of game I'm telling you about is what's called a grinder. We were lucky we had our best pitcher to go again on three days rest because the guy on the mound for the Cubans had all his stuff and was giving us fits.

We had a 2–1 lead going into the stretch half of the seventh inning, and then a gal who was one of the most popular singers in the country woke up the crowd with the way she sang the Cuban national anthem. The first two guys up for them both hit doubles off the right field wall, and they scored two runs in the inning to go ahead 3–2. In the eighth, we had two on and two out when our center fielder hit a low line drive the Cuban center fielder came racing in for and tried to snag with a dive before it hit the grass. It fell in front of him, took a bounce and rolled most of the way to the wall. Both runners scored and our guy had a triple, but we couldn't bring him home.

We got past their half of the eighth with no problem and took the 4–3 lead into the last of the ninth. I had a left handed reliever ready on the mound to throw to their first batter, a left handed hitter, and he got him on a grounder to short. They had a righty up next, so I brought in our best right handed reliever in the bullpen. He went to a full count on the hitter, but then walked the guy on a pitch the ump could've called either way. The Cuban pitcher was due up next, so I figured we'd see a pinch hitter and I was waiting to see what side he hit from. All of a sudden there was a lot of noise coming from the stands behind first base, and then I saw Castro himself come through the gate in front of the box seats and onto the field. Up to that point I hadn't thought about him at all, and had no idea where he'd been sitting. He was dressed in a fatigue uniform and holding a shopping bag in his hand. The Cuban team's manager came running out and led Castro back to their dugout. It took about five minutes, as the noise in the stadium kept getting louder when more people found out what was going on, and then Castro came back onto the field. He was wearing the team's shirt and cap, and had traded in his boots for a pair of spikes. But he still had on his fatigue pants.

As everyone watched, Castro went over and began talking to the home plate umpire. Then the ump called both of us managers over. He said Castro told him he hadn't played any baseball or even swung a bat in several years, and he wanted to take some batting practice before he pinch hit. How did we feel about that, the umpire wanted to know. Well, the Cuban manager said that Fidel—he called him Fidel—had played for the team before he went off to fight, it was an honor to have him back, and he certainly was entitled to take some batting practice. I wasn't sure what to do. I'd never heard of anything as crazy as this happening, but the umpire obviously hadn't ruled it out. While I hesitated, he said if the two managers disagreed, he'd have to make the call. I figured he wasn't going to go against what he knew fifty-five thousand fans in the park wanted, so it wasn't going to matter what I said. The ump proved my feeling about him was right when he took me aside and reminded me we were dealing with the country's Prime Minister and its great hero of the revolution. He thought instead of his having to make the decision, I should agree Castro could take batting practice before getting into the game.

"If you reject his request, he will not forget you," he said, "and when Fidel does not forget you, your troubles begin immediately."

That did it for me. I had to remember there were twenty-two college kids in a foreign country who were my responsibility, and we were there to impress Castro in some way, not get him mad at us. So I told the umpire I agreed and gave Castro a big smile when the ump translated it into Spanish.

I was asked to take all our players off the field, and I did. Our pitcher was allowed to throw on the side and keep loose, but the rest of us sat in the dugout and watched Castro swing at what the Cuban manager was throwing him. He was rusty as an old gate at first, but you could see he was an athletic guy and after a while began to make solid contact with some of the balls he swung at. Finally, about fifteen or twenty minutes later he dropped the bat at the plate and showed he wanted the two managers to join him. He spoke in Spanish, and the umpire told me what he said.

"We don't have a trophy to give you if you win the game," he told me. "We were sure we would never lose,"—and he laughed a little when he said that—"but I've been told of your affection for the convertible in front of the Presidential Palace. If you win, everyone on your team will be allowed to sit in the car, two at a time, for five minutes, but the car will not be moved. Maybe at another time in the future you'll have that chance. But if our team wins the game, you will have to give me your baseball uniform because I see we are the same size and perhaps I will wear it on different occasions." When the ump finished speaking, Castro smiled at me and held out his hand to confirm the deal. I smiled back and we shook hands.

Our team took the field again, and the Cuban manager sent up a pinch hitter, but it wasn't Castro. It was a left handed hitter, and I felt I'd been outsmarted by not having a southpaw get loose also while Castro was taking his swings. The batter jumped on the first pitch and drove it off the low wall in right field, just missing a home run and ending the game right there. That gave the Cubans runners on second and third. With the crowd on its feet and roaring, Castro came to bat. In a normal situation I'd have given him a free pass to set up a double play and end the threat, but I felt pretty confident about getting him out. Well, Castro watched the first five pitches go by, three balls and two strikes, without taking the bat off his shoulder. Our guy was firing them in, one fastball after another, and Castro looked overpowered. The pitches he'd seen in batting practice didn't come close to the speed of those he was looking at now. He didn't step out of the batter's box once. It was almost like he was in a trance. I was thinking the Cuban manager probably wished Fidel had never left his seat in the stands, and that he was going to either strike out looking, or walk if he was lucky, without ever taking a cut. What worried me was he'd swing late and get just enough bat on the ball to hit one of those sickening flares down the right field line that lands on the chalk with three fielders each a step away from reaching it. On the next pitch he almost did what I was thinking, but I could see right away it was slicing foul off to the right and would land in the lower boxes out there. At that point he stepped away from the plate for the first time since getting set in the box, took a few hard practice swings and then pointed out to left field. I couldn't believe it. I wondered whether he knew about Babe Ruth doing that years ago, or was making it up himself. My pitcher turned around and looked at the outfield like he was expecting to see a loose beach ball out there. Then he raised his hands as if he was saying

"What's he pointing at? What's going on?" I hollered out to him to forget it and shouted "Whiff this guy, throw it by him." The seventh fastball in a row left the mound and almost reached the catcher's glove. I think in the next twenty seconds we made Fidel Castro a bigger hero in Cuba than what the revolution did. I couldn't tell you whether he had his eyes open or not, but he hit the pitch no more than twenty feet off the ground out to left field, 330 feet away into the bleachers, right in the direction he'd pointed. When the ball landed, the crowd made the loudest noise I ever heard in a ballpark anywhere. It was "Fidel, Fidel, Fidel," and they never stopped shouting his name. He stood at home watching the ball until it left the park, like Manny Ramirez always does when he knows it's gone. I watched him make his home run trot around the bases, and when he rounded third he looked my way and gave me one hell of a big smile. Then he pointed to his cap, his shirt and his pants, reminding me I owed him my uniform. I clapped my hands a couple of times just to show him I appreciated what he'd pulled off.

The bus took us to the airport on Monday morning after we'd had a late breakfast. I asked Mr. State Department what he thought of the game, and he told me he missed it. He looked up an old friend and they went to a museum and to dinner. It didn't surprise me. When we passed by the Presidential Palace, I had one more look at the Roadmaster and then put it out of my mind. A couple of weeks later I got a note from the Secretary of Latin American Affairs and he congratulated all of us on a good showing in Cuba. He let me know he was aware we had really won the series the way it was set up because we beat them three out of the first five. He also figured Castro couldn't hate us all that much since we'd made him a great baseball hero. He was wrong on that one.

So, like I told you, Emo, when I began this story, fifty years have gone by since we played that game. And now, out of the blue, Castro thinks of me and sends me an anniversary present. If you want to see it, let's go in the garage. I had the delivery guys put it in there. Watch your step. Here, let me put on the light. Surprise, huh? Now you know what a 1954 Buick Roadmaster Convertible looks like. Beautiful, isn't it? Imagine how I felt when it arrived. Go ahead, the hood opens easy if you put your fingers where the "BUICK" letters meet the top of the grill and push up. There you go. Yeah, I was shocked myself. Now we both know why this gorgeous automobile sat in front of the Presidential Palace so many years and never moved a foot. Who would've ever guessed there was just a big empty space under the hood?

CATCH ME, CATCH ME

"Trying to sneak a fastball past Hank Aaron is like trying to sneak the sunrise past a rooster."

—Joe Adcock

MORE THAN FORTY years have flown by since I last saw Catch Me, Catch Me. I was a member of the Iroquois then, a social and athletic club started by some of us in our early teens who lived on three adjacent streets in town.

We were one of a handful of clubs whose members spent most of their free time at Franklin Field. Our primary adversaries, from other streets in the same general neighborhood, were the Rangers, Blackhawks, and Devils. We opposed each other regularly in baseball and football, and in the winters when the huge field was intentionally flooded and iced over, some of the teams played hockey. Once in a while a fight broke out during these encounters, but it didn't cause any more lingering animosity than what already existed simply by virtue of our belonging to one club or another.

Catch Me, Catch Me, whose real name was Norman, "Normy" to us, had no attachment to any of the clubs. That's not because he wasn't a good athlete. Tall, wiry and strong, he had biceps we all envied, and he could throw a baseball or kick a football farther than any of us. He was a pitcher, a left-hander, with easily the best stuff of anyone I knew who played ball at Franklin Field. He tried to get into the Rangers at one time, but the club president, who also pitched most of the team's games, blackballed him. After that, I guess Catch Me, Catch Me decided to stay independent rather than risk the embarrassment of being rejected again.

The problem was that until he got to high school, Catch Me, Catch Me didn't have the chance to pitch in many games. He was much too good for any of the neighborhood clubs playing each other to waive the "no ringers" rule when he was around, except when a team was unable to put nine guys on the field. Even then, he was restricted to an infield or outfield position. The only time he could pitch was in an occasional pickup game when no club's pride or record was at stake.

For a while, Normy also got the chance to show his skill on Sunday mornings in the summer when guys in their twenties and thirties got together for a weekly game. He waited patiently until replacements were needed in the late innings for those who had to get home, and was sometimes allowed to finish out the contest on the mound. But that stopped when enough players complained about being embarrassed by a fifteen-year-old kid.

There were two things that distinguished Catch Me, Catch Me at the field. For one, he was the only player there who wore even part of a baseball uniform. This was years before Little League got started, and it imbued him with a special status. An uncle of his had given him a shirt that said "Tigers" on the front, in orange letters, with the number "19" on the back. Normy told us that his uncle had played minor league ball in the Detroit organization. Soon afterwards, his long, dirty blonde hair could be seen flowing out from beneath the black baseball cap with the Detroit "D" on the brim that he purchased at a Fenway Park souvenir stand.

The other thing setting him apart was that he always carried two baseball gloves with him. One was his own, a regular fielder's mitt for a lefty. The second was a catcher's glove for a right-hander because most of us threw that way. Whenever he saw someone he knew, he extended the catcher's glove and virtually pleaded, "Catch me, catch me." Two of Normy's upper teeth on the same side of his mouth were chipped in the same place, giving him almost a smile within a smile whenever he spoke. He was prepared for rejection, which was the usual result. Most of us were afraid to try and catch him without a mask, chest protector and shin pads. But if he detected even the slightest hesitation, he pounced.

"You've got to see what my new fast ball can do, it's amazing," he would say, or, "I've been working on a curve that can drop two feet." At that point he had all but put the catcher's glove on the other person's hand, still imploring, "Come on, catch me, catch me, just for a while." That's how he acquired his nickname.

It was hard for me to turn him down, despite knowing that I was going to be nervous and straining on every pitch. It didn't matter that he always announced what he would throw next. His was the fastest baseball I'd ever catch from that sixty-foot, six-inch distance he immediately marked off with the roll of measuring tape he always carried in his pocket.

There was also the realization that if I didn't react quickly enough to a pitch that broke at the last second or landed in the dirt in front of me, I could easily get hurt. The well-padded catcher's glove would take care of my hand, but there was no protection anywhere else. Still, Normy had made it clear to everyone that he was going to be a major league pitcher some day, and what he could do on the mound with a baseball was overwhelming enough to convince me he'd reach his goal. There was always the thought in the back of my mind that someday I'd be able to brag that I caught his pitches when we were kids.

Things improved dramatically for Catch Me, Catch Me when he got to high school. Although the rules didn't allow him to play for the varsity in his freshman year, he performed better than any other pitcher in the intra-squad games held during the tryouts. The freshman team played a fourteen-game schedule. Normy started eight of those games, completed seven and won them all. He averaged fifteen strikeouts each time out. I was the third baseman on that team, and it was because of me that everyone else got into the habit of calling him Catch Me, Catch Me, and rhythmically shouting the name every time he got two strikes on an opposing batter.

In our sophomore year, Catch Me, Catch Me was the star of the team. He had grown taller and broader, and a weightlifting program gave him more strength in his shoulders. There was greater velocity on every pitch he threw, and he quickly established himself as the ace of the pitching staff. The varsity played two games against each of the other nine teams in our high school division. Normy got the chance to face all of them and to pitch twice against our archrivals from Mattapan. For the second year in a row he went undefeated and maintained his fifteen strikeouts per game average. Until the final game of the season, he pitched at least eight innings every time he took the mound. His fame spread quickly around school, and the ten rows of stands on the first base side of the baseball field were usually filled with friends shouting his nickname whenever he played.

The first meeting with Mattapan, at our field, fell in the middle of the schedule. It was a squeaker all the way. Both Catch Me, Catch Me and the pitcher for the visitors had each allowed just one hit going into the last half of the ninth inning. Normy was a terrible hitter, but with one out he somehow connected on a long drive to right center field that split the outfielders. He raced around the bases, past a teammate coaching at third who froze in indecision, neither waving him on nor signaling him to stop, and scored the only run of the game after a collision at home caused the catcher to drop the ball.

The sound of "Catch Me, Catch Me" from our bench and from the bleachers behind us accompanied him all the way. Watching him run 360 feet at full speed, Mr. Levine, the school's track coach, decided on the spot that there was a place for Catch Me, Catch Me on his team. Normy told me later that the coach had all but ordered him to come out for indoor track in the fall. Little did he know he'd also be running track during the next baseball season.

It happened that suddenly. The last game of the year was the rematch with Mattapan. Normy found himself dueling the same pitcher he had beaten earlier with his home run. In five innings he had already notched nine strikeouts and was leading by the one run we had just given him, courtesy of my double, in the top of the sixth inning.

The second out in Mattapan's half of that inning was his tenth "K" of the contest and the last pitch Catch Me, Catch Me ever made in a baseball game. He screamed as he let the ball go and then fell on the ground in obvious pain. The coaches of both teams ran out to him, comforted him as best they could and sent one of the players to the school to call for an ambulance. We could hear its siren begin to wail many blocks away from where we were, and then watched silently as Normy was lifted into the van on a stretcher. It turned out that he had completely torn his rotator cuff, although we never heard it called that back then. Someone with that injury was always described as having "thrown his arm out." Catch Me, Catch Me was told never to use his left arm to throw hard again. For the record, we held on to the lead to win that last game and were division champions, but without our star pitcher we were near the bottom of the heap in my junior and senior years.

Coach Levine found that Normy's speed and stamina made him a natural miler. He took to the training, and by the middle of the indoor season brought excitement to every race he ran. His nickname seemed even more suited to his new sport. Many of his friends in school began attending the meets, and the cry of "Catch Me, Catch Me" filled the gymnasium whenever he raced the twelve laps around the track in the mile competition.

Mr. Levine insisted that Normy stay in training during the three-month hiatus between the indoor and outdoor track seasons. Except for school vacation weeks, he reported to the coach after classes every day for the exercises and practice runs that had been scheduled for him. I never heard him complain about it, probably because he could see the steady improvement himself. Track was now the only way he could show off his athletic ability, and he decided to make the most of it.

By the time the outdoor season began, Normy was the best miler our school had ever produced. His times were fantastic, prompting one of the local newspapers to run his picture above the caption, "Four Minute Miler?" That was a huge exaggeration, of course, since he was usually twenty seconds above that threshold. But in competition he was always so far ahead of the pack that the race was over, for all intents and purposes, when he still had much of the final lap of our quarter mile track to complete.

The roar of "Catch Me, Catch Me" from the students in the stands and the other athletes in the track's infield grew louder and louder as each of his races progressed. Then he added a new wrinkle to the excitement. I still recall the first time Normy glanced over his shoulder at his distant pursuers as he was still far from the finish line and hollered a taunting "Catch me, catch me." We loved it.

And that became the routine. No one ever came close to beating him during the rest of his high school career. As his times for the mile improved, his following grew larger. The reward for those who encouraged him by shouting his nickname came that moment during the final lap when he signaled his victory by turning his head to those running behind and called out, "Catch me, catch me."

I'm certain that the last time I ever saw Normy was at the senior prom. By that time I knew he was soon leaving for the Army in order to satisfy his commitment and save some money before starting college. He was disappointed that the colleges to which he applied for a scholarship to run track had very little financial assistance to offer him. We wished each other well and shook hands on the thought that we'd meet up again at a class reunion. I attended all of them, from the first, held ten years after graduation, to our 40th reunion in May. Catch Me, Catch Me never came to one.

What brought all this to mind was the story that ran last week in the business section of the Times. Seeing Normy's name in large bold print caught my eye, and the few details of his past that were included, along with a photograph, assured me that the article was about my old baseball buddy and classmate. The essence of the report was that he had found a unique way to siphon millions of dollars from the Wall Street securities firm where he worked, and had created a software program to alert him immediately if anyone's suspicion about missing funds led to the checking of certain records. Having apparently discovered that such an investigation was in its initial stage, he took a two-week vacation leave and used it to flee the country with his wife. The only thing authorities now knew for certain was that his flight had landed in Zurich ten days before the incriminating evidence pointed in his direction. It was assumed that the investment firm's money was resting comfortably in one or more Swiss bank accounts.

For my part, I could only picture Normy looking out the window of that plane, watching New York City fade further into the distance every second and, with a smile of victory on his face, whispering the words, "Catch me, catch me."